# BETRAYAL
# in
# BLUE

Mark M. Bello

Copyright 2018 Mark M. Bello

All rights reserved. No part of this book may be used or reproduced by any means, graphic, electronic, or mechanical, including photocopying, recording, taping or by any information storage retrieval system without the written permission of the author except in the case of brief quotations embodied in critical articles and reviews and other noncommercial uses permitted by copyright law.

This is a work of fiction. All the characters, names, incidents, organizations, and dialogue in this novel are either the products of the author's imagination or are used fictitiously.

Because of the dynamic nature of the Internet, and web addresses or links contained in this book may have changed since publication and may no longer be valid. The views expressed in this work are solely those of the author.

8Grand Publications
7115 Orchard Lake Road #320
West Bloomfield, MI 48322

Published September 2018
First Edition

Printed in the United States of America

ISBN: 978-1732447103
E-ISBN: 978-1732447110

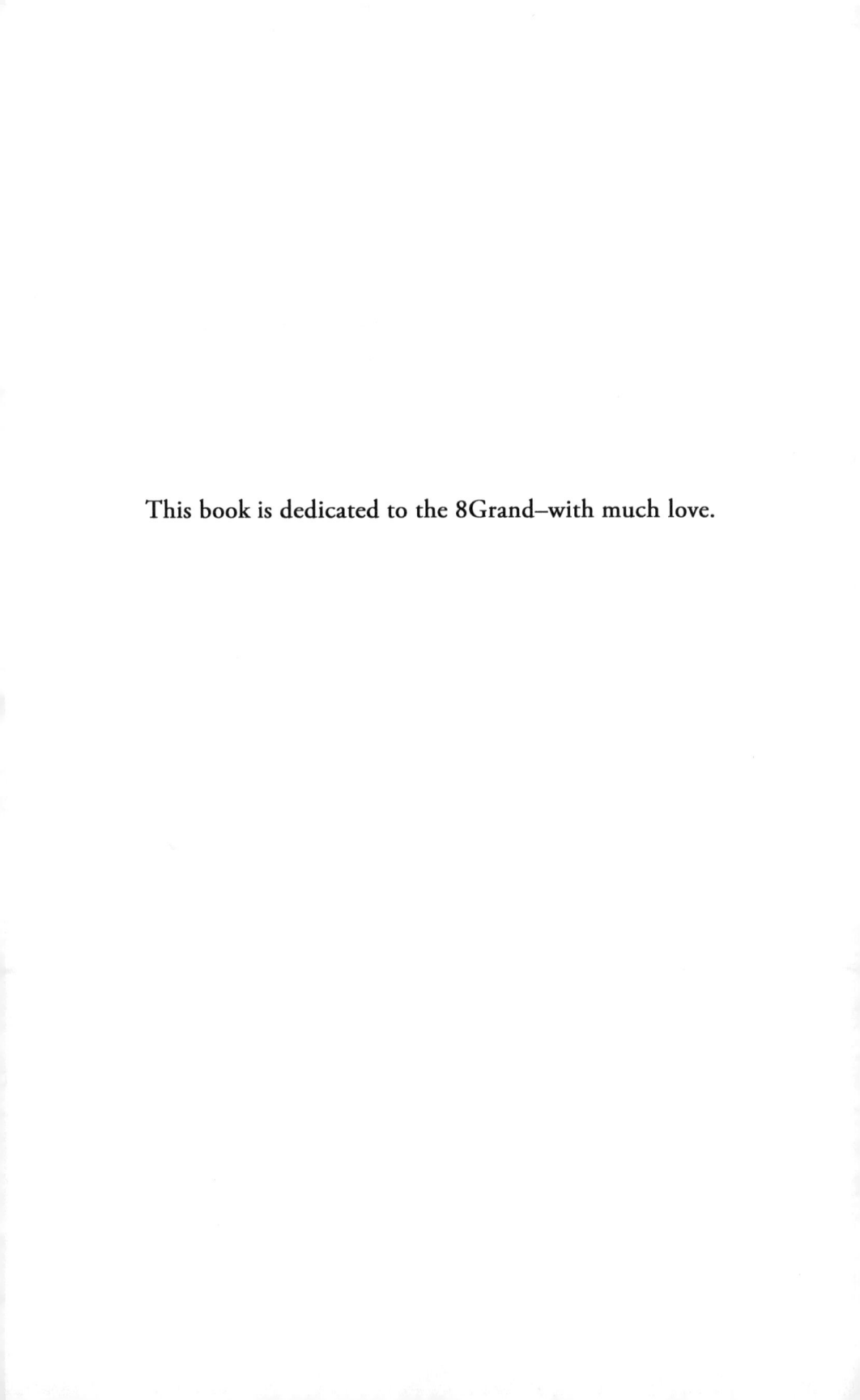

This book is dedicated to the 8Grand–with much love.

This book would not have been possible without the contributions of Christine and Alexander Borrello. Thank you for your valuable advice and input. *Betrayal in Blue* is a far better novel because of you. I sincerely appreciate your assistance.

# PROLOGUE

*ATTENTION FREEDOM BROTHERS:*
*BVI A.M. DB / SARIN CAMEL-COP OP*
*DARK WEB ONLY*
*—SUPREME WHITE KNIGHT*

Noah Thompson rushed into the office of Captain Jack Dylan and handed him the message, direct from a search of the dark web.

"Sarin in Dearborn? Are you shitting me?" Jack pounded his desk. His morning coffee spilled all over the burglary file he was studying. Coffee was everywhere, flowing across the desk and dripping onto the floor. Jack didn't notice. He was staring at the two-sentence message.

"What do we know, Noah?"

"We don't have any details, Jack," replied Noah, Jack's and the Dearborn Police Department's technology guru. "What you see is all we have. We've decided DB, together with 'camel-cop' means that Dearborn, cops, and Muslims are the principal targets. This is probably some sort of revenge plot for the Blaine situation."

"We can't take this lightly, Noah. We need to gather the team immediately."

# PART ONE—TERROR

# Chapter One

The men around the table became quiet as they absorbed the news. They were an elite unit of Dearborn Michigan police officers, a task force that achieved some notoriety for bringing down a group of white supremacists after one member bombed the local mosque and an Islamic museum. In the process, the task force exonerated and rescued Arya Khan, a young Muslim woman falsely accused of murdering the mosque bomber and who, later, was held hostage by these homegrown terrorists.

Their leader was Benjamin Blaine, head of the "The Conservative Council" and an icon/exemplar for numerous, similar groups. After their capture, trials, and many plea bargains, Blaine and seventeen others were now serving multiple life sentences in a Michigan prison.

"What do we know about sarin gas? How is it released? What kind of damage does it cause?" Jack Dylan's mind was racing as he addressed his elite group of cops.

"According to my limited internet research, sarin was developed by the Germans in 1938. No surprise there, I guess," replied Noah.

"Go on…"

"It has been associated with acts of terror in the past, as you probably know. There was the Japan subway attack in 1995 which resulted in twelve deaths, fifty injuries, and five thousand afflicted with temporary blindness of some sort."

"Keep going, Noah," said Shaheed Ali, Jack Dylan's right-hand man. Shaheed was lieutenant on the task force and its only Muslim. He and Arya Khan became "an item" following her rescue. Their relationship was the talk of the task force. Shaheed refused to provide the level of prurient detail his nosy and obnoxious colleagues were interested in, which caused them to be more curious and more obnoxious. Such was life in the brotherhood in blue.

"It was used more recently in Syria last April, where more than ninety civilians were killed by the Syrian air force rockets of Bashar al-Assad. United Nations weapons inspectors have confirmed this incident. This stuff is lethal, guys. Sarin is a clear, colorless, tasteless liquid. Exposure to as little as a couple of drops of it in liquid form might cause death. It is incredibly volatile, turns to gas at room temperature and can penetrate the skin. It attacks the nervous system, over-stimulating nerves that control muscle and gland functions. Sarin is almost thirty times deadlier than cyanide, if you can believe that.

"A victim might inhale or ingest it or might be exposed to it through skin or eye contact. It can remain on an affected person's clothing for thirty minutes or so, which will not only expose that person but all the people he or she comes in contact with for that period." Noah stopped and surveyed the room. His colleagues were digesting the information, in stunned disbelief.

"What happens to someone exposed?" Shaheed asked.

"The victim will first experience a runny nose, chest tightness, and eye problems. After those initial symptoms, the person becomes nauseous and begins to drool as he or she loses muscle control in the mouth and throat. The next progression is full-fledged vomiting, loss of body functions, perhaps twitching, shaking, and jerking. Finally, the victim chokes, convulses, and dies from asphyxiation. The whole thing is over within minutes of exposure," replied Noah.

Jack rose and began to pace around the room, thinking, indifferent to the presence of the others, virtually ignoring them, muttering to himself. He was a distinguished-looking middle-aged man who was graying at the temples. Being a no-nonsense cop, he took this threat very seriously. Because of Arya Khan, Shaheed Ali, and the events of last year, Jack became a better cop, someone more aware of racism and bigotry in his community, and someone whom the citizens respected.

Suddenly, he stopped pacing and sat down at the head of the table, eyeballing his colleagues.

"These internet ramblings are obviously not enough to do anything with at the moment." Turning to Noah, he said, "Noah, you and your team continue to monitor all internet activity. We need more details. Shaheed, I want you to investigate all white supremacist or nationalist groups in the area. I know the activity among such groups has been increasing over the past year. Look for which groups are most active in the Detroit Metropolitan area and which have close ties with Blaine and The Conservative Council. We are still recovering from the last incident. We have to stop this plot if that's what it is. We have to stop it cold before it gains any traction."

"Got it, boss," replied Shaheed.

"And by the way, Shaheed, get together with Noah and investigate whether or not the threat may be foreign rather than domestic. Sarin may have been invented in Germany, but its recent use has been limited to Middle Eastern countries and Islamic terrorists. The noise on the web could be a smokescreen for all we know. Better to be safe than sorry."

"Understood."

Jack turned from his men and gazed out onto Michigan Avenue. It was a dreary spring day. The nasty weather mirrored how he was feeling after hearing the news of another potential terrorist attack in his beloved city.

The leaves on the trees were in bloom. Dark clouds still blanketed the sky. A storm recently passed. Jack could hear an occasional angry horn as drivers weaved in and out of stop-and-go traffic.

Commuters with their morning cups of coffee hurried along the sidewalks and streets of the city. The enveloping fog was eerie, like a tightening vice, given the possibility of a sarin gas attack in Dearborn proper. Was the fog a sign of evil about to descend on the city? Jack was startled out of his deep, trancelike state by Shaheed Ali.

"Boss? Jack? Earth to Jack?" Shaheed said, amused.

Jack shook himself back into the meeting and immediately turned to Andy Toller, a new cop on the task force. His primary talent was research and operational planning. Andy replaced Asher Granger, once a good cop and a trusted friend. Granger, it turned out, was more invested in the white nationalist agenda than being a loyal officer of the law. Ultimately, Benjamin Blaine killed him after Asher attempted to betray Blaine.

"Andy," Jack continued, "I need you to get me everything you can on a black-market distribution of chemicals. If someone wanted to smuggle sarin gas into the city, how would they do it? Where are the obvious and less obvious points of entry? How would they weaponize it? Talk to narcotics officers in all local police departments. Talk to undercover operatives and snitches. I want to get a handle on the situation before making any decisions involving the Feds and Homeland Security. Got it?" Jack was determined -- all business.

"Got it, boss. Glad to be of service," said Andy, pleased to be seeing some action and excited to prove himself to Jack and the others.

"Anybody have anything to add?" Jack asked, looking around the room. Silence.

"Then let's get to work. Sarin…shit! We must stop these guys…again."

The men nodded, stone-faced. Was it déjà vu all over again?

## Chapter Two

The Free America Party was a white supremacist/white nationalist organization headquartered in Lexington, Kentucky. An evil bigot and anti-Semite by the name of Barton Breitner chaired the organization. It was not a large group, but it was an active and angry one, livid over the recent events in Dearborn. Bart was a disciple of Benjamin Blaine, and his group was a splintered faction of the Conservative Council. Retribution for the Council's downfall was the reason for the Party members' meeting on a dark, foggy morning in Howell, Michigan.

Howell is Livingston County's seat, located northwest of Detroit and southeast of Lansing, nearly halfway in between Michigan's largest city and its capital. It's a small city, home to numerous festivals and events. People travel to Howell for its famous holiday parades. The city even placed second in a national newspaper's "10 Best Main Streets" contest.

But Howell is also known for a dark side -- in particular, its long association with the KKK. A white supremacist leader and Michigan Grand Dragon named Robert Miles regularly held KKK gatherings on his Howell farm. Miles died in 1992, but "gatherings" have continued well into the twenty-first century.

During Miles' lifetime, few ever questioned or criticized his behavior or rhetoric. Over the last several decades, citizens stepped up, and the dark perception of their city began to change. Still, many knew the history. Miles' legacy and Howell's "split personality" were important symbolic reasons why Breitner chose to hold the meeting there.

Fifteen middle-aged white men crammed around a small table in a conference room at the Belview Inn on Barnhardt Drive. Breitner led the meeting. He was much younger than the eighty-five-year-old Blaine, and his identity as a white nationalist was far less transparent.

While Blaine and his men were unkempt, long-haired bikers with multiple tattoos (including swastikas) all over their bodies, Breitner and his group looked and dressed more like businessmen or professionals on a casual-dress retreat. Breitner, as an example, had well-groomed dark hair and was physically fit. In his khakis and polo shirt, he looked like a country club member who just completed a round of golf. Breitner had an authoritative air, a presence that defied disrespect. With Michelob in hand, Breitner addressed the group. The moment he stood, the room fell silent.

"We all know what happened to Ben Blaine, and I'm certain most, if not all, of you are aware of the parties responsible," he said. They nodded in agreement.

"I refuse to allow their actions to go unpunished. So, I've called all of you here to discuss our revenge strategy."

Breitner chose the participants carefully. All were very dedicated to the cause, loyal to him, and would blindly follow his orders, even those that imperiled their own life.

"What's the plan, Bart? What do you have in mind?" a member asked.

"Have all of you familiarized yourselves with sarin gas?"

Breitner looked around the room. Confused looks abounded. All read the memo and recognized sarin as a chemical weapon, but they struggled to imagine how they could access it. Only one man, unnoticed at that moment of revelation, seemed shocked at the mention of sarin.

"Sarin has been used in the Middle East, most recently by the Syrian government against the rebels. It's a gas that attacks a person's nervous system and causes almost immediate nausea, headaches, and blurred vision. Those exposed convulse, lose consciousness, and die shortly afterward. It all happens pretty quickly."

"Damn," replied one stunned attendee.

"So, what's that got to do with us?" another asked.

"What if I told you I could get my hands on enough sarin to wipe out the entire Dearborn Police Department and every worshipper at a certain Dearborn mosque?" Breitner replied.

"How do you plan to accomplish that?"

"I have a lead on a supply of the gas that was supposed to be destroyed. As luck would have it, some brilliant bureaucrat decided to keep and store it in a secure warehouse in Virginia. A single guard stands on duty at any given time. One of the guards happens to be one of us. He has no record, and he is willing to look the other way either while we take what we need or help us confiscate the gas," Breitner replied.

Every single member sat in stunned silence. They weren't shocked Bart Breitner would use sarin gas on American citizens. They were shocked it was so readily available and guarded by someone loyal to Breitner.

"Sarin?" One of them shouted. "Guarded by a solitary man in Arlington who is one of us? God Bless America!"

"This is perfect," said another. "We pretend to overwhelm the guard, knock him out or something, and that way, he might still be in play if we ever need him again." Breitner and the others liked the idea. But the man, who was previously aghast at the mention of sarin, spoke out as the lone voice of reason.

"What do any of you really know about this?" he asked. "I was in Iraq and Syria, and I've seen what this type of stuff can do to people. I'm probably the only one in this room who knows firsthand how dangerous chemical weapons are. I saw a whole lot of suffering. It is a terrible way to die. I get the whole revenge thing, but we must draw a line somewhere. How do you plan to contain it so innocent people don't get hurt? Isn't there some other way?"

To an outsider, he seemed to be speaking common sense. To the group, he came across as a skeptic. Breitner, however, remained diplomatic.

"Of course, there are other ways, Stone," replied Breitner. "But we have access to this stuff now, and these assholes need to answer for

Ben. We're working on the issues, Stone. We won't pull the trigger until we have all the answers. Having said that, if a few civilians must die for the cause…"

Jonathan Stone was not intimidated and would not be silenced considering the seriousness of the group's contemplated actions. He answered with a hostile tone that surprised the others in the room.

"What does that mean, Bart? How do you define a 'few civilians'? Five? Ten? You can't just fly off the damn handle without considering all the consequences, Bart. I've seen lots of death in my life, caused a lot of it, too, and I sure as hell don't care about cops or camel jockeys dying. But these chemical weapons…you guys have no idea what you're talking about, let alone what you're dealing with."

Breitner was done listening to Stone's bullshit. This was war, and the rules of war applied. "Shut the fuck up, Stone. I did my damn research, and I don't have time to hear you run down every scenario. You're worried about casualties? *This is about casualties.* If some others go down too, that's a grim reminder not to cross us. We have access to the stuff now, so *now* is the time to act."

But even Bart Breitner could not silence Stone. He was terrified of the group's contemplated actions. "I've got to be honest, Bart. I'm not a big fan of this plan. If we carry it out, the guys you choose to release the gas better really know what they are doing."

With a contemptuous smile, Breitner replied, "You've got some balls, Stone, I'll say that for you. You've also got the experience. Great! You get to lead the release team. Now shut up and listen."

Another man decided to change the subject. "What's the timetable? Who do we have in D.C. or Virginia besides the guard?"

"We do this ourselves," replied Breitner. "We'll drive to Virginia, grab the stuff, and transport it back here. The Virginia cops or the Feds will think something is about to happen in Virginia, and the local cops will have no idea the shit is about to hit the fan in Dearborn. As to the timetable, I would like to get my hands on the gas sometime in the next thirty to sixty days. We don't have to hit the mosque or the police station that quickly, but I want to have the sarin ready for when we do. Let those cop fuckers try to guess what we're going to do and when and where we are going to do it."

"Sounds like a plan," another said with a sinister smile crossing his face. "I like it. I can't wait to see how much heat there is after the local cops or the Feds discover the stuff is missing. Afterward, we can monitor their movements and observe where their efforts are directed. I'll bet they fall all over themselves thinking this is for a terrorist act in D.C. or Virginia. Their priority will be to protect the President and the Congress. No one would ever dream it's in a truck headed for Dearborn."

"Exactly," replied a smiling Breitner. He continued: "We keep this on the down low. We'll be crossing four state lines and driving on toll roads. There will be more traffic cams than usual. If they suspect anything, we're screwed. I suggest renting a small van–indistinguishable, with fake plates and the works. We have our guy in Arlington leave us another – larger, different, but just as nondescript – to pick up the gas from the warehouse. Then, we load it back into the van we go out in and dump the Arlington one. As soon as the cops realize the gas is missing, they will be looking for suspect vehicles around Virginia. By the time they figure anything out, given the small chance they do, we'll have already made it back."

"We will need about four to six men. Do we have any volunteers?"

Every hand in the room but one, Stone's, shot up in support. Breitner noticed Stone hadn't volunteered. *Is he going to keep challenging me? Will he be a problem?* Breitner looked directly at him.

"Don't worry, Stone. You've already won your place on the team. For the rest of you, we'll draw straws. Peterson, you make some contacts to get us an untraceable van and plates."

"I'll take care of it," replied Peterson.

"Then we have the beginning of a plan. Remember, limit communication over the phone and internet, but if you do, use the codes we have established. Peterson, Stone, the straw winners, and I will all meet back here tomorrow. The rest of you can check out and go home. We will notify you if and when we need you. And of course, we will need all of you when we implement the plan to release the sarin, got it? This meeting is adjourned."

Revenge was at hand. No one at the table noticed the look of terror on Jon Stone's face.

# Chapter Three

A couple of days later, Jack and his team were sitting in the conference room reassessing the sarin threat. No new information developed, but Jack insisted on constant updates out of caution. His intercom buzzed. It was the Chief.

"Jack, may I see you in my office?"

Jack proceeded over to Chief Acker's office and sat down beside the desk. Across from him were two serious-looking individuals -- a man and a woman, in dark suits. Jack noticed the man first. He was clearly the younger of the two and despite a false air of confidence, must have been new to this line of work. With his hair neatly combed and his new suit, he was evidently trying to compensate for his age and inexperience. Jack turned to the woman. She was alluring yet intense, arguably more severe than Jack himself. Closer in age to Jack, she was at least ten years her partner's senior. In stark contrast to her partner, she exuded the confidence of someone with much more experience. With her hair pulled back in a messy bun and subtle wrinkles in her jacket, she was a mirror of Jack's own stress. He knew that look. *What was going on?*

"Jack," said Acker. These are Agents Clare Gibson and Pete Westmore. They're with the FBI's Detroit Field Office."

*Great -- Feds, I should have known.*

"Nice to meet you both," he replied, respectfully. "To what do I owe the pleasure?"

"We've recently discovered your community has been linked online to a potential sarin gas threat," replied Gibson.

*Well, shit.*

Gibson continued. "A few days ago, a cryptic message appeared on a dark web forum commonly associated with domestic terror groups and white supremacist organizations. There was mention of both the gas and Dearborn, particularly police officers and, we believe, the Muslim community. After what you all faced last year, the bureau felt it was in everyone's best interest to inform you."

"What's the risk assessment, Agent Gibson?" asked the Chief. Thankfully for Jack, the task force was a unique unit in the Dearborn Police Department, and unsubstantiated evidence didn't require the Chief's approval. Up to now, Jack chose to leave the chief in the dark.

"We have placed your city on our alert list, but, according to information gathered thus far, the risk seems minimal. Larger cities see these kinds of threats all the time, and given Dearborn's ethnic composition and recent history, it isn't at all surprising. We will keep watching for online details, and our office will be standing by if necessary. All we ask is you remain alert and notify us if anything seems off."

"Well, thank you very much for informing us," replied Chief Acker. "Captain Dylan is the head of our new terrorism task force. The force keeps tabs on any significant threats to the community, and Jack's team is more than willing to work with you. Aren't you, Jack?"

Jack's mind was spinning for the past several minutes. In fact, he missed most of what the agent and the Chief said.

"Jack?"

"Huh?"

"Your team will stay connected with the bureau, right?"

"Oh. Of course, we will Chief. We can handle it, Agent…um…" Jack stuttered.

"Gibson. But please, Captain, you don't need to do anything. We're uniquely qualified to handle any significant threat that may develop. Dearborn and its police department only need to do what they normally do. A higher level of vigilance is probably wise."

*What we normally do? Handling terrorist threats have become the new normal.*

"Our card," said Westmore, handing Jack a business card.

Jack took the card and eyed Westmore. *Young guy. Recruit? Just along for the ride?*

The two agents stood and headed for the door. Jack was reeling as the Chief thanked the agents again and showed them out. Jack was startled from his thoughts as Acker returned to his office.

"Well, Jack. Let's hope nothing comes of this, but you still better alert your team."

"Right, Chief." Jack returned to the conference room wondering what to do next.

\*\*\*

After a week of silence, Noah detected some new online chatter. He barged into Jack Dylan's office, interrupting a meeting with Chief Acker.

"Oh, uh, sorry. I didn't know you were busy, Jack. I'll come back later."

"Hold on, Noah. Chief Acker and I want to hear what you've got. The sarin thing is exactly what we're discussing," Jack said.

"Yes, Thompson," said the Chief. "Have a seat and tell us what you've found."

"There seems to be some connection here between Dearborn and Arlington…Virginia, I think."

"What makes you say that?" Jack asked.

"Because both cities came up in the same conversation, although I couldn't make out the context."

"What exactly was the message, Noah?" Jack asked.

"Well, it wasn't much, but these two guys were talking about a meeting in Howell and when they would be driving out to Arlington to pick up 'the stuff.'" Noah paused.

"Virginia?"

"They didn't *say* Virginia, Jack. They said Arlington. There are Arlingtons all over the United States. It could be Texas, but it could be anywhere. My guess would be Virginia. If for some reason our government got ahold of sarin gas from Syria and wanted to store it somewhere as a temporary, pre-destruction measure after it reached our shores, where would they store it? Near the nation's capital or in Texas somewhere?"

"But they never actually mentioned Virginia, correct Noah?"

"No Jack. They said Arlington and only Arlington."

"Then, just so we're certain about the location, here's what I want you to do, Noah. Put together a small team of tech guys. Find out how many Arlingtons there are…"

"Whoa. Stop, Jack," Chief Acker interrupted.

"But Chief, we have to know which…"

"It's great Noah found some more intel, but we promised Agent Gibson anything we learned would be turned over to the FBI."

"I know Chief, but I'm not going to provide any half-assed or unverified intel. That's not how I run my team. If they knew about Arlington, then the threat is credible, and they would have told us. The fact they haven't speaks volumes. We know something they don't. Rather than waste time sharing information and risk duplicating efforts, we'll find the correct Arlington for them and give the Feds a head start finding the gas."

Acker pondered the suggestion. "Alright, Jack, I'll go along. I trust you."

Jack was surprised Acker bought his thinking.

"But you let the Feds know the minute you narrow the location down."

"Of course, Chief."

"This Arlington thing sounds like a promising lead. Follow it up. Leave no stone unturned. Aside from the FBI, alert adjacent community units if necessary. We are all in. Find these guys and stop this madness."

Acker left the office. Once he was out of earshot, Noah asked, "We aren't calling the Feds, are we, Jack?"

"Nope."

# Chapter Four

Noah Thompson assembled the best tech team he could find. They identified at least thirty-seven different Arlingtons in the United States. All of them were cities and villages except Arlington County in Virginia. Though Noah and his team could not officially rule out any of the thirty-seven, the only two that made reasonable sense by size and location were in Texas and Virginia. Due to its proximity to D.C. and coastal ports, Noah continued to believe Virginia was the best bet. Logic was a computer nerd's best companion.

The group continued to monitor web chatter, but there was virtually none -- nothing narrowing down the possibilities by anything more than gut instinct. Frustration was palpable. Instinctually, Noah felt Virginia made the most sense. But Jack wanted certainty, not gut instinct.

Searching the dark web brought its own set of unique challenges. Its users utilized The Onion Router (or TOR) and other anonymity networks to access largely unrecognized sites while leaving a minimal IP footprint. Governments worldwide have tried, for years, to take down dark web crime with mixed success, often reluctantly using TOR themselves to do so. It was far less common among local law enforcement, but not every city was Dearborn and not every techie was Noah Thompson. Noah even created his own enhanced TOR, which he not so cleverly called ThOR (Thompson's Onion Router). His network allowed the team to go on the dark web under encryption, just like regular users, while also being able to track IP footprints left by others. Noah's past use of ThOR proved it could crack any shield of anonymity. He believed if anyone were leaving behind information about the sarin attack, he'd find it. Yet, they ran ThOR for days, and nothing turned up.

As Noah was about to wrap things up for the day, one of his team members excitedly ran into his office.

"It's Virginia, Noah! We're positive!" Oliver Levine exclaimed. "There were messages exchanged between two IP addresses, one in Howell and one in Arlington, Virginia. There wasn't much chatter, but the person in Arlington confirmed renting a black cargo van. I presume that's how they plan to transport the sarin."

"This is terrific, Oliver. You guys have made my day. I was not looking forward to my daily briefing with Dylan. Thank everyone for me. Rounds at McShane's, I'm buying."

"We'll take you up on that, Noah."

\*\*\*

On his way out, Noah stopped by Jack's office where Jack was meeting with Shaheed.

"Guys, we confirmed Arlington, Virginia. I'm buying rounds at McShane's. You coming?"

"Thanks, but I'll pass," Jack replied.

"I might come over in a bit," Shaheed answered.

"Alright. See you tomorrow, Jack." Noah turned the corner and left.

Jack paused before continuing. He and Shaheed were debating whether to release their information of the threat to the public.

"I'm telling you, Shaheed. The Muslim community is in serious danger. I can't fathom not telling them. The mosque has already been attacked once. We can't allow another. It is our duty to protect them."

"Jack, I understand. Not only am I a cop, but I'm also Muslim, and I live in Dearborn. I understand the risks, probably more than anyone. Just the same, I wouldn't do it. We can't confirm this attack is going to happen. All we have is some dark web chatter."

"And you believe the chatter is harmless? Are you seriously willing to take that chance?"

"Of course not, but the FBI knows about the threat, and I'm sure they are on top of it. Besides, what do you do when they catch wind you warned everybody and started a panic over potentially nothing? You want to deal with the wrath of the Feds?"

"We are a hundred steps ahead of the FBI on this!"

Shaheed just stared back.

"Okay, maybe only a few steps, but it's a lot more than they have. Tell me, if we could prove the threat was fully credible and currently in development, would you agree the mosque should close for a few days as a precaution?"

"Yes, but that's up to Imam Ghafari."

"As a member and not as a cop, would you want to be forewarned of the closure impeding your religious practices and informed of why?"

"Yes." Shaheed could tell where Jack was going and had to admit Jack's determination was admirable. "If you can convince the imam of the threat and the need to warn everybody, then, by all means, go ahead."

"Thanks."

***

The following Friday, Jack Dylan attended an evening of worship at Imam Ghafari's Mosque of America.

Jack stood off to one side and listened as the imam introduced him to the congregation. He was well known for leading the mission that captured Benjamin Blaine and freed Arya Khan. Imam Ghafari praised Allah for delivering Jack to the community. Jack was going to be a "guest speaker" for the evening.

By Islamic tradition, the men and women of the congregation would worship in separate rooms, but for this "pre-worship" event they were gathered in the same prayer hall. Imam Ghafari considered Jack's message to be *that* important.

Per Shaheed's suggestion, Jack consulted Ghafari about whether or not to warn the community, and after careful consideration, the imam shared Jack's sentiment. He believed erring on the side of caution was vital to the safety of the community even if it scared or angered the people.

As Jack scanned the congregation, he was mindful some of those in attendance were Syrian refugees. These brave souls left everything in their home country, immigrating to Dearborn to escape threats akin to those they were now facing. *How ironic is that?*

"Thank you, Imam Ghafari. My friends and neighbors, I have come today, on your day of prayer, because I have something serious to discuss with you. The Dearborn Police have reason to believe there may be a terrorist threat targeted at our city, and your community in particular."

The congregation let out an audible gasp. The congregation's fear was palpable.

As Dylan continued, they were quiet and attentive.

"We do not have any specifics yet, but after what happened last year, I take all threats, big or small, specified or unspecified, very seriously. We are working diligently to determine the credibility of the information we have found. If we believe the mosque to be at any significant risk, we may close it for a few days as a precautionary measure. I understand that may interrupt your worship, but it is a last resort and in the interest of your safety. We don't want you to be alarmed, but we *do* want you to be observant. If you see something, even the smallest thing, you need to say something. Call the Dearborn Police or the Crime Watch Hotline immediately. Even Imam Ghafari will know what to do."

"Captain Dylan? Arya Khan here." Arya Khan stood. She was dressed in a full *burqa*, and unrecognizable to Jack.

"Yes, Arya? It's nice to see you. I wish it were under different circumstances," replied Jack.

Addressing the congregation rather than pointedly pressing Jack, Arya said, "Brothers and sisters. Captain Jack Dylan saved my life. He saved our city and our community. He cares about us. The captain is part of the same task force as Shaheed Ali, who many of you know. Please listen to what Captain Dylan has to say and take it very seriously."

Another shouted anonymously, "Do you know anything more than you have told us, Captain Dylan?"

"No, I'm afraid I don't. As I said, the threat is unspecified. But it might be a matter of importance. We simply don't know enough yet."

"What do you want us to do, Captain?" Jack recognized the voice as Arya's. He found her presence and her questions comforting.

"I want you to be careful. I want you to pay attention. If you see something that doesn't seem quite right, call the police, call the hotline, or call the Imam. Call all three, if you prefer. But please, don't ignore anything you see or hear that does not seem quite right."

The back and forth went on for a few minutes more, and it became apparent to the congregation Jack knew very little other than the fact an unspecified internet threat alerted the police to the possibility of some type of attack. Jack Dylan would stay all night to answer questions, but he didn't know much more than what he'd already told them. Imam Ghafari called a halt to the frantic and repetitive barrage of questions. He signaled this evening's special session was over, thanked Jack for coming, and watched the women retreat to a separate room for the traditional *Salah*. During prayer, a general sense of uneasiness permeated both rooms. The congregation was warned. Jack fervently hoped those warnings would prove unnecessary.

***

After prayer was over, Arya Khan and her parents strolled over to Jack. Her parents, Hamid and Riah Khan, loved Jack.

What couple wouldn't be grateful to someone who helped save their daughter's life? The fact Jack didn't believe Arya's original story and arrested, jailed, and nearly tried her for murder was all but forgotten.

"Anything else we should know, Captain Dylan? Anything else you want to tell the 'crime virgin?'" Arya chuckled. 'Crime virgin' was a term Jack used mockingly to describe her during the Blaine investigation.

"Arya, the captain deserves your respect," admonished Riah.

"Mama, Jack knows I'm kidding. Don't you, Captain?"

"Yes, Arya. I know, and I'm happy to hear you joke. Your life could have turned out very differently, you know."

"I know. I will always be grateful to you, Shaheed, and Zack." Zachary Blake was the prominent Metro Detroit attorney who represented Arya during her trial. Zachary's investigative and courtroom skills not only brought about her acquittal but also helped prevent her parents from being deported.

"Thank you, Arya. Have you spoken to Zack recently?"

"No, I haven't heard from him in a quite a while."

"Well, if you do, tell him 'hello' for me."

"I will, Jack. Is there anything I can do to help beyond what you asked of us? I'd like to be involved."

"No, Arya -- just pay attention. That goes for all of you. Pay careful attention. I don't want a situation like what happened last year to happen again, now or anytime in the future."

"Believe me, Jack. After last year, we take *everything* seriously."

"I'm glad to hear it. I have to run," said Jack, more abruptly than he intended. "It was good to see all of you. Next time, hopefully, it will be under better circumstances."

He walked away, leaving Arya and her parents alone. Arya scanned the area intently but saw nothing of concern. She noticed her parents doing the same.

"So, what do you think?" Arya asked her father.

"Only a year ago, a white supremacist bombed our mosque and our museum, kidnapped and tried to kill you. Now, we have a new 'unspecified threat.' What am I supposed to think? I love you, and I praise Allah you are safe and have found a wonderful man like Shaheed. But I worry about these things, Arya. I worry about the future. We must be vigilant."

"Aw, Papa. I love you guys, too. I will be vigilant, I promise. I will be vigilant."

\*\*\*

Zachary Blake sat in the library of his Bloomfield Hills home, pecking away on the keyboard of his MacBook Air, preparing remarks for a television interview on gun control. As he was wrapping up work, his private cell phone rang. Someone from Dearborn was trying to reach him. Since his very public victory with Arya, Zack received many new clients from the area. He answered the phone.

"Zack Blake."

"Zack, it's Arya Khan. I hope I am not disturbing you."

"Arya! So nice to hear from you! You aren't disturbing me at all. How are you? How are your folks?"

"Everyone is fine, Zack, you?"

"Everything is great. What can I do for you?"

"I just wanted to make you aware of a meeting I just attended. Jack Dylan came to the Center to advise us there might be a terrorist threat against the city."

"What kind of threat?"

"Jack wasn't specific, but he told us to be alert, an 'if you see or hear something, say something' sort of thing."

"Sounds like good advice. How can I help? Has someone been arrested?"

"I don't know, Zack, call it woman's intuition or whatever, but can you please reach out to Jack for me? There is more to this than meets the eye."

"I don't understand. This sounds like a police matter."

"I understand, Zack, but something isn't right here. I have a bad feeling."

"Well, I have a hectic week, but I will try to make some time to call Jack, okay?"

"Thanks, Zack. I appreciate it."

"No problem. Call me anytime." Zack's wife, Jennifer walked into the room and put her arms around her husband's from behind his chair. He looked behind and smiled.

"Bye Arya," he said into the phone.

"Arya Khan?" Jennifer asked.

"Yes, she's concerned about Jack Dylan and some kind of threat in Dearborn."

"Not again!"

"Apparently, just some chatter. Arya's worried about Jack for some reason. Woman's intuition, she says."

"Never discount woman's intuition, Zack. That is real."

"I never discount a woman's anything, dear. The world would be a better place if a woman were in charge. I'll reach out to Jack after this interview. For now, I'm exhausted."

Zack pulled her close and kissed her.

"I thought you were exhausted, "replied Jennifer, blushing.

"I am," he replied, innocently. "Let's go to bed."

***

Jack Dylan sat alone in his office, burning the midnight oil. It was one week after his address to the Mosque of America congregation. Jack was gravely concerned. Every day, he checked in with Noah. There was no chatter, not a word on the dark web about sarin gas or a potential attack on Dearborn.

Jack feared silence wasn't a good sign. The eerie calm before the storm reminded him of last year and Ben Blaine.

"Benjamin Blaine," he muttered. *Glad that asshole is locked up for the rest of his miserable life.*

But Jack was not naïve. He knew there were thousands like Blaine across America, spurred to action by the sinister rhetoric of a racist president. Either way, they were equally as dangerous, perhaps more so.

"Sarin gas…" he said to no one in particular. *Sarin is very nasty stuff.* He was terrified of the potential harm this could cause in his city.

"Not on my watch," he muttered. Jack returned to his desktop and the mountain of paperwork he neglected for weeks, on his desk. The phone rang, startling him. He looked down at the telephone. The receiver read, "Caller I.D. blocked." Jack picked it up in the middle of the third ring.

"Dearborn Police. Captain Dylan speaking."

"Jack Dylan? Captain Jack Dylan?" an imposing voice asked on the other end.

"Speaking," Jack replied amiably. "How may I help you, sir?"

"I am almost assuredly risking my life to place this call, Dylan. Before we continue, you need to arrange some serious protection."

Jack sat straight up in his chair. This man, whoever he was, immediately captured Jack's complete attention. "Keep going. I'm listening."

"Protection, Dylan, I need guaranteed protection first. If I'm going to help you, it comes with a price, and it is not negotiable. I want the complete protection package, relocation, the total nine yards. I've got to fucking disappear."

"Well, don't you think any protection you get should depend upon what you have to tell me?"

The man paused, thinking. To Jack, the seconds of silence seemed endless. "Well…" he finally said, "what if I was to tell you a shitload of sarin gas is heading your way and I know the how, when, where, and why? Would that qualify for the protection I'm asking for?"

As Jack quickly stood, his wheeled chair pitched forward, and he stumbled, almost falling to the ground. Papers flew all over his desk.

"Who are you? What do you know and how do you know it?" Jack's mouth spouted as questions as rapidly as they could form in his mind.

"One thing at a time, Dylan. Again, my information comes with a price. Complete immunity and witness protection."

"But I don't have that kind of power. We would have to get a federal prosecutor involved, perhaps the FBI. Where's the sarin gas coming from?"

"I've got nothing to say until we have a deal in place. Mark my words; we don't have a lot of time. This shit is going down fast, and if you stall, even a little bit, it will be too late to stop it."

"I'll do what I can. One way or another, I'll get it done. How much time do I have? How do I get ahold of you?" Jack lamented the fact he was alone. He wished Shaheed or Noah were there to record or, better yet, trace the call.

"You have a week, maybe less. Stay by the phone. I will call you when my deadline is closing. When I do call, you better have what I need, or you will never hear from me again."

"I'll get it done. I promise. At least tell me who you are. Who's behind this plot? Hello? *Hello?*"

As he waited frantically for a response, Jack heard an audible click followed by a dial tone.

# Chapter Five

Since the "hit" on Virginia was identified through ThOR, there was scant chatter or information. Now, out of the blue, Jack got a call. *Was it a coincidence?*

Picking up his phone, Jack summoned Shaheed to his office.

"Some serious shit is about to go down, and it involves the sarin gas issue," said Jack. "I don't want to lose control of the situation, but I am afraid we are going to need the local Feds."

"What's up, Jack? Did Noah find more information?"

Jack shared with Shaheed the recent call and the request for full immunity.

"I agree with you, boss," said Shaheed. "If for no other reason, we don't have the authority to grant immunity."

"No choice but to call Gibson, then, I guess." *Shit!*

\*\*\*

Agent Clare Gibson was out of the office, so Jack was transferred to her boss, Ernest Cobb.

"Captain Dylan, my receptionist said it was a matter of some urgency. What can I do for you?"

"I got an interesting call today regarding the potential sarin gas threat on the Dearborn community."

"I'm listening," replied Cobb.

Jack proceeded to tell Cobb about the call and request for full immunity.

"What is the caller's name?"

"He didn't say. In fact, he didn't give me a lot of details. I told you everything I know."

"What's his motive for calling you, then?"

"As I said, he wants full immunity and protection. He says he won't release any more information until I can guarantee the immunity package. Beyond that, I have no idea."

"We need more, Jack. When do you plan to hear from this guy again?"

"He wasn't specific on that either. He just said a week, maybe less."

"Ok, we will get on this immediately," said Cobb with a sense of urgency in his voice. "I'll send someone over later today to put a tap on your phone. We want to be ready when he calls. I also will have Agent Gibson meet with you to discuss, in advance, what we need you to say to this guy when he calls. We can't have any slip-ups. If this guy is serious, we need to locate the sarin and find out who is orchestrating this plan without media involvement. In the meantime, I will contact Homeland and give them a heads up. If this escalates, we will need them."

Jack was relatively certain if there was a supply of sarin gas somewhere in the United States, it was, most likely, in Arlington, VA. But the exact location, when it was to be stolen, and whether it would cross state lines after the theft, were still unknown. Those were questions only the mystery caller would be able to tell him. He hoped to keep the investigation from the Feds, but with the recent developments, he needed them -- for now.

## Chapter Six

The U.S. Attorney's Office in Detroit serves approximately 6.5 million people in the Eastern District of Michigan's Lower Peninsula. If actions are filed against the United States government in the district, the U.S. Attorney defends the government in federal court. The department also brings civil actions on behalf of the United States and coordinates with local and community law enforcement agencies like the Dearborn police and courts to prevent and/or reduce crime. The office is heavily invested in those tasks.

However, crime prevention and reduction were tough tasks in the current tumultuous political climate. Once Ronald John, an unconventional maverick, assumed the presidency, he fired every U.S. attorney in the country. Cleaning out his predecessors' political appointees hampered the effectiveness of the office, but to RonJohn, the symbolic house-cleaning gesture was important. These abrupt terminations were made for political reasons, and were more symbolic of John's mandate to change Washington. They might have had a devastating effect on federal law enforcement but had no practical or political effect at all. That was because President John failed to appoint successors to those he terminated. As a result, in almost every case, the first assistant assumed his or her former boss's position.

In the Eastern District of Michigan, that first assistant was Daniel Wolfe. As fate would have it, Wolfe was the perfect federal prosecutor for Jack, Cobb, and company. Wolfe was a career government man, having first served as a trial lawyer and chief appellate lawyer at the Oakland County Prosecutor's office. He left Oakland County for an appointment as chief of the U.S. Attorney's Criminal Division. Wolfe would easily understand Jack's dilemma and his need for immunity, protection and relocation deal for the mysterious whistleblower.

Jack Dylan, Shaheed Ali, and Clare Gibson entered the lobby of the mid-rise building in the 200 block of Fort Street in the heart of the downtown business and legal districts. Cobb came through. He got them the meeting with Daniel Wolfe and sent Gibson as his surrogate. Closing the deal was up to Jack and Clare.

The group signed in at the guard's desk. They were checked in by the guard and directed to a bank of elevators.

"You can take those elevators to the seventh floor," he said casually, "or if you're adventurous souls, you can take the steps." He pointed to a door marked "Exit" in the corner of the lobby.

Jack chuckled and thanked the guard as the group turned and walked to the elevators. The old elevator threatened to stop several times on the way up, but it eventually arrived at the seventh floor, which was entirely devoted to the U.S. Attorney's Office. A round receptionist desk sat in the middle of the well-appointed lobby. A female receptionist sat in the center and was talking on the phone as they approached.

After finishing her call, the woman looked up and gruffly addressed the group. Each provided his or her name, and Jack indicated they had an appointment with Mr. Wolfe. The receptionist picked up the phone and announced the group's arrival into the receiver. After a few minutes, a tall, thin, distinguished-looking gray-haired man wearing an expensive gray suit appeared at the door of the anteroom. *Anyone could have picked this guy out as the attorney,* thought Jack.

"Welcome, my friends, glad you could make it on short notice," he said. "I'm Daniel Wolfe. Come on in. Can we get you anything? Coffee, tea, water, soft drinks?"

Gibson and Shaheed motioned no; Jack asked for a cup of black coffee. Gibson introduced the two police veterans to Wolfe.

"Sandra?" Wolfe said to the receptionist. "A cup of black coffee for Captain Dylan here?"

"No problem, sir," she replied, much more pleasantly than she treated his visitors. She knew whose ass to kiss.

The group followed Wolfe into his windowed office. Before them sat a large executive desk and a terrific, panoramic view of downtown

Detroit. Jack walked to the window, complimented Wolfe on his fantastic view, and gazed out at the city he called 'home' for most of his life. The city was undergoing rapid redevelopment, especially in the sports and entertainment district along Woodward Avenue. The district was home to all four major sports teams. As an avid sports fan and a lifetime resident of the Detroit area, Jack was proud and impressed.

As he turned toward the others, Jack could not help but notice Wolfe's uncluttered desk. *This is a far cry from the mess in my office. How do other busy people keep their desks so clean? What's their secret?*

At that moment, Sandra walked in with Jack's coffee. Wolfe asked her to hold his calls and invited everyone to be seated.

"Again, welcome. I understand we might have some trouble brewing in Dearborn."

The visitors agreed Gibson would do most of the talking, at least at the beginning of the meeting. "That appears to be true, Dan. I wish it weren't, but this appears to be a serious threat."

"From our telephone conversation, I understand the Dearborn Police have been monitoring chatter about a sarin gas attack of some sort. Things were quiet until, out of the blue, Jack Dylan here gets an anonymous phone call suggesting an attack of some type is imminent. Does that about sum things up?"

*No nonsense,* thought Jack. *He gets right to the point. I like that.*

"Yes, Dan, that's about it in a nutshell. Jack took the call. He can explain it to you better than I can," replied Gibson.

"And this caller wants blanket immunity for a crime yet to be committed?"

"Yes, sir, that's correct," replied Jack.

"Call me Dan."

"Sure, Dan." Jack liked Wolfe. He made Jack feel very at ease and seemed to understand the importance of the situation without engaging in the usual political crap.

"Have you been able to narrow down the potential list of terrorist groups on our watch list? More importantly, why would this guy call you?"

"I have no idea other than an educated guess, or a cop's hunch if you will."

"All well and good, but not nearly enough to grant blanket immunity to a potential terrorist. How do you know he's not playing you?"

"I think this guy has seen combat in the Middle East, Iraq, maybe Syria. There was an underlying fear in his voice like he encountered sarin or something like it in his past. Someone who has witnessed, first hand, the effects of this stuff on human beings, would be terrified of what might happen."

"So, why doesn't he just come clean now, and we can stop these guys in their tracks before anyone gets hurt?" Wolfe inquired.

"Because he doesn't trust us, and he's terrified of something or someone. I am certain of both. Whoever our whistleblower is afraid of, there is probably no limit to what this bad boy would do to him if he discovered the caller's identity. I watched the white nationalist Benjamin Blaine kill Asher Granger, one of my officers turned traitor, in cold blood."

"An immunity deal depends upon the information. If the information is reliable and the operation is successful, we can consider immunity. Not before."

"I told him this same thing, but it's a non-starter. He wants a deal in place *before* he spills his guts. He wants to disappear, sooner than later. If I don't have what he wants when he calls, we'll never hear from him again and, worse, we leave the city at the mercy of a terrorist with a supply of chemical weapons."

"That's not the way it works, Jack."

"I understand, Dan, but that's the only way it will work in this case," Jack pleaded.

Gibson spoke up. "Dan, I've been involved in these kinds of investigations long enough to know every case and every criminal is different. If Jack is right, I don't think we have any choice. Hell, we don't even know if Jack's caller belongs to a terrorist faction or not.

What's the downside in closing the deal? If nothing goes down, no harm no foul. But if he's been telling the truth and we can prevent a sarin gas attack on U.S. soil…" Clare stopped, abruptly, to let the consequences of doing nothing sink in.

"It's hard to argue with your logic, Clare. But even if I agree, I still need to run it by the big guns in Washington. I'm sure you understand."

"Of course, I understand. But how long will this take? We don't have much time. Will it have to go to Attorney General Parley? Surely this does not reach the President." Clare knew Jack didn't want the President involved. The whole Arya Khan affair severely damaged Ronald John's presidency. Neither John nor Parley had love or sympathy for the citizens of Dearborn or its cops.

Wolfe understood the concern. "I don't think this goes that far. To be sure, there is a national security issue here, but not many of these negotiations reach the upper echelon."

"Good to hear. I have it on good authority Parley has no love for Detroit, or Dearborn either," said Gibson.

"What exactly is the timetable?" Wolfe asked.

"We need this yesterday," replied Clare. "Jack is supposed to get a call from this guy sometime within the week."

"Then you guys need to get the hell out of my office and let me get to work," said Wolfe with a smile. "I offer no guarantees, but there are still some rational people left in the Justice Department. If approved, documents by mid-day tomorrow, Clare?"

"That's great, Dan, thanks," said Gibson.

Wolfe escorted the visitors out and immediately returned to his office.

*Wolfe took this seriously, and Gibson seems willing to work with us. Maybe we can stop a potential attack,* Jack thought.

They took the elevator down to the lobby, signed out and thanked the guard. There was stone silence as they exited through the revolving door. Once outside, Jack turned to Gibson and asked her to thank Cobb for getting them in to see Wolfe on short notice.

"Good meeting, would you agree, gentlemen?" Gibson asked, turning to Jack and Shaheed.

"As good as we could have expected," Shaheed replied.

"Okay, then. Once we receive the docs from Wolfe's office, we will set up a remote office at your place and set up a surveillance and tech team for the call."

"Excuse me..." Jack replied, agitated.

"Come on, guys. This is a federal matter. It involves a terrorist threat and the transfer of chemical weapons across state lines. The FBI has jurisdiction and will be taking over the case. Surely you expected this. We're grateful for the tip and your work so far. We're counting on your continued cooperation."

"Gibson, there is no chance you are freezing us out of our own investigation. This guy called *me*, specifically. And if I can actually arrange a meeting, it is *me* he is going to expect at the meet. We have the best local terrorist task force in the state. We have this, Clare."

"Sorry, Jack, it's a federal matter, and Fed trumps State. You want to stick around? We could use the backup, but this will be our show, our equipment, our trace, our men and women. And if there is a meeting, I will be right there with you."

"No way...No way, dammit."

"You got Cobb involved and asked for our help with Wolfe. The boss stuck his neck way out for you, and now it's his neck on the line. It's our agency and our rules. Are you in or out? Make a choice."

Jack sighed. He didn't like being pushed around like this. Jack felt betrayed. But he also knew Gibson was right. In a turf battle with the Feds, the Feds *always* win. *Besides...*

He extended his hand to Gibson. "We're in," he replied. *We have all the intel.*

\*\*\*

After parting company with Clare Gibson, Jack and Shaheed walked in silent thought toward the parking lot. Shaheed spoke first.

"So, what do you think, Jack?"

"Wolfe took the threat seriously. We'll get the deal…"

"But?"

"You heard her. She wants us to take a back seat, a subordinate role. This is *our case*. We are good at this stuff. Besides, Shaheed, I'm still not comfortable with how Parley and the President will feel when they hear the attack is expected in Dearborn."

"But it's directed at cops. They are all for 'law and order.'"

"I know, but it's *Dearborn*. Those two don't have to search their memories very far to remember what happened. Neither was happy about how the Khan case got resolved, and we were a big reason why it resolved the way it did. To top it off, Shaheed, you're *dating* the woman they blame for the whole mess!"

"How would they know *that?* Besides, I think you might be underestimating Parley, Jack. His early record on racial justice may be spotty, but this is a homegrown terrorist threat."

"Maybe so, but past actions speak louder than any moderate tone he has adopted lately. According to Wolfe, this immunity deal will never reach either of their desks, anyway. And I can handle Gibson." said Jack. "You hungry? Bucharest Grill on Michigan Avenue is supposed to have terrific Middle Eastern food."

"Lead the way, boss. You buying?"

"Sure."

The men changed direction and walked toward Michigan Avenue. Because it was halfway between lunchtime and dinnertime, they were seated immediately. They ordered drinks, and when they arrived, Jack proposed a toast.

"To immunity," replied Shaheed, holding up his glass.

"To beating the Feds to Arlington," said Jack.

Shaheed almost choked mid-sip. "Amen, Jack. Amen." The two men laughed, held their glasses in the air, and then brought them to their lips. They finished their drinks, ordered another round, and enjoyed a fabulous meal while discussing their planned subterfuge. They also watched the last few innings of a rare afternoon Detroit

Tiger's game and shot the breeze with other suffering fans, critical of the team's poor play this year and its wholesale trades of prominent players. The meal was a welcome respite from the looming threat of disaster to come. And the Tigers beat the White Sox, the other shit team in their division, on a walk-off home run by Miguel Cabrera. Perhaps there was hope for the world.

# Chapter Seven

Two days later, half a dozen cops sat in the squad room waiting for the telephone to ring. Jack Dylan, Shaheed Ali, Andy Toller, and Noah Thompson were present, as were Ernest Cobb and Clare Gibson. Andy and Noah were ogling Gibson, but she seemed to be either oblivious or indifferent to the attention. Jack figured she was used to it. *She is nice looking, though.*

Noah was impressed with the advanced tracking and recording equipment the Feds provided for the call. He was equally impressed with the tech who introduced him to the equipment. Noah was a quick study and was engaged in assuring both the principal and backup recording devices were operating correctly.

Suddenly, the phone rang. The trace was set, and everyone simultaneously picked up respective receivers. *Game on!*

"Dearborn Police Department, Captain Jack Dylan speaking." The others were breathless, their hands cupping their receivers.

"Do we have a deal?" the caller asked, immediately getting down to business.

"It depends on the information. If terrorists are planning to release sarin gas or anything like sarin, and your information prevents such an attack from happening, you will get everything you asked for."

"In writing? Guaranteed?"

"In writing and guaranteed by the U.S. Attorney's office."

"If I agree to meet with you, will you bring the written immunity deal?"

"What's your name?"

"Leave that blank. I'll fill it in at the meeting."

*This guy is careful, and...terrified.* "Will do," Jack replied. "When do you want to meet?"

"8:00 a.m. sharp. Jefferson Marina. There will be a sailboat docked in front of Sinbad's Restaurant.

The name of the boat is *Jillian's Dream*. If you're not there, I'm sailing away without you."

"I'll be there," replied Jack, "with the U.S. Attorney and the written immunity deal."

"You and the lawyer, no one else or the deal's off."

The phone clicked, and the dial tone sounded.

"I was supposed to be at the meeting," Gibson complained.

"You heard him, me and the lawyer, no one else. How could I say I was bringing a Fed? If you want this to work, you're going to have to trust me." *Just like I planned it, no FBI.*

***

The following morning, Dylan and Wolfe sat on the dock in front of Sinbad's Restaurant. *Jillian's Dream* was tied to the pier, not more than ten feet away. At 7:55 AM, there were no signs of life. The previous evening, Noah contacted the Secretary of State and the U.S. Coast Guard to inquire about the boat's registration. It was registered to a Jillian Stone of Eastpointe. However, when they ran a background check on her, they hit a brick wall. There was no driver's license, no automobile registration, no Social Security number, and no record of any Jillian Stone anywhere in the state. *It was clear someone didn't want to be found,* Jack concluded.

Jack looked at his phone: 8:00 a.m. sharp. He directed his attention back to the boat and noticed a tall, well-built, middle-aged man was emerging from the cabin. Jack figured him to be around forty years old, six feet tall, 185 pounds. He had a weathered face, like someone who spent too much time in the sun. He was dressed in white shorts and a dark-blue polo shirt. *'Rugged' is the word that describes this guy,* thought Jack.

The man looked directly at Jack and waved him and Wolfe over to the boat. The man scanned his surroundings and motioned for them to climb aboard. Dylan and Wolfe complied, and without any exchange of words, the man started the boat and backed it out of the dock.

Turning the wheel, he headed in the direction of Lake St. Clair. After motoring off the dock and into the wind, the man raised the sail and killed the engine. Still, nothing was said.

Finally, fifteen to twenty minutes after they left the dock, the man spoke.

"Did you bring the agreement?"

"I've got it right here," replied Wolfe. And for the first time, the man noticed the briefcase. *Sloppy,* he thought. *He could have a listening device or, worse, a weapon in there. I've got to be more careful.*

The man took the briefcase, searched it, and pulled out two copies of the agreement and a pen. He found nothing else but a couple of yellow legal pads and began to carefully scrutinize one copy of the agreement. Silence again descended on the lake. Daniel Wolfe already signed the document.

The man finished reading, grabbed the pen, and executed both copies of the agreement.

"Gentleman, my name is Jonathan Stone. I am a proud member of Bart Breitner's Free America Party."

Jack presumed some connection to white nationalists but shuddered at the mention of Breitner's name. He ran across the name and exploits during the Benjamin Blaine investigation. *This guy's as crazy as, if not crazier than Blaine. If Breitner actually got his hands on sarin gas...* Jack's thoughts were interrupted as Stone continued.

"Bart called a party meeting two weeks ago. He proclaimed we would avenge the capture and imprisonment of Ben Blaine by releasing sarin gas at Dearborn Police headquarters and the Mosque of America."

Jack shuddered again. The color drained from Wolfe's face.

"How does he plan to get his hands on the stuff?" Jack asked.

"Apparently, there is a secure government-owned warehouse full of the stuff in Arlington County, Virginia. Bart said something about the government seizing the stuff from the Syrians and wanting to get it out of the Middle East, so terrorists could not get their hands on it."

"So, how do you get into a heavily guarded government facility and steal sarin gas?"

"It is not heavily guarded, and even though it's supposed to be a secure government building, we just happen to have someone on the inside," replied Stone calmly.

"What?" Wolfe was incredulous. "How is that even possible?"

"He's one of the guards. He has no record and no ties to any white nationalist group. He's completely clean," replied Stone.

"Can security really be that lax where a chemical weapon is being stored?" Jack asked, speaking more to himself than anyone else.

"It can, and it is," replied Stone. "Apparently, very few people know the stuff is stored there. The Feds thought keeping things low profile would create the impression there is nothing worthwhile located in the storage facility. If we didn't have that guard stationed at the location when the sarin was delivered, we would never have known about it, and the stuff could have stayed under the radar for years. We're renting a couple of vans to drive down there, collect the gas, and bring it back."

That story squared perfectly with the internet chatter Noah uncovered.

Jack decided to play the role of an angry law enforcement officer. He didn't have to do much acting. He *was* an angry law enforcement officer.

"This sounds like a fucking dream for you guys! Why would you tell me any of this? Your friends will come after you if they find out you talked, and all that's at stake are the lives of some cops and Muslims. And we know you hate both, right?"

"You're right about my feelings for cops and Muslims, but I did three tours in Iraq, Afghanistan, and Syria, and I saw first-hand the effects of sarin gas exposure on human beings. I hate the camels and you fuckers just as much as the next nationalist, but sarin…man…that's a bright fucking red line for me. I can't be a part of that. I can't know a sarin gas attack is about to happen and not do something to prevent it."

"A white supremacist with a conscience? Why don't I believe you, Stone?" Jack continued to taunt the man, much to the chagrin of Daniel Wolfe, who was scared Jack would blow the deal and leave Dearborn vulnerable to an attack.

"I don't care if you believe me or not," replied an emboldened Stone. "I have a signed immunity, relocation, and identity change agreement either way, correct Mr. Wolfe?"

"You do indeed, Mr. Stone."

"That's all I care about now," said Stone. "If you guys are stupid enough to ignore my warnings, all those deaths will be on you. Even if I am lying, what do you have to lose by showing up? Man hours? A few dollars, perhaps? But if I'm right…" He sailed the trial balloon directly over their heads. The next few moments of silence were deafening.

*Of course, we must see this through,* thought Jack. "Okay, Stone, assume we believe you. What else can you tell us?"

Stone spilled his guts, laying out every detail: the location of the warehouse, gaining access with the guard, where Breitner's men would be stationed, and even his own role in the plot. The more Stone talked, the more Jack and Dan Wolfe believed every word that came out of his mouth and the more terrified they became.

An hour later, they returned to the dock. As Jack was about to step off the boat, he turned back.

"One last question, Stone. Why me? Your conscience gets to you, and you choose to call one person, and it's me?"

"I know who you are, Jack. I read the news about your case last year. I may not like how it turned out, but I have to admit you get the job done."

Jack looked at Wolfe, amused. *Wonder what Stone would do if I told him this operation belongs to the Feds?*

# Chapter Eight

A stealth joint task force surrounded the Arlington warehouse and waited patiently for signs of activity. The team was made up of high-ranking FBI agents and Virginia SWAT team members. The Dearborn anti-terror task force was not on the scene. Despite the vehement protests of Jack Dylan, the FBI froze Jack and his elite team out of the operation.

The joint task force was taking no chances. All federal and SWAT operative were wearing the latest in mobile *HAZMAT* garments, which protected them from a gas attack but allowed them more freedom of movement.

It was after 4:00 AM, and there was a slight chill in the air. They were on the scene for well over an hour and were becoming increasingly uncomfortable. *The life of a stakeout officer,* thought Clare Gibson as she hunkered into a corner with Ernest Cobb.

A lone armed guard, presumably the traitor, patrolled the walkway in front of the warehouse. SWAT circled the place more than once, and other than the guard, saw no activity. They possessed the latest technology. Several officers carried handheld Doppler radar devices enabling them to 'see through the walls.' All was clear inside.

At precisely 4:15 AM, consistent with Stone's statement, a moderate-sized moving van could be seen approaching from the access road. The truck stopped at a cross street, turned, and disappeared. The men looked at each other in mild disbelief until they heard the gears grind and saw the back end of the truck reappear. The guard scanned his surroundings and waved the truck backward until it was almost flush against what resembled a residential automatic garage door. The guard scanned the area a second time before opening the garage door with a hand-operated remote device. Five men, including Jonathan Stone, exited the vehicle from all sides and the cargo hold.

*Twenty-five elite law enforcement officers against six racist assholes. Four to one; pretty good odds,* thought Clare. Team leaders carried old mug shots of Bart Breitner, as it was essential to confirm Breitner was present before commencing with the operation. *Cut off the head of the snake . . .*

Suddenly, from the obscured opposite side of the truck, there was Bart in the flesh, walking directly into the garage before Clare, Cobb and the others could register his presence. The operatives could hear someone barking out orders from inside the garage. There was no way they were going to risk the possibility of even an ounce of sarin left that warehouse. It was time. The team leader gave the green light.

A muffled shot to Cobb's left brought down the guard. The others were inside the warehouse, but it was unknown whether or not they were armed. Surely, Breitner had a massive stockpile of weapons, but Stone wasn't privy to discussions regarding preparations and methods. FBI and SWAT operatives advanced on the building in total silence.

Team members reached the fallen guard and peered around the corner into the garage. The men inside had waistband handguns, but none of them were drawn. They had yet to move a container. The SWAT leader gave the signal, and all hell broke loose. Agents began pouring into the warehouse from all doors. A couple of the terrorists pulled weapons and got off a shot or two in the dark, but they were immediately put down by return fire. The rest of the men raised their hands in immediate surrender. It was over before it even started. The SWAT leader gave the all clear, and the others abandoned their hiding places and descended on the warehouse. Clare Gibson and Ernest Cobb approached the garage door, swung to the right, and entered the warehouse. Given their number and appearance, it seemed the containers were untouched and undamaged.

*Thank God!* Clare envisioned multiple ways for the mission to go south, officers ambushed and killed, gas released, innocent civilians dead or dying. Thanks to the number and skilled efficiency of federal and local law enforcement, there were only two deaths. Among those injured, the most serious was a gunshot wound suffered by the nefarious warehouse guard.

Air quality specialists were dispatched into the building to test whether any sarin was inadvertently released. Although doubtful, it was better to be safe than sorry. Once the team received an all-clear signal from the air specialists, Gibson, Cobb, and others removed their *HAZMAT* gear and began searching every inch of the warehouse.

Gibson approached the group of supremacists who had their hands raised or who were in the process of being handcuffed by a couple of officers. Clare gave a slight nod of thanks to Jonathan Stone, who ignored her. When the officers finished and the wounded were attended to, five handcuffed men were led out of the warehouse.

"Wait!" Cobb shouted, looking up and down at the mug shot he carried. "There are only five. Where's the sixth guy?" He glared into the faces of the five men and back down at the photo. None of these men were Breitner. He was there—they saw him walk into the warehouse, plain as day—but there was no sign of him now. Cobb directed the men and women to open every door and search the warehouse from top to bottom. Bart Breitner vanished into thin air. *How could a man disappear from a warehouse surrounded by a large force of elite operatives?*

***

The following day, Jack was in the FBI's Detroit office enduring a painful briefing from Clare Gibson. *How could they fuck this up?* Jack thought. But, he felt a small measure of glee at the FBI's ineptitude. Clare was mobilizing an interstate manhunt for Bart Breitner. Jonathan Stone was in federal custody and would be processed for witness protection. His secret participation went undetected. However, before he could begin enjoying the fruits of his new beginning, Gibson needed to debrief by him. She threatened to revoke Stone's witness protection status if he refused to provide information about Breitner's escape and current whereabouts. Jack was permitted to sit in as an observer.

"Where does Bart live?"

"I don't know."

"Where is the group's headquarters?"

"We don't have headquarters, per se.'"

"Where, 'per se,' do you meet, then?"

"Various places."

"Where did you meet for the planning of the sarin attack?"

"I already told you guys that. We met at the Belview Inn in Howell."

"Howell? Why Howell?"

"Symbolic reasons. At least that was Bart's explanation at the time."

"Symbolic? What the hell?" Clare didn't get it.

"History of the Michigan Klan and all that sort of shit."

A light bulb went off in Clare's head. "Oh, of course. How many people were at the meeting?"

"I'm not sure, maybe fifteen to twenty or so."

"Do you know any of those guys or their whereabouts?"

"Some."

"Why are you making this so difficult, Stone? You got what you wanted. If you want to start your new life sooner rather than later, you better start giving us some names and addresses and start doing so right now!" Clare was running out of patience with this bigot.

"These guys are friends of mine. They didn't do anything except attend a meeting. I don't rat on my friends."

"Your agreement calls for you to disclose all relevant information, everything you know. Since you have admitted you know some of these guys and their whereabouts, you'd be violating the agreement by not providing full disclosure. Want to spend the next ten to fifteen years in prison, Stone?"

Jonathan Stone took a huge breath in and let it out slowly. He looked up and around, his eyes darting from Clare to

Jack and back again, deep in thought. *Can I legally avoid disclosure? Would they really revoke the agreement? Am I willing to risk prison for these guys?*

At that moment, with those scary thoughts weighing heavily on his mind, he realized they had him firmly by the balls. So, Jonathan Stone capitulated. He spilled his guts.

"This won't be traced back to me. You can't do that, right?" Stone was jittery.

"No, Stone, this will not be traced back to you. You have held up your end, and we will hold up ours. Is there anything else you want to tell me?"

"Can't think of a thing."

"Okay. Hang tight. I've got to talk with Cobb and find out where we go from here. Can you babysit for a few minutes, Jack?"

"You sure a lowly Dearborn cop is up for the assignment, Gibson? After all, we aren't the big, bad FBI." Jack couldn't resist picking at the scab of the botched operation.

"I'll take the risk," she replied, rolling her eyes. She left the room and slammed the door.

Jonathan Stone locked eyes with Jack Dylan.

"If there is anything you didn't tell her, now is the time to stick it to the FBI, Stone."

"I didn't see you in Arlington."

"That's because we weren't there. The FBI kicked us off the operation."

"You kept your word to me, even though they shit on you? You are a straight-up guy, Dylan. Shut up and let me think for a minute." Stone closed his eyes and appeared to search his memory. Suddenly, they opened.

"As a matter of fact," he said, "it so happens I *do* remember something. It might be important, or it might not. But, it is exclusive to you. Share it with the Feds or don't, I could give a shit."

Jack was dubious, but he wanted to scoop the FBI. "So, what is this big revelation?"

"Bart used to brag about some place he had up north. He mentioned a boat he docks in front of the downtown business district and said the fishing was great. He also said we could all go up there for some R&R after this was over. He called it 'hiding in plain sight.'"

"'Up north' describes every place north of Flint. Can we narrow it down? Upper or Lower Peninsula?"

"I don't think it's in the U.P. Bart said we could get there in about four hours via I-75."

"Well, gee, Stone, that's informative. Let's see if I can help you."

"Okay."

"Petoskey? Traverse City? Charlevoix or Gaylord?" Stone shook his head. "How about the west coast along Lake Michigan? Ludington? Frankford? Manistee?"

"Manistee! I think he said Manistee."

"All right, Jon Stone! Now, this is between you and me, right?"

"Always fun messing with the Feds," he said. Stone gazed down at the ground. He was conflicted, happy to be free, but stung by the fact that freedom was achieved by ratting out his pals.

At that moment, Clare Gibson returned with Ernest Cobb and another federal cop who identified himself as a U.S. Marshall.

"Gather up Mr. Stone here and take him to your office for relocation, Marshall," Gibson directed. She turned to Stone. "They are waiting for you, Stone. Have a nice life. Why don't you use this opportunity to venture down the path of the straight and narrow?"

"I'll think about it," replied Stone, with a touch of defiance.

*Sure you will,* thought Jack.

The Marshall took out a pair of handcuffs and motioned for Stone to hold his hands out in front of him. Stone followed his silent orders and permitted the cuffs to be applied. This was more for show than for safety, After all, Stone had an immunity deal. He was guilty of no crime, but he also did not protest. If Breitner or any of his men were watching, it was essential to treat Stone like a criminal.

"Marshall, please make sure to provide us the details of his relocation including his new name, rank, serial number. I want his ass available to me if I need him," ordered Cobb, with arrogant authority. "And when you're done with that, get his ass out of here."

# Chapter Nine

Jack Dylan was conflicted. He was pleased a terrorist plot was stopped and no harm was done to his community, but he was pissed Breitner escaped and his task force received the brush off from the Feds. Shaheed Ali, at Jack's instruction, called Imam Ghafari and Arya Khan to deliver the fabulous news that the immediate threat to Dearborn was over. However, he also warned this incident, on the heels of the Blaine incident, should serve as a stark reminder "our people need to be vigilant."

While Jack was pleased with the success of the mission, he was uneasy, on edge because Breitner escaped capture. Jack would not rest until he'd hunted Breitner down and brought him to justice. *How could a man "disappear" amidst all those elite law enforcement officials? Would things have been different if we were in charge?*

Crime scene techs determined Breitner escaped underground, through a sewer drain below the warehouse. *Smart move, asshole. You planned this escape and let the others take the fall. I will hunt you down, tough guy. I will find you...*

Jack called Shaheed, Andy, and Noah into his office. He previously shared the Manistee revelation with his three subordinates and swore them to secrecy. As they took seats around the small conference table, he asked them for an update on 'Project Manistee.'

"The best lead we have, boss, is Manistee, the boat and the dock on Lake Michigan," Andy explained. "We have limited resources without reaching out to the local police, but we have cultivated and retained a couple of local private investigators. I'm not particularly comfortable. These guys may not know the difference between sarin and a fart, but I'll keep an open mind. They're all we have at the moment. I sent them Breitner's photo, and I'm waiting to hear back."

"Did you tell them how dangerous this guy is? What's their background, Andy?"

"They're small-town P.I.'s, former cops, which is good. They claim to know the town and everyone in it like the backs of their hands. I made it clear what kind of person we were dealing with. I believe they got the message."

Jack was not convinced. "We can't leave this to chance, Andy. Make sure they're up to snuff. I want Breitner found." He glared at Andy and the others.

"I understand, boss, but without local law enforcement or the Feds, we have minimal access. These are good guys, well connected. If Breitner is in Manistee, we'll find him."

Jack softened a bit. "What's the head honcho's name, the private eye?"

"Emmit Thorn."

"So, a former cop, eh? What's his history? Always been in Manistee?"

"Yes, boss."

"Stop calling me boss. Have you got his number?"

"I do, Jack, but we had a nice long chat, and I think he got the message loud and clear."

"Manistee is the best lead we've got, and Breitner is a slippery bastard. I want to talk to this guy and make sure he knows how serious this thing is."

"This is not on you, Jack. We weren't in Arlington. This is all on the Feds and Arlington SWAT. Don't beat yourself up."

"Just give me the damned number."

Shaheed opened a file, pulled out a piece of paper and read a number to Jack.

"Anything else, boss? Andy asked.

"No, that's it for now," he muttered as if a million miles away.

The three men rose, exited, and started toward the squad room.

"What was that?" Noah asked as they walked away.

"He is really pissed and who can blame him? They kicked us off the case and let that bastard get away. Jack's afraid Breitner might try something else," replied Andy.

"His plan failed, but guys like Breitner never stop. He'll try something again." Shaheed replied.

"I've never seen Jack like this," said Noah.

"You haven't known him for as long as I have. He takes this stuff to heart, but that's also what makes him a great cop," replied Shaheed. "He'll be good to go when the time comes."

"I sure hope so," added Andy.

*\*\*\**

Jack Dylan continued to stare at the phone number. He picked up the desk phone and dialed. A man answered, "Thorn Investigations, how may I help you?"

"I'm looking for Emmit Thorn," replied Jack.

"This is Thorn. To whom am I speaking?"

"This is Captain Jack Dylan of the Dearborn Police. How are you doing today?"

"Captain Dylan, nice to hear from you. I've heard a lot of good things about you from your colleagues. What can I do for you?"

"I know you spoke to Lieutenant Ali this morning. I understand he told you about our situation."

"He did," replied Thorn.

"I want to make sure you know this is a terrorist situation, Mr. Thorn. This man, Breitner, is likely armed and dangerous and has already gone to great lengths in an attempt to commit mass murder."

"Call me Emmit, and I'll call you Jack if that's okay. Ali filled me in, Jack. I am aware of how serious this is and why we can't alert the locals," replied Thorn.

"Thanks, Emmit. This guy planned to bomb our headquarters, who knows who's next?"

"I'm on this, Jack. I promise. I will let you know as soon as I hear anything. If your guy is here, my people will find him."

"How many men do you have to put on this?"

"Two currently. I am lining up two more to back them up."

"That's not enough! This guy is a terrorist! He's an extremely dangerous man. Think Bin Laden, Emmit!"

"I can't do much more, Jack. Keep in mind this is a very small town. But, I can assure you my men are highly skilled, and we know how to do our jobs."

Jack softened. "Thanks, Emmit. I appreciate what you're doing for us. I know you're at risk with the locals. Keep me posted, please."

"Will do."

Jack hung up the phone. *This guy seems fine, but he and four others aren't nearly enough. They don't know what Breitner is capable of. Do they appreciate the threat? I've got to get to Manistee.*

# Chapter Ten

Jack Dylan sat alone in his office. His recent conversations with his staff and the Manistee private eye did not inspire confidence. Jack wanted results. He decided to take matters into his own hands and called Shaheed into his office.

"What's up, Jack?"

"I'm taking a little time off."

"Now? With Breitner on the loose?" *What's going on?*

"I'm tired. I'm aggravated. I need a little time to myself."

"Come on, Jack. That's bullshit. Talk to me."

Jack studied Shaheed. *Can I trust him? I can't have him going over my head to Acker.*

"Jack?" Shaheed was becoming nonplussed.

"Can I count on your discretion, Shaheed? I need to know I can trust you. After Granger…"

Asher Granger was a former member of the task force, a good cop and a trusted advisor to Jack. However, he also had a dark side as a disciple of Ben Blaine. During the mosque bombing and murder investigation the previous year, Granger showed his true stripes. He turned on the task force and began feeding Blaine information about the investigation. He helped kidnap Arya Khan, and when his own capture became inevitable, he tried to give himself up. Blaine shot and killed him for his traitorous actions. *A traitor to both sides, the ultimate asshole…*

"Jack," said Shaheed, interrupting Jack's thoughts. "I'm not Ash Granger. You *know* that. Talk to me, man."

"I'm going after Breitner."

"Whoa, what does that mean? Alone? You're a *cop*, not a vigilante. Besides, I thought Thorn was on this."

"I talked with Thorn, and I don't get the sense he has enough manpower or understands the threat level. He knows Manistee, and that's a huge plus. He's competent and confident, and I'm sure he's an asset, but he has no idea what he's dealing with. If he or one of his guys finds Breitner, a huge *if*, someone will most likely end up at the bottom of Lake Michigan. I have to get up there."

"We have no jurisdiction in Manistee, Jack. You are crazy to do this without the Feds or the locals, and you are nuts to do anything without Acker's okay."

"You and I both know Acker's a 'by the book' kind of cop. He'll never sign off on this."

"Exactly."

"Which is why I have to do this alone."

"Come on, Jack. Be reasonable. Let's run this up the chain of command."

"Acker will never approve, and even if he does, we would have to deal with some Barney Fife type cop up in Manistee, and *he* would never agree. I'm screwed either way."

"Who's Barney Fife?"

"He's an old television character…oh…never mind. The point is this situation is way beyond anything these guys up north have ever seen."

"What's the plan, Jack?"

"I'm going to take some time off and go undercover. These guys don't know me, and Breitner has never seen me. I need to become one of them, blend into the crowd and do something interesting that captures his attention. I'll hide out in the open and wait to be contacted. Your friends dress like your enemies, and your enemies dress like your friends. Ultimately, it appears these guys want to eliminate anyone who is not white and Christian. They want to wipe racial diversity off the face of the earth. This is not a negotiation. It is a mandate, a calling for them. If they had the support and armament, we would already be at war with these animals. I'm going to play their game, and when the time is right, I'll take them all down."

"Take me with you, Jack. This guy tried to gas my people."

"A Muslim does not exactly fit into the Manistee demographics. If *you* go, you will be noticed. Besides, I need you in charge while I'm gone. Keep the pressure on, and keep looking for Breitner. We still don't know for sure he's in Manistee or anywhere near Manistee. I'm doing this because it's the only viable lead we have."

"This is not safe, Jack. You need backup."

"I have to stay under the radar, but I'll figure out a way to communicate -- burner phone, email at the library, shit like that. And if there is any serious heat, I'll call in the cavalry. I promise."

"This is crazy, Jack. You can't do this."

"Assuming Bart doesn't know we turned Stone or discovered his connection to Manistee, we have a small window of surprise. This only works if we keep it small, away from the locals and the Feds, for as long as possible. Meanwhile, you promised to keep your mouth shut."

Shaheed paused and sighed. "I must be as crazy as you are. Okay, Jack, but promise you'll call at the first sign of trouble. I'll have the whole task force out there, ASAP."

"I enjoy living, and I'm not stupid."

"Don't underestimate these guys, Jack. Don't consider them to be unsophisticated. They carefully planned every step of the sarin attack. These guys know what they are doing."

"I won't, Shaheed. And thanks, I appreciate the support."

"What do I tell Chief Acker?"

"Tell him I needed some R&R."

"In the middle of the Breitner thing? He won't believe me, Jack. He's not dumb."

"Tell him whatever you want. I looked for him to ask for some time off and he wasn't around. I have time coming, and I don't need to explain myself to everyone. And, Shaheed, we didn't have this conversation."

"It's your rodeo, Jack. Please be careful and remember we are here for you if you need us. Can I loop in Andy and Noah?"

"As long as they agree to keep things between us bros in blue. I'm counting on the support of my team when the time comes."

***

A half-hour later, the phone rang in Jack's office. The caller I.D. screen displayed a Bloomfield Hills number. Jack picked up the receiver.

"Jack Dylan."

"Jack, it's Zack Blake."

"Zack, how's my favorite defense lawyer?"

"I'm good Jack, you?"

"Things could always be better. What's up?"

"A while ago, I got a strange call from Arya Khan. This is the first chance I've had to call you. Believe it or not, Arya's worried about you."

"About me? Why?"

"She said you addressed her congregation a couple of weeks ago to advise people about some threat to the community. Arya's 'woman's intuition' told her to worry about you."

"There was a threat to her community, but we have taken care of it. The threat has been neutralized, and everything is good, Zack. I promise."

"Does Arya know?"

"Yes, we've communicated with Arya."

"I believe you. I told her I would reach out and now I have. Call me if you need me."

"I will, thanks."

## Chapter Eleven

A week later, Jack Dylan was sitting on a lounge chair, sipping a beer outside the Bay Shore Hotel in Manistee. It was late May. The wind off the lake was rather chilly at that time of year.

The hotel was perfect for someone looking for R & R. From his room, Jack could see the beach, pier, and boat dock lining Lake Michigan. The hotel was quiet, tranquil and a short drive from the downtown area.

During the week, Jack met with Emmit Thorn and his team. The collective strategy was to chat up the locals and inquire about professional fishermen who might be available to take them out fishing. Typical of most small towns, the people were cordial, even friendly. Although Jack received a few helpful tips and learned a lot about bluegill and perch, he found no sign of Breitner. Thorn and his team had no luck, either. Jack began to question the strategy. *Maybe Bart's not here after all.*

As Jack sipped his beer, a young man approached and asked if the lounge chair next to him was taken. Jack politely told the man it wasn't.

"Where you from?" the young man asked.

"Detroit area," Jack replied. "You?"

"Lansing"

"You work for the government?"

"Sort of. I work at Capitol Airport. I'm an air traffic controller."

"Yeah? Hear that's a stressful occupation. This seems like a good place to relax," said Jack with a smile. "I'm Jack Manning, by the way."

"Alan Berger. Nice to meet you."

"Nice to meet you, too, Alan."

"What do you do, Jack?"

"I'm an engineer. Right now, though, I'm looking to have some lunch and then, perhaps, hook up with one of those fishing junkets. Care to join me for lunch?"

"Sure. I was just about to have lunch, myself, but, if you don't reserve a lounge chair, they run out real quick."

"Throw a towel on it and it's yours."

They walked into the hotel dining room and were seated at a table for two. Both ordered coffee and began studying the menu.

"So, Alan, how often you come up here?"

"About once or twice a year. As you mentioned, air traffic work can be very stressful. A few guys from work like to come up, relax and do a little fishing. The other guys are back in their rooms. We had a little too much to drink last night. The weather is nice this time of year, and the fishing is great."

"Yeah? I'm still hoping to fish. I haven't had much luck finding the right fishing expert who does charters."

"We had a great time the other day and a big catch too. We always use the same guy when we come up here. We're going out again tomorrow if you want to join us."

"Thanks. I might take you up on that, Alan."

"I've got to warn you though. This guy, Robert, the boat owner, is a strange dude, but we go with him because he's a great fisherman."

"Strange how?"

"I don't know…strange…sometimes he seems to be mad at the world. Don't get into politics or religion with him, that's for sure. This last trip he was really in a foul mood."

"Why?"

"Apparently, some deal went bad."

*This sounds promising.* "What kind of deal?"

"Hell if I know. But, man, can he fish!"

"Where do I find this dude?" *Could this be Breitner?*

"You don't need to find him, man. I told you. My friends and I have a reservation tomorrow. You're welcome to join us. The boat is docked about a mile, give or take, up *Bay*

*Shore*." Berger pointed north. "He owns his own fishing business, and his boat is beautiful."

"Is there money in that?"

"Money in what?"

"Fishing." *Talking to this guy is like having your teeth pulled!*

"Sure, especially in the summertime. In winter, you don't need a boat. You can ice fish in a shanty. I think this guy has a shanty, too."

"Where do I find this dude again?"

"On his boat, I guess."

*OMG!* "Do you remember the name of the boat?"

"Sure."

*I'm going to shoot this guy right here, right now!* "So, what's the name?"

"It's the '*White Knight*.'"

*Why does that sound familiar? 'White Knight?'* "Alan, I would *love* to go fishing with you and your friends tomorrow. Are you sure Robert or your friends won't mind?"

"Nah. Robert charges by the charter. One more guy won't matter and, besides, my guys are cool."

"What's it cost to go fishing with this Robert guy?"

"Alone?"

"No, with you and your friends."

"About three hundred bucks for the day."

"Set it up. My treat."

"I told you, Jack. It's already set up, but you can throw in a fifty and bring some beer."

"I'll do better than that. I'll cover the whole trip *and* bring the beer."

"That's very generous, Jack. Thanks."

*If this fisherman is Breitner, this information is priceless.* Jack took a swig of coffee and stood. "I enjoyed our chat. I've got to run an errand. What time tomorrow?"

"9:00 a.m. sharp."

"I'll meet you right here tomorrow morning at 7:30."

"See you tomorrow."
And with that, Jack turned and disappeared into the crowd.

# Chapter Twelve

Jack walked up Bay Shore, looking at every boat and boat dock he passed. If for some reason Alan was a no-show, Jack still intended to go fishing with the man who owned the *White Knight*. After strolling the dock for a mile or more, he came upon the boat, securely tied to the dock. Jack was quite surprised at its size and grandeur. Jack expected a piece of crap, but was, instead, looking at a first-class commercial fishing boat with all the bells and whistles. The boat was a beautiful forty-footer, It was more like a party boat than an everyday fishing boat.

*How does a guy like Bart afford a boat like this? Does bigotry pay that well?* He realized there was a great deal he needed to learn about Bart Breitner.

Jack saw no signs of life and decided to take a closer look. He approached the boat, and suddenly, a man appeared from the berth. *It's Breitner!* Jack had no place to go, H could turn and walk back to the hotel, but he was concerned Breitner would notice his abrupt about-face and become suspicious. If he continued forward, he might have to engage him in conversation. If Jack merely stood there, looking as foolish as he felt, that would be as bad as an about-face. Jack started walking toward the boat. The closer he got, the more he knew it was the terrorist in the flesh, no more than twenty feet away.

*Look at that asshole! Not a care in the world! Today, I fish; tomorrow, I blow up a mosque. Smart, hiding in plain sight.*

If Jack Dylan was Captain Ahab, Bart Breitner was Moby Dick. Jack felt exhilarated, as Ahab must have felt when he finally encountered the great white. He would approach with caution and test the waters. He was alone, and he sensed extreme danger, but this was a tremendous opportunity he could not pass up.

"Afternoon." Breitner noticed Jack and was being 'friendly.' Jack, startled at the overture, looked up and saw Bart Breitner staring up at him, waiting for a response.

"Good afternoon."

"Something I can help you with?"

"Ah…no, not really. I'm going fishing tomorrow with a guy named Berger, and he mentioned this boat. He said it was less than a mile from the Bay Shore Hotel, where I'm staying, so I thought I'd come over and take a look."

"So, you're my customer? Want to come aboard? Look around?"

"Sure, if you don't mind. But if you're busy or something…"

"If I were too busy, I wouldn't have offered."

*Not too busy-nobody around to torture or murder? I should shoot this bastard right here, right now!*

As Jack approached the boat, Breitner extended his arm and hoisted Jack aboard.

"This is a beautiful boat," exclaimed Jack.

"It's a forty-six-foot Trojan," replied Breitner. "You and your friends will have a good time tomorrow. There are two large staterooms and two heads, both with showers. Are you going to have women on board? Great place to get laid; the ladies love it down there."

"I'm just a guest of Berger's. I don't know what he's got planned."

"I'm just sayin'. Would you like to look around?"

"Sure."

"I'm Robert, by the way. Robert Bright. But you can call me 'Bert'. My friends call me that."

"Thanks, Bert. I'm Jack Manning." The two men shook hands. Breitner turned and started moving things from one place to the other.

"Need some help?" Jack asked.

"No, I'm fine. Make yourself at home. I'll be done in a few."

Jack strolled around the boat's perimeter. It was bigger than he'd first thought, with a stylish design and a modern interior. The salon was huge and had open access to the galley. A hard-bottom inflatable raft hung from a cradle. There was a hard-surfaced awning, a tackle center in the cockpit, several fishing rods and rod holders, and a vast storage area. A person could live very comfortably on this boat, which was more of a yacht.

Breitner came up behind Jack, startling him.

"Sorry," said Breitner. "I didn't mean to sneak up on you like that."

"That's okay. You went off one way and came back another. I just wasn't expecting it." Jack and Breitner looked over the bow. "She's a beauty, isn't she? Two seven-hundred-and-fifty-horsepower diesels are pushing this thing to thirty knots, even more, if I really want it. "

"She's beautiful, alright."

"Would you like a beer?"

"No thanks. I just ate lunch."

"I *always* leave room for beer. Mind if I have one?"

"Not at all."

Breitner pulled a beer from the cooler, twisted it open, and took a swig. "So, what brings you to Manistee, Jack?"

Jack decided then and there to begin his undercover adventure. "I needed some quiet R & R. Just to relax, catch up on my reading, go fishing, and scuba diving. A get away from some of the scumbags I work in the big city."

"What big city is that?"

"Detroit."

"Detroit? What do you do?"

"I'm an engineer with Ford Motor Company in Dearborn, just outside of Detroit."

"Dearborn?" Breitner's ears perked up at the mention of the city.

*Was it a mistake to mention Dearborn?* "Yeah, you know it? It's a multicultural community, lots of mosque-goers if you know what I mean. Came to Manistee to breathe some clean, fresh air."

"How do you mean?"

"Let's just say I am tired of sharing my city." *Am I speaking your language, asshole?*

Breitner smiled. "I know exactly what you mean. Sounds about right."

"I needed to get *far* away if you get my drift. No phones, no computers, no email, no one to get ahold of me and bother me."

"You should buy a boat and become a fisherman. That's exactly how I live when I'm out here. Just my boat and some of the best lakes, rivers, and fishing in the whole world."

"Sounds wonderful, but don't you ever feel isolated from the real world living up here?"

"I don't. I mean I have a phone and a computer, like everyone else. But not when I'm out here. Out here, I don't want to be connected."

"No phone?"

"I carry one, but only use it for emergencies. Who the fuck needs technology on a fishing boat, anyway? All you need on a fishing boat is a rod, reel, and some bait."

"I like your style."

"But I'm doing all the talking. What's your story?"

"I told you. I'm an engineer at Ford and damned tired of all the bullshit. I needed a break, a breath of fresh air if you will. I say hell yes to making America pure again."

"Well, Jack. That is an interesting philosophy you've got there. But, I've got to be honest with you, man. You sound like a bigot to me."

*Back up the truck a bit, Dylan. You're coming on too strong!* "I don't know about that. I don't mind if non-whites go to school, get an education, work hard, climb the ladder, and do well. I like anyone willing to work hard. But in my experience, and I've got a lot of it, these people want to whine and cry about how society treats them, and they want us white boys to step aside and give them things. In my world, if you want something, you go out and earn it."

Jack paused and looked at Breitner, who was studying him again, sizing him up. "I'm sorry, Bert. I don't know you that well. I don't know your politics or how you feel about this shit. I'm out of line. I didn't mean to go off like that."

"Well, I'd be more careful if I were you. Today's politicians are falling all over themselves to promote 'diversity.' You can get yourself in real trouble talking to people like that."

Jack looked down at his watch and pretended to be in a rush. "Shit, I've got to get back to the hotel. I'm supposed to meet a girl for lunch and drinks."

"No problem. Bring her with you tomorrow; no charge." Breitner smiled. "I enjoyed our conversation. We'll talk more tomorrow." He reached out his hand to shake Jack's. Jack took it, and the two men engaged in a bit of 'who has the strongest handshake' male bonding. Jack climbed up onto the dock.

"Thanks for the tour, Bert. I'm looking forward to tomorrow."

"Me too, Jack. Have a nice time with the chick."

"Thanks, I fully intend to."

"I want details."

Jack chuckled. "You got it. I'll see you tomorrow."

"See ya, Jack. It was nice meeting you."

"You, too."

Jack walked away. He could feel the eyes of the terrorist boring into him. Was it his imagination? *Did I say too much? Did I go too far?* Time would tell, but Jack was buoyed at the prospect of infiltrating the Breitner inner circle. *This could be huge.* He paused. *Or it could blow up in my face!*

# Chapter Thirteen

The following morning, as Jack was preparing for the fishing trip, he was questioning his judgment. *Am I crazy to go on this trip? Should I notify local law enforcement? If I do that, I won't get to Bart's comrades, some of which might be hanging out in Manistee somewhere. No...I've got to see this through.*

It was 7:30 AM when he walked into the dining room. Alan Berger was there with his friends. Berger saw Jack and called him over.

"Guys, this is Jack. Jack, this is Marty, Chuck, Evan, Mark, and Gib. Jack, these are the boys."

"You will be tested on the names," Evan said, laughing. *Or was it Chuck?*

"Ready for some good grub and some great fishing?" Alan asked.

"Ready when you guys are."

"Great. Let's eat quickly and get the hell out of here. Hey, Jack, Alan says you're treating all of us to the boat and the fishing. If that's true, we appreciate it," offered Marty.

"It's true, and it's my pleasure, uh..."

"Marty," Marty said with a laugh.

*Real funny,* thought Jack.

Alan and his men were surprisingly enjoyable company. Jack felt safe in their numbers, which was the reason he'd wanted to tag along with this group in the first place.

When they finished breakfast, they agreed to return to their separate rooms, and meet in front of the hotel in five minutes. Ten minutes later, they were walking along the boardwalk, heading toward the *White Knight*.

When they arrived at the boat, Breitner was emerging from below, a carbon copy of the day before. He welcomed everyone aboard, asked for his money, and Jack handed him three one-hundred-dollar bills.

"Everybody ready?" Breitner appeared to be in good spirits as he pocketed the cash.

After some preparatory odds and ends and a few minutes of priming, the boat pulled away from the dock.

Bart was an excellent fisherman, host, and teacher. They fished Lake Michigan and the Manistee River, and it was clear 'Bert' knew the waters and was astute at locating great spots to fish. To Jack's surprise, he was a pleasant, very knowledgeable and patient captain, willing to help anyone land a fish when his assistance was necessary. Jack was dubious when Alan heaped praise on Bert, but the praise was earned. Bart Breitner, aka 'Bert Bright,' was the real deal.

According to legend (Alan Berger), if there were only one fish in Lake Michigan, Bert Bright would find it and catch it. He had a keen desire to put his customers on fish. Jack learned much about fishing in the Great Lakes and Manistee and was surprised to discover he was having the time of his life. Bart seemed to know precisely how, when and where to catch different species of fish. He had an uncanny ability to locate them and what lures to use to entice a strike.

Within the first hour, the men landed four fish and three different species, salmon, steelhead, and trout. They also lost an Atlantic salmon (Bert identified it for them), right at the net. The fish fought spectacularly, tail walking for more than thirty feet. Bert said he'd been fishing for many years but never saw a salmon do the tail walk that far before. At the end of the epic battle, the fish won, dislodging the hook and swimming away.

Six hours later, after catching their limit, eight drunk, stoned fishermen and their captain, pulled the *White Knight* up to the dock. Bert showed them how to clean the fish expertly, and all in attendance thoroughly enjoyed dining on the various species, barbequed exquisitely by 'Chef Bert.' Finally, after a solid eight hours together, the adventure was coming to an end.

"Thanks, Bert. We had a great time," said Chuck.

"And let's have a round of applause for Jack for paying for this fabulous day." Everyone applauded. "We're going to go back to the hotel, fry some more of this fish, and find some girls, Jack. Care to join us?"

"I'll be along, still enjoying this evening sky. You guys go. I'll catch you later."

Jack stood on the dock with Breitner.

"Something on your mind, Jack?"

"Not really, Bert. I just wanted to thank you for a wonderful afternoon. I learned a lot today." He wasn't kidding. He learned more about fishing in one day than he learned in his lifetime. To his dismay, though, the angry version of the man Alan described did not present himself.

"It's a lot of fun when you know what you're doing and where to do it."

"And provided you know the right people."

"Sure there's nothing on your mind, Jack?"

"Well…as long as you mention it…I was wondering…."

"Wondering what, Jack? Say what you want to say already or be on your way."

"Don't take this the wrong way, Bert, but Alan told me you might be someone who could help me find guys who believe America needs some help. Alan says you're pretty hyped up about this shit."

"What are you getting at, Jack?"

"Alan says you're kind of angry about the way things are."

"What does that mean?"

"People coming over here, not doing things the right way, taking our jobs, that kind of thing."

"I guess you could say I'm angry about some things. Probably talk too much too, especially when I'm drunk. What else did Alan say?"

"Not much. He tells me you're passionate about America and how things should be."

"Well, I am."

"How should things be?"

"America first, America pure, if you know what I mean. President John has the right idea. And I'm not alone in feeling that way. But, for most people, it's all talk. The country needs some action if you ask me."

Alan Berger forgot his tackle box. He told an inebriated Gib to keep going and promised to catch up. Then, he turned and began to walk back toward the *White Knight*. He saw Jack and Bert chatting on the dock and was about to shout out a greeting when he heard what Jack asked Bert. He was intrigued. The two men didn't see him, so he ducked behind a shed and listened in.

"I couldn't agree more," replied Jack. "So, what kind of action do you have in mind?"

"We can demonstrate, exercise our First Amendment rights, and more if people have the guts and the resources. There are things we can do."

"What kinds of things?"

Breitner studied Jack, not sure what to make of this guy. Most of his people were vetted and tested, under fire. He'd never recruited anyone he didn't know well. *But my gut tells me he's a good guy.*

"I might be able to share some ideas, Jack. I've got a busy day tomorrow, but I'm available in the evening. Why don't you meet me here around 8:00 p.m. and we can talk some more? Work for you?"

"Sure, Bert. Sounds good." *What the fuck am I doing? The plan was never to allow myself to be alone with this guy.*

"See ya tomorrow, Jack."

Bert turned and hopped on the boat, disappearing into the cabin. Jack started walking away. *Shit! What am I going to do now?*

As Jack walked down the boardwalk, Alan Berger peeked out from behind the shed to see whether Bert Bright went below or was still on the boat's deck. Bright was nowhere to be seen. He waited for Jack to walk further away and then took off after him. *What the fuck was that about?*

# Chapter Fourteen

"Dearborn Police Department, Detective Squad. Lieutenant Ali speaking. How may I help you?"

"I have a collect call from a Jack Dylan. Will you accept the charges?"

"Yes, put it through, please." Shaheed heard an audible click.

"Shaheed?"

"Jack! Why haven't you checked in? What's going on? Is everything all right? Did you locate Breitner? Have you checked in with our guys in town? Talk to me, man!" Shaheed was both frantic and relieved at the same time.

"Whoa, whoa. Take a breath. I'm fine, and I found Breitner. Yes, I've talked with Thorn and his guys. I like them, but not sure yet whether they are front line guys if you know what I mean."

"You *found* Breitner? What are you going to do?"

"I'm not sure which is why I'm calling. I want to discuss things with you."

"Talk to me, Jack. We're here to help."

"We've met. We got along fine. I was on Breitner's fishing boat with a bunch of guys. He goes by an alias, but he's definitely Breitner. I'm meeting him again tomorrow evening to talk about making America a better place for bigoted white dudes. I think he *likes* me. If he's alone, maybe I can take him down. If he's got men in Manistee, I will definitely need some support. Maybe we can get in there and bring the whole thing down. Who knows? Or we can call the locals or the Feds, tell them we've found the guy, and let them get involved and make an arrest. I'm not sure which way to go."

"Your infiltration idea sounds dangerous to me. I say we get Breitner, now. What's a group without its leader? I'd call in the Feds, sooner than later." *Cut off the head of the snake…*

"But, so many things can go wrong if I call in the troops. Breitner is a slippery bastard. He escaped the Feds in Arlington. He knows the nooks and crannies of this town and could easily escape again."

"Sounds like you've already made up your mind."

"No, actually, I haven't. I keep going back and forth. That's why I called."

"Assuming you don't call in the cavalry, what's your next move?"

"For now, all I've got is the meet on his fishing boat tomorrow night. You should see this thing. It must have cost a fortune. We had a great time. I learned a lot about Great Lakes fishing, caught some salmon and trout. We even had a nice conversation. It was a strange feeling."

"Sounds to me like you're planning to meet him alone."

Jack didn't respond.

"Jack, this is way too dangerous. You promised not to do anything stupid, and this idea is the epitome of stupid. What if he's onto you? Have you considered that possibility?"

"He doesn't know me. As I told you, we spent the whole day together, and he doesn't have a clue."

"But this thing can go wrong in so many ways for so many reasons I can't count them all. You have no backup, and the locals don't know you're there or that you're a cop. I hate this whole situation, Jack."

"Tell me how you really feel," Jack replied caustically.

"You asked for my opinion."

"What if you, Andy, and Noah drove up here tonight? Noah could wire me, and we could record the whole conversation. You guys would monitor the whole thing, and if there is any trouble at all, you'll be my backup. And, if necessary, you guys can call in Manistee's Barney Fife. How does that sound?"

"Still not a fan, but it's better than meeting him all alone. What do we tell Acker?"

"Nothing unless he asks, and if he does, we're working a case."

"If the shit hits the fan, we're all standing in the unemployment line."

"It's worth the risk to bring down Breitner."

"I hope that's true, Jack. I'll grab Andy, Noah and whatever equipment I can swing, and we'll try to get up north by suppertime. Where are you staying?"

"Bay Shore Hotel. It's famous up here. Google it or ask Siri. You can't miss it."

"We'll see you in about five hours, and Jack?"

"Yeah?"

"Don't do anything until we get there."

"Jack?"

"Yeah?"

"Promise me."

"I promise," replied Jack.

"See you soon."

***

Five and a half hours later, the four Dearborn veteran cops met in Jack's hotel room to plan the next day's events. When the meeting was over, everyone's role in the operation was defined. Jack would meet with Breitner at the boat as scheduled. The only difference was he'd be wired. Andy would provide covert, on-scene backup and follow Breitner wherever he went, beginning that evening. "Load up on the coffee," suggested Jack.

Noah would handle the tech part, which included wiring Jack up and monitoring his activities with Breitner. The men asked about the wire's range, and Noah assured this was the latest and greatest technology. Because a dark-skinned Muslim would stand out in Manistee, Shaheed would hang back with Noah and provide backup wherever he was needed. The men adjourned for a few hours of sleep (except for Andy, who was given directions to the *White Knight*). Jack called the front desk and requested an 8:30 a.m. wake-up call.

The men went to their separate rooms, and Andy headed out, picking up a cup of free coffee before strolling through the front door. He walked the boardwalk as Jack did earlier. There was very little activity. Most of the businesses and restaurants were closed. A few bars, with very few customers loitering around, remained open. One of those establishments happened to be within shouting distance of the *White Knight*. There was a group of men sitting on the boat deck drinking cocktails. Most of them appeared to be very intoxicated. Andy looked down at the mug shot of Breitner, looked back at the boat, and observed a very drunk man who might have been Bart. He and some other men were conversing quite loudly, but, at this distance, he had to strain to hear what they were saying. Andy took out his camera phone and tried to video the event, but it was too dark to record faces and too far to pick up clear audio. *Are they planning another attack?* The man who would be Breitner stood and began to speak. Andy strained to listen. He wished his colleagues were here and that he was close enough to hear him clearly.

"We . . . avenge . . . Blaine . . . fall . . . sarin . . . everything within our power . . . bring them down . . . rain fire . . . can't stop use . . . terror." The man was very drunk, shouting, staggering, and slurring his speech.

". . . Made us bleed . . . their turn . . . meet . . . maker . . . betrayal . . . Virginia . . . revenge on all . . ."

The meeting broke up, and the men dispersed. Andy immediately called Shaheed and told him what he heard.

"Should I continue surveillance?"

"Yes, Andy, follow him, but keep your distance and keep me on the line." Andy followed Breitner as he headed up the boardwalk, further from the hotel.

"What's he doing?" Shaheed asked.

"He's coming up the street right now. I'm going to hang back a bit. Wait a second . . . I think he's being followed."

"Followed by whom?"

"I don't know. The vehicle is a black Hummer. The monster looks like a fucking tank."

"What's happening now?"

"He ducked into Kilwin's."

"Kilwin's? He wants a frigging ice cream cone?"

"Not sure, but four guys just got out of the Hummer and followed him in. Unless they all happen to want ice cream, something is definitely going on."

"Can you identify any of the Hummer guys?"

"No."

"Get the plate off the Hummer."

"It's a vanity plate. Fuck, you won't believe the number."

"What is it?"

"PURE USA."

"Fitting."

"I'm going in."

"What does that mean, going in?"

"I'm suddenly in the mood for ice cream."

"Be careful. You have no backup. Don't pay these guys any attention. Stay off their radar."

"I'll be careful."

Andy walked into Kilwin's. The store was quiet. In fact, Breitner and his group were the only other customers. They ordered and paid for double-scoop cones, exited the store, and sat down at some ice cream tables situated in front of the shop, where they immediately got into a heated conversation.

Andy quickly ordered a one-scoop waffle cone with Mackinaw Island Fudge ice cream, paid, then hurried out the door to catch the conversation. He sat down at a table as far from the men as possible, while still close enough to see and hear them. He could even cell phone video the meeting.

"The new guys are a little green, but they're committed," Andy heard Bart say, still slurring his speech.

"What's the plan?" asked one of the men.

"No plan yet. We are just testing the waters to determine whether to avenge Blaine and Arlington. It appears we agree we can't let up. They will have to silence every one of us before we capitulate."

"Patience is a virtue, but whatever the plan, count me in," said another. The others nodded their affirmation.

"You are all invited to offer suggestions and ideas, new guys, fresh perspective -- you know what I mean? We need a solid plan. We cannot survive another Arlington."

"Understood," said the Hummer driver. "When shall we meet again?"

"Today's Tuesday. How's Friday evening on my boat?" Breitner replied.

"Works for me." Again, the rest of the men nodded their assent.

Breitner rose. Apparently, the big cheese decided the meeting was over. "See ya Friday." He dumped his cone and staggered up the boardwalk, alone.

Andy was conflicted. *Will I be noticed if I get up and follow Breitner?* He decided to stay but keep Bart in sight, figuring he was returning to his boat.

"That guy has a screw loose," said Hummer man. "His anger over Blaine and the other stuff is going to land all of us in the slammer or, worse, dead."

"That's why we need to come up with a great plan."

"Or get the hell out of Dodge."

"Can't do that. In for a penny, in for a pound."

"Not if the consequences are prison or death."

"Cross Bart, and he'll find you. You'd be as good as dead anyway."

"Shit, what a fucking nightmare!"

"That it is. What choice do we have now?"

"This better be the greatest fucking plan in the history of plans."

"Nothing more we can do tonight. Get some sleep. We'll meet up tomorrow."

They rose, walked to the Hummer, and drove off.

Andy resumed surveillance on Breitner, some distance away. He called Shaheed. "Something's in the works, but no definitive plan yet. If we don't do something to stop this, a real shitstorm is coming."

"Make sure he boards the boat, then head back to the hotel. Maybe Jack's meeting with Bart will give us more to go on."

"There's dissension in the ranks, which is good, I guess, but I've got a bad feeling about all this."

"Me too, Andy. Me too."

# Chapter Fifteen

Jack walked the boardwalk and reached the *White Knight* at precisely 7:50 p.m. the following evening. Breitner was there, sitting on the boat deck with four other white guys who looked like vacationing tourists. This group scared the hell out of Jack. You could easily identify Blaine's guys. They *looked* like white nationalists, but not these Breitner boys. These guys were your next-door neighbors, wife, two-point-five kids, a dog, a nice car, and a house in the 'burbs.' A conversation was underway, but the men stopped talking as soon as they saw Jack approach.

"Jack Manning, this is everyone. Everyone, this is Jack," said Breitner. They exchanged greetings, fist bumps all around.

"Wow, that was quick."

"We don't fuck around," replied one of the other men.

"You work for Ford, Jack?" one of the men asked.

"Yep."

"Now, there was a nationalist! I sure wish he was still around."

"Who?"

"Henry Ford."

"Ford? Why?"

"Because he hated Jews and loved Hitler; my kind of guy."

"Yeah, he was a real peach."

"You disagree?" The man eyed him with sudden suspicion. Shaheed, listening in on the wiretap, squirmed in his seat.

"I agree with his attitude toward the Jews, got no use for Jews. But Hitler wanted to control the world. He would have attacked the United States. America first."

"I see what you mean. Hard to argue with that logic."

"We are discussing a situation, Jack," said Breitner.

"What kind of situation?"

"Looking to even a score."

"I'm not sure I understand."

"No, you wouldn't. I'm not sure what to do with you."

"What do you mean?"

"Have you ever been in trouble with the law, Jack?"

"Never been caught, if that's what you mean. I stay off the radar. I'm no saint, just never been caught."

"What's the worst thing you've ever done?"

"Come on, Bert. This is not something I'm comfortable talking about."

"If you were caught doing whatever it was would you have gone to prison?"

"Yes."

"What was it?"

"Shit, Bert, come on."

"Out with it, Jack."

"Drugs."

"Buying or selling?"

"Both."

"What kind of drugs?"

"Meth lab."

"How long ago?"

"Long time. I've been on the straight and narrow since I got my degree and went to work."

"Must have taken a lot of planning to manufacture and sell meth and keep it on the down low."

"Strategic planning is a specialty of mine. That's most of what I do at work. I basically traded covert planning in the drug world for strategic planning in the corporate world."

"Good to know. We might need your services."

"Happy to help if I can. What's going on?"

"Revenge. Like I said before, looking to even a score."

"Revenge for what?"

"You came clean with me, so I'll come clean with you," said Breitner. "A few weeks ago, some of the boys and I planned an event that would have wiped out a whole bunch of cops and a shitload of camel jockeys."

"Shit!"

"Shit is right. Guess where?"

"New York?"

"What city has the most camel jockeys? I'll give you a hint. You work there."

"Dearborn?"

"Correct, Dearborn."

"What happened?"

"Nothing. *That's* the problem. Someone tipped off the cops, and the plan was derailed before it got started. Two of my men were killed, and the rest were arrested. I'm the only one who got away."

"Hmm…I didn't hear anything on the news."

"That's because the cops kept it hush-hush."

"Kept what hush-hush?"

"What do you know about sarin gas?"

"Sarin? Not sure…wait…isn't that the stuff from Syria where that dictator gassed his own people?"

"That's the stuff."

"Okay, what about it?"

"We found out there's a large quantity of the stuff stored right here in the good ole' USA."

"You're kidding me."

"I don't have a sense of humor."

"So, what happened?"

"We tried to steal it. Somehow, the cops and Feds figured it out. A lot of our guys are going to prison. One got shot."

"I'm really sorry about your guys, Bert, but what does this have to do with Dearborn?"

"Ever hear of Ben Blaine?"

"Name is familiar, but I can't place it," Jack pretended to search his memory.

"Involved in the Dearborn mosque bombing last year?"

"Yeah, that was a big deal in Dearborn, front page news. This Blaine guy was a white supremacist, right? He wanted to kill Muslims and cops. It didn't turn out very well if I recall."

"Blaine is a friend of mine. He's in prison for life. We want revenge for that too."

"I don't blame you, but wouldn't you be better off laying low for a while?"

"No. That's what they expect me to do. I want to do the opposite of what they expect. I want my revenge Jack, and you know Dearborn well. You offered to help. Still interested? If so, here's your chance."

"I *do* know Dearborn."

"Any of you guys come up with anything?"

No response.

"Let's continue this on Friday. Stay on topic, men. I need some fresh ideas."

When Bart rose, the men knew they were being dismissed. They rose and stepped off the boat and onto the dock.

"Good to meet you, Jack. We'll come up with something, Bert," said one of the men. "See you Friday."

"There will be hell to pay if you don't," replied Bart as they walked away, leaving Jack and Breitner alone.

"Want a beer, Jack?"

"Sure, Bart..."

"Wait. What did you just call me?"

"Bert." *Oh shit!*

"Oh shit," said Shaheed, in his room, listening with Noah.

"No, you said Bart. Why?"

"Bert, Bart. Simple mistake. No big deal."

"But it is a big deal, and I think you know it is."

"Why are you getting so bent out of shape over nothing?"

"Don't think so, Jack. I'm not buying it. I knew there was something about you. You're a little too eager to help for my taste, too many questions and not enough answers. That's why I brought you here and told you all that shit. I wanted to see your reaction. And that's also why I wanted to get you alone. You're good man, really good! I've got to hand it to you. Now, who the fuck are you, really, Jack?" Breitner pulled a gun from the back of his shorts and pointed it at Jack Dylan.

"Whoa, Bert. What the fuck? You're scaring me, man. Please put the gun down. Come on. I got confused, that's all."

"Turn around, slowly, no sudden movements."

"Seriously? Why? Stop pointing that gun at me and let's talk this over."

"I will not ask you again. Turn around." Jack did as Bart commanded.

"Bert, please. This is stupid. Why are you doing this?" Jack began to walk forward, away from Bart, looking for an exit of some kind.

"Hold still, Jack. If you take one more step, I swear I'll shoot you."

"Shoot me because I screwed up your name? This can't be happening."

"Don't move, asshole." He cocked the gun, and Jack stopped in his tracks.

Shaheed jumped on the horn and called in the cavalry. He called 9-1-1 and told the operator there was an officer in danger and to get every patrol car in the area over to the dock in front of Shirley's Bar & Grill.

"Stay put while I frisk you," said Breitner. Jack had no choice but to let him, up to a point. Breitner felt around and came across the wire, which he viciously yanked out of Jack's shirt. On the other end, Shaheed heard a high-pitched wail and promptly lost the signal. Jack was alone with the terrorist.

Suddenly, Jack lunged forward and threw his body into Breitner with all the force he could muster. Breitner fell backward, banging his hand against the wall. The gun dropped to the deck.

Jack lunged for the gun, retrieved it, and turned back to Breitner. He was gone. Not knowing how many weapons were on the boat,

Jack dashed for cover behind a wall. After a few short moments, he peeked around the corner and saw no one. The faint sound of a siren could be heard in the distance.

Jack slowly moved forward toward the front of the boat, still no sign of Breitner. He stepped onto the bow and peered down into the cabin. He saw Breitner standing at the threshold, less than four feet away, holding a grenade, his fingers surrounding the pin.

"Drop the gun, Jack."

"No fucking way, Bart."

"Honest mistake, Dylan?"

"You knew all along?"

"Of course I knew all along. You think I'm stupid?"

"No, I think you're crazy, and I'm taking you in, Breitner."

"Over my dead body, Dylan."

"If need be. I have no problem with that."

The sirens were getting louder.

"You're not taking me alive, Jack, and you aren't getting out of this alive either."

"Put down the grenade, Bart. You hear the sirens, don't you? Be sensible. No one got killed in Virginia. The attack on Dearborn was aborted. All you're guilty of right now is conspiracy to commit a terrorist act, which you can probably plead out. That's a lot better than dying or going to prison for murdering a cop, don't you think? Give it up, Bart."

"Fuck you, Dylan. Why don't you drop the gun?"

The sirens sounded louder now. The cops were almost there. *If I can keep him talking a little while longer…*

"I'm not dropping the gun. You hear the sirens, don't you? It's over, Bart. You're not getting out of here…"

Manistee squad cars pulled up to the dock, and several Manistee police officers ran toward the boat. Shaheed, Andy, and Noah followed shortly behind.

"Bye-bye, Dylan," said Breitner with an ominous look as he eyes glaring at Jack. "See you in hell, buddy."

He pulled the pin and tossed the grenade at Jack.

Jack hesitated a second before jumping onto the bow and diving into the water. The grenade exploded, sending boat debris flying in all directions. The policemen were thrown backward by the blast as the debris rained down. All hell broke loose.

# Chapter Sixteen

Five Manistee police officers rose from the ground, staggering and shell-shocked. They brushed boat debris off their uniforms and shook their heads, clearing the momentary shockwaves. As they approached the wreckage, the officers observed sections of the boat and other debris strewn around the boardwalk, the dock, and floating in the water. Suddenly, Jack Dylan's head emerged from the murk. The officers immediately pulled their weapons and trained them on the man in the water.

"You! In the water! This is Police Chief Christopher Alexander of the Manistee Police Department. Don't move!"

"If I stop moving, I'll drown," replied Jack, continuing to tread water.

"Funny guy," replied Alexander. "Get your ass out of the water now!"

"Don't shoot. I'm coming out," said Jack.

Shaheed, Andy, and Noah came up from behind Alexander. Three police officers whirled and trained their weapons on them, as well.

"Whoa, whoa, whoa," said Shaheed, reaching for his badge.

"Hands in the air now! Keep them up where I can see them. Who are *you*?"

"I'm Lieutenant Shaheed Ali of the Dearborn Police Department. I'm the one who called 9-1-1. The guy in the water is our Captain, Jack Dylan."

"Keep your hands up where we can see them," one of the officers commanded.

Alexander focused on Jack. "Get out of the water now! Don't make me ask you again."

"I'm coming, I'm coming. Give me a break. I might be injured.

Jack climbed onto the dock, shook himself off, and raised his hands.

"Keep your hands where I can see them." Jack sighed and raised his hands higher.

Shaheed approached Alexander. "May I please show you my credentials, Chief?"

"Left hand, very slowly, Ali," warned Alexander.

Shaheed followed orders and gently removed his badge and credentials. He moved forward and handed them to Alexander. The other cops continued to train weapons on the rest of the Dearborn contingent. One by one, each was granted permission to remove and hand over their badges and credentials. The last to do so was Jack Dylan.

"So you're their captain? What the hell happened here, Dylan?"

"I was undercover, hunting down a terrorist. He was plotting the murders of hundreds of people. I tracked him here and tried to arrest him, but he pulled out a grenade and exploded the boat. He blew himself up, and he tried like hell to take me with him. See all that crap in the water? That's what's left of him and his boat."

"Why were you on his boat?"

"As I said, I was undercover."

"You men are out of your jurisdiction. Notification to the local police force of a sting operation in their town is common courtesy. Why weren't we informed?"

"The situation was very fluid. It developed rapidly. There wasn't time. Besides, you have to understand who this guy was…"

"I don't care who he was," roared Alexander. "It looks to me like he's dead, his boat's destroyed, and you're all that's left. That's what I see."

"This guy was a terrorist, Chief. Have you or any of your men ever dealt with a terrorist? Do you have the resources to do so?" Jack's condescending attitude was not helping his cause.

"Sure, wise guy. This 'catch the bad guys' stuff is way over the heads of us country cops, right? From where I'm standing, this looks like you had some sort of agenda. You stalked this guy, and you killed him. I'm taking you into custody on suspicion of murder, Dylan. Turn around." Alexander pulled out his handcuffs.

"You have got to be kidding me, Chief," said Jack.

"Do I look like I'm kidding?" Alexander replied, holding out the cuffs. "Should I add resisting arrest to the list of potential charges? Perhaps I should arrest your colleagues here, as well. Perhaps this was a conspiracy to commit murder."

Jack needed to be certain Shaheed, Andy, and Noah were not sent to jail. They needed to be available to help clean up this mess he'd created. *Wait until Acker finds out about this. Crap! Maybe I should let Alexander kill me.*

Jack stepped forward and turned around, placing his hands behind his back. "No need for that, Chief. I'll come quietly."

As Jack was being handcuffed, he scanned his surroundings. Several people must have heard or seen the explosion. Now they were all standing around witnessing Jack's arrest.

"Someone should interview all of these people while they're here. They are all potential witnesses."

"Damn, Dylan, you are one condescending bastard. One more word and I'll put you in solitary. Come along now. Let's get to the station for processing."

"Aye, aye, Chief." Jack Dylan was incapable of curbing his attitude toward the Manistee policeman. Luckily, this time, Alexander ignored him.

Jack was placed in a squad car. Chief Alexander told Shaheed that he and his men could follow the vehicle to the station. The three men piled into the unmarked police vehicle and followed the local cops back to the station. Jack was processed and tossed into a cell. He continued to wax sarcastic despite Shaheed's constant warnings to shut his mouth.

Chief Alexander contacted Chief Acker at a number provided by Shaheed. Acker was livid Jack not only duped him and the Dearborn and Manistee Police Departments, but he also defied the Feds and interfered with a federal investigation. Acker called the Detroit office of the FBI and informed them of the situation. FBI representatives were dispatched to Manistee, and Chief Alexander eagerly offered to help them in any way he could.

Shaheed sensed what Jack hadn't yet come to terms with: Dylan was about to face federal charges for stalking a victim and murdering him. He would probably be charged with murder in the first. If convicted, Jack Dylan faced mandatory life in prison without the possibility of parole. Drastic action was required, and Shaheed knew with absolute certainty the one person he needed to call.

# PART TWO—PRE-TRIAL

# Chapter Seventeen

Zachary Blake just finished delivering a serious ass kicking to a pro-insurance company legislator on a legal radio program. Zack was well aware that in the constant conflict between loyalty and service to policyholders versus allegiance and service to *stockholders*, the stockholders would emerge victorious every single time. It didn't surprise him the *carriers* always put profits ahead of policyholders. He could not understand, though, how elected officials could take pro-insurance stances against the citizens who elected them. *Carriers don't vote, dammit. People do!*

Zack hated insurance companies. He was pleased to use his recent fame to make appearances like the one on the legal talk show or to donate large amounts of money to causes that benefited victims rather than carriers. Public appearances always included reasoned and effective attacks on the insurance lobby.

His extraordinary public courtroom successes made him famous, a household name in both civil and criminal legal circles. First, there was the Tracey clergy abuse case. Zack won a hard-fought, nine-figure verdict against powerful forces in the church, intent on covering up the disgusting crimes of a rogue priest. That outstanding result led to his retention in the Arya Khan murder case, where his stellar legal work freed an innocent Muslim woman, falsely accused of murder. Zack was a newsworthy public figure, and people were interested in what he had to say.

As he was about to open a file and return to work, his private phone began to ring. Caller ID displayed an unknown number, which was not uncommon following the Khan case. Curiosity got the best of him, and he answered the call.

"Zachary Blake. May I help you?"

"Zack?"

"Speaking."

"Zack, this is Shaheed Ali."

"Hey, Shaheed, nice to hear from you. How is everything in Dearborn?" Zack remembered Shaheed from the Khan case. He was Jack Dylan's second in command, a good guy as far as cops go.

"Right now, Zack, I'm not in Dearborn. I'm up north, in Manistee. Jack Dylan is about to be charged with murder in the first."

"What? How is that even possible? Tell me what happened."

Shaheed proceeded to tell Zachary Blake the short version of the story. Zack probed him with questions, which Shaheed very patiently answered. The two men paused for a moment.

"Has he been formally charged?" Zack finally asked.

"I don't think so, but things could change at any moment."

"Is there any chance he's guilty?"

"As I said, he went there undercover, without color of authority, to catch a terrorist. But there is not a chance in hell Jack Dylan murdered anyone. Jack says the guy blew himself up and that's enough for me. No way is Dylan a cold-blooded murderer."

"Listen to me, Shaheed. Tell Jack I'm on my way and not to utter a word until I get there. I've got timeshare ownership in a small jet, and I can be there in a couple of hours. Okay?"

"Okay, and Zack?"

"Yes?"

"Thanks a lot."

"Thank me when we get Jack out of this mess." Zack hung up the phone and sat back in his ergonomic desk chair. *Jack Dylan charged with murder*, he ruminated. *Could he possibly be guilty?* Zack recalled how callously Jack treated Arya Khan when she was first accused. However, when he received sufficient proof of Arya's innocence, Jack worked diligently to free her. Afterward, he tracked down the men who framed her for murder. *He can be a prick, but he's a fair and honest cop. I can't see him as a cold-blooded murderer. Jack thought the mosque bomber was a coward. Even if he could kill someone, he'd never use an explosive.*

Zack picked up the phone and telephoned his wife, Jennifer. She knew Jack Dylan's history, and when she heard the story, Jennifer told Zack he had no choice but to go to Manistee and do whatever he could to help. She knew the game. Zack could be gone a couple of days, a couple of weeks, or, worst-case scenario, a couple of months. Jennifer was right, though. Zack had to go and help this man.

Two hours later, Zachary Blake walked into police headquarters in Manistee and asked to see his new client. The desk sergeant checked Zack in and directed him to a lobby area with several rows of hard plastic chairs. Zack placed a call to Shaheed Ali and told him where and when to meet him. Shaheed wanted to come down to the station, but Zack advised against it. Attorney-client privilege would not apply if Shaheed witnessed conversations between Zack and Jack. Instead, Zack asked Shaheed to book him a room at the Bay Shore and to text him directions.

"Mr. Blake?" A heavyset man in a cheap suit was standing in front of him. His badge read 'Chief Alexander'

"Yes, sir?"

"You're here to see Jack Dylan?"

"I am."

"You from around here?"

Zack handed him his business card. "No, my office is in Bloomfield Hills, near Detroit. May I please see my client, Chief?" Zack was not in the mood for small talk.

"Sure."

"Has he been charged?"

"No. We're still investigating. I'd *like* to charge him with being a complete asshole."

"Sounds like Jack," replied Zack. "But that doesn't make him a murderer. If it means anything, from someone who knows the guy and knows his commitment to the rule of law, he couldn't commit murder. Dylan is a good...no, a *great* cop."

"Good to know, Mr. Blake, but if the evidence points to his guilt, the fact he's a cop won't mean shit. Murder is murder around these parts, cop or not."

"I understand. May I see him now, Chief?"

"Right this way." Chief Alexander pointed to a door off to the left of the lobby. Zack followed Alexander to the door, a buzzer sounded, and the door clicked. The two men entered, passed a small squad room, a couple of jail cells, and came upon a small, locked room. Another buzzer sounded, and the door to the room opened. Inside sat Jack Dylan, dressed in an orange prison-issued jumpsuit.

"Blake," exclaimed Jack. "Boy, I never thought I'd be happy to see a defense attorney, but am I glad to see *you*, man! These guys have this all wrong."

"Shut up, Jack," replied Zack.

"Why is my client dressed in prison garb? I thought you said he wasn't charged."

"He jumped in the lake during the explosion. He was brought into headquarters soaking wet with no change of clothing. These were the only dry clothes we could provide on short notice. If someone brings him a change of clothing, he's welcome to wear those."

"Okay, Chief. Can we have the room?"

"Sure."

Alexander left Zachary Blake alone with Jack Dylan.

"Thanks for coming, Zack. You're the only defense lawyer I trust. Shaheed told me he was calling you. I'm in deep shit here, man."

"I'll do the best I can to get you out of this mess, but you have to stop antagonizing the locals, Jack."

"But they are *morons*, Zack! Why would I kill the guy? I'm a sworn officer of the law. But there's an even *better* reason."

"What's that?"

"I wanted to work undercover and convince the guy I was sympathetic to the cause. I wanted to bring down his whole organization. To do that, I would have had to infiltrate the group. I was on to something and killing Bart Breitner would not have facilitated that agenda."

"Hang on a second. I'll be right back." Zack knocked on the locked door, and Chief Alexander unlocked and opened it.

"I presume the crime scene is secured?" Zack asked.

"Yes, Mr. Blake, it is. It's complicated since much of the evidence is floating in Lake Michigan. The Coast Guard has a man there, and so do we. There are cameras on the dock, and we're monitoring those," replied Alexander.

Zack did not respond. He was staring into space.

"Mr. Blake? Anything else?"

"No, that's it for now." Alexander left the room and closed the door. His footsteps could be heard walking away down the hall.

"Satisfied, Jack?"

"No, I'm not satisfied at all, dammit! Please, Zack, get me the hell out of here."

"Let's keep a level head, shall we? Getting you out of here may not be so easy, Jack. I need to hear the whole story. Don't leave anything out."

"We need to get Eric Burns and his team up here right away," replied Jack. Eric was a crime scene investigator and processor for the Dearborn Police. His stellar forensic work helped free Arya Khan.

"We'll get to that, Jack. We'll need Micah Love and his team up here, too, when the time comes." Micah was Zack's private investigator. His team helped Zack win the Tracey and Khan cases. Micah and Zack became quite a pair, and their combined efforts produced legendary results in many high-profile cases. "For now, I need you to tell me everything that happened."

Jack told Zack the entire story, from when he'd first heard about a potential sarin gas attack on his city, to his team's investigative work in finding those responsible. Jack carefully recounted every detail, from Stone's immunity deal to the Arlington fiasco, to the Manistee undercover operation, and, finally, to the boat explosion.

"I swear to God, Zack. I didn't kill him."

"You're a cop. Your story is plausible. But you came up here without authority after being taken off the case by the Feds. You don't advise the locals, and you appear to be obsessed with Breitner. How would you see it if you were them?"

"They don't like me, and they don't know what the fuck they are doing. That's how *I* see it."

"Maybe they don't like you because you came here undercover and conducted a criminal investigation as a private citizen and not a cop."

"Whose side are you on here, Blake?"

"I'm on *your* side, Jack, but locking heads with the locals is not helping your cause. Look where your own stupid behavior has landed you. Can you tell me anything useful? Did anyone see you on the deck when the grenade exploded?"

"I didn't notice, but that doesn't mean there wasn't anyone there. We recently finished a planning committee meeting. The other guys just left. Some of them might have still been around. Or, maybe, someone will grow a conscience."

"Maybe…did you get any names?"

"No, but I can describe them reasonably well."

"Anything else?"

"Yeah! A guy named Alan Berger invited me on a fishing trip with Bart. He seemed to know him pretty well, but under an alias, Robert Bright. He went fishing with 'Robert' many times. He even warned me about 'Bert's' temper. He may know more."

"Sounds worth exploring. What else?"

"How about common sense, Zack? Killing Bart Breitner is the exact opposite of what I was looking to do. If anything, I'm an idiot for underestimating the man, but not a *murderer*."

"Don't beat yourself up, Jack. Besides, maybe, after the investigation, they'll come to their senses. They haven't even charged you with a crime yet. I'll talk to Alexander and see whether I can get you out of here. Ask for professional courtesy or something. Can I get you anything before I go?"

"No, I'm good, Zack. Thanks again for coming. I really appreciate it."

Zack knocked on the door again. This time, another local cop opened it and led Zack back into the waiting room, where he found Shaheed, Noah, and Andy talking with Alexander.

"Hi, guys," Zack greeted pleasantly. "Anywhere we can go and get a cup of coffee?"

"There's a Kilwin's down by the crime scene," offered Alexander. "You can get some coffee and visit the crime scene at the same time."

"Thanks, Chief. Will you keep us posted on the investigation, please? Not officially, but as a courtesy, one officer to another?" Shaheed asked.

"As much as I am able, I certainly will," replied Alexander, looking Shaheed over. "You're certainly more pleasant and polite than he is," he continued, nodding over to the lockup where Jack was housed.

"Jack Dylan is now represented by counsel, Chief. Please direct all inquiries or developments directly to me, please," Zack requested.

"Not a problem, Mr. Blake."

Zack almost responded, 'Call me Zack, Chief, but didn't. *Keep it professional,* he decided.

The four men walked out together, leaving Alexander to deal with Jack.

"Which way to Kilwin's?" Zack asked.

"That way," replied Shaheed, pointing up the street.

"Lead the way," replied Zack.

They walked a short distance up the dock until they reached the shop. Across the way was the obliterated boat and damaged dock, cordoned off with yellow crime scene tape. The men skipped Kilwin's and walked over to the scene. There was a Coast Guard cutter on the water and a squad car parked at the dock, with an officer sitting inside.

Zack walked up to the squad car and signaled for the officer to lower his window. The officer obliged.

"My name is Zachary Blake. I'm the attorney representing Jack Dylan, whom I presume you know. Do you mind if I look around?"

"Chief said you might be coming. Look around, if you want, but stay out of the taped-off area," replied the cop indifferently.

"Thanks," replied Zack. He walked up, as close to the destroyed boat as possible and looked out into the water. *It's possible someone was out on the lake or coming to shore at the time of the explosion.* He looked right, then left. Everything was closed, probably as a result of the blast. *Stores, bars, and restaurants mean people. Which ones were open at the time of the explosion? Did anyone see or hear anything? Can I trust the cops to find them if they exist? No, absolutely not.*

He made a mental note to call Micah and request he send a team to Manistee as soon as possible. He turned to the others.

"What do you guys make of this?" he asked no one in particular.

"Not much to go on," replied Andy. "It would be nice if someone found a nice big piece of the grenade with Bart Breitner's prints all over it."

"That would be nice. Of course, that assumes his prints are in the system. We sure aren't going to be able to fingerprint him going forward," said Shaheed.

"Maybe the divers will find something useful," said Noah.

"It's possible, I suppose. But we can't count on that," replied Zack. "It would be nice, though." He scanned the area again. "What time did this happen?"

"Around eight, eight thirty last night," replied Andy.

"We need to find out which stores were open," said Zack, continuing his scan of the surrounding area.

"When we arrived after the explosion, I noticed the Kilwin's ice cream shop was open. So was the pizza place directly across the street from the explosion, but I don't know if anyone was there or saw anything."

"That's a start. Let's head into both places and see whether anyone knows anything. You guys are not here in any official capacity, and I don't want you getting into it with the locals. I'm his lawyer. I'm expected to be a pain in the ass. If you notice someone or something or have a question to ask or point to make it would be better to do it through me. Jack has made you persona non grata."

The men split up. Some went into the ice cream store, and others into the coffee shop. They talked with the managers of both, as well as several employees, all of whom worked the evening before. Everyone heard the explosion, some even ducked for cover at the ferocious sound, but no one saw anything. Finding someone who was walking along the boardwalk or sitting outside at the time of the blast would be a challenge.

The men reassembled at Kilwin's. Zack ordered four coffees. They sat in silence, sipping their brew. Zack was deep in thought, contemplating Jack Dylan's fate. *The first nonpartisans to observe the crime scene were the cops who arrived within seconds of the blast. And they immediately determined Jack Dylan murdered Bart Breitner. Things do not look good for Jack. Things do not look good at all.*

# Chapter Eighteen

"Love investigations. May I help you?"

"Hi, this is Zack Blake. Who's this?"

"This is Ginger," came the reply, the voice of a seductive-sounding young female. "How may I direct your call, Mr. Blake?" She made "How may I direct your call?" sound like "Would you like to meet me for drinks?" Micah Love had a proverbial revolving door of beautiful women rotating in and out of his receptionist chair for as long as Zachary had known him.

Micah Love was an extraordinarily talented private investigator. He and Zack had a falling out a few years ago when Zack's life was in the toilet, and he stiffed Micah on a couple of investigation invoices. A couple of years later, though, the investigator took a big chance on Zack, who, at the lowest point in his career, landed the Tracey clergy abuse case. The two men exposed a vast conspiracy to cover up the clergy's abuse of children, and when the case was finally over, Micah and Zack were multi-millionaires. Micah and his team were also a significant factor in exonerating Arya Khan. Today, there was almost nothing these two men wouldn't do for each other.

"Micah Love, please?"

"Please hold, Mr. Blake. I'll page him."

"Thanks, Ginger."

Zack could not help wondering what Jessica, Micah's girlfriend, thought of Ginger. The line clicked.

"Zaaaaaackkkkkk, buuuudddddy, how are you, man?" Micah was in a jovial mood.

"Hey, Micah. So, what's Ginger like?"

"What do *you* think?" Micah asked.

"Never mind me, man. What does *Jessica* think of her?"

"She's fine with anyone I hire as long as I behave. Can't be too careful these days.

"Too careful must be terribly difficult for you, Micah," Zack quipped.

"Is this a social or business call?" Micah asked, getting down to business.

"Business, Micah, serious business. Remember Jack Dylan?"

"The Dearborn cop? Did not like him much, but don't like or trust cops on general principle. What about him?"

"He's been arrested in Manistee."

"That's not good. What did he do?"

"I don't think he did anything, Micah. But I'm up in Manistee now, and this is a serious situation. There are no charges yet, but I believe they are inevitable. I'm guessing Jack is going to be charged with murder in the first degree."

"Whoa! Who has he supposedly murdered?"

"Another Blaine-type supremacist. Ever heard of Bart Breitner?"

"Name is vaguely familiar. First Blaine and now Breitner, it's not a good time to be a white supremacist. Perhaps they should find another line of work? How can I help?"

Zack gave Micah the *Reader's Digest* version of the story. "I'm going to need serious investigative and forensic help up here, Micah. The majority of the evidence is floating in Lake Michigan. Witnesses have yet to be identified, and most are probably tourists. The local cops don't have the latest technology, they don't seem to like big-city interference, and they don't like Dylan. I've got my work cut out for me."

"I am at your service, buddy. Can this guy afford me?"

"I've got you covered, man. You know that. May I send the jet for you?"

"Fancy."

"Only the best for you. City Airport?"

"That would be great. If not, Oakland County works."

"Thanks, Micah."

***

Twenty-four hours later, Micah Love and his forensic and investigative teams landed in Manistee. Zack was there to greet them. After they checked in at the Bay Shore, the men met in the hotel's conference room. Jack Dylan's Manistee nightmare was a pleasant dream of unexpected business for the Bay Shore Hotel.

"Have they charged Dylan with a crime yet?"

"This morning."

"First-degree murder?"

"Yep. Eventually, I think it will get reduced to second-degree, but if you follow the Manistee cops' theories, Jack carefully planned it all. He lied to his boss, came to Manistee without authority and without letting the locals know he was here, stalked Breitner, gained his trust, and then killed him at his first opportunity. Malice aforethought plus careful planning equals murder in the first. I think we can easily defeat the 'careful planning' part, which probably gets the charge kicked down to second-degree."

"Sounds right. What are the other theories?"

"Jack lied to his boss. That's not contestable. But he did it to conduct an undercover operation and reduce the risk of blowing his cover. Still, he kept his closest advisors in the loop. The plan was to befriend Breitner and infiltrate his organization. He wanted them to believe he was a nationalist, then expose them, shut them down and put them all in prison. If that was Jack's goal, and he shared that goal with his closest advisors, why would he murder Breitner before gaining any information?"

"I can work with that. Do we have any evidence to support it?"

"We have Jack's team here with us. They were aware he was undercover here, and they're willing to testify he's doing police work, even if it was 'off book.' In fact, Jack talked to his second-in-command, the evening before the explosion. Why would he do that if he planned to kill Breitner?"

"I get it. It goes to motive and planning, what any cop would do. Jack planned to infiltrate and prevent an attack. He did not come to execute the guy."

"Exactly."

"But we need more. Forensic evidence would be helpful. The victim's fingerprints on a grenade part or something like that."

"That would be nice, but not very likely."

"Never know until we get over there."

"What's the likelihood that we can obtain that type of evidence?"

"Any evidence we examine will have to be after the arraignment and after the locals collect and process it."

"Maybe they can be persuaded to let us assist. One of my guys is a superb criminalist and forensic specialist. I'll offer his services."

"Probably a non-starter, Micah. Neither the locals or the Feds like Jack very much these days."

"When's the arraignment?"

"Tomorrow morning."

"Point me to police headquarters, and I'll go sweet talk the chief, what's his name?

"Alexander, Christopher Alexander."

\*\*\*

A half-hour later, Zack, Micah, and Matt Jordan, Micah's crime scene specialist, were standing in the lobby of Manistee police headquarters, waiting for Alexander.

"What's he like?" Micah asked.

"A little to the right of Buford T. Justice," replied Zack, referencing Jackie Gleason's classic portrayal of a country cop in *Smokey and the Bandit*.

"I love Buford T. Justice. If I were an actor and I could choose to play only one part, it would be Buford T. Justice."

"Great role, Micah, but Buford is not the type of cop you want if you are trying to prove your client's innocence."

"Suppose not."

A door opened, and Alexander walked out into the lobby. Micah started chuckling. *Buford T. Justice!*

"What's so funny?" Chief Alexander asked. He disliked Micah even before introductions were made.

"Nothing, Chief. I told Micah a joke right before you walked in."

"Oh, it must have been hilarious."

"Want to hear it?"

"Pass. I'm busy. What can I do for you?"

"Chief, meet Micah Love, my investigator, and his *CSI*, Matt Jordan. We were hoping to get permission to examine the crime scene."

Alexander ignored the two men. "As soon as we release it, you can have at it."

"We were hoping to offer assistance in processing it. Matt here is an expert in his field, and all local protocols will be strictly observed. Your team and the Feds will keep the lead."

"We're fine. The Feds are on their way. They will provide all the assistance and all the 'expert' forensic guys we could possibly need. Your man is welcome to process the scene when we're done," Alexander repeated. "And I'll make all of the evidence we process available to your team just as soon as the judge so orders."

"Chief, be reasonable. This is a fellow cop we are talking about, and evidence could be floating further and further away, as we speak."

"We have the crime scene fairly well contained, and we have a team out there right now gathering evidence."

"Anything you are willing to share, Chief?" Jordan asked.

"Not at the moment. Soon enough," replied Alexander.

"Can I go out there and observe Chief?" responded Jordan.

"I can't stop you. Don't get in the way and don't interfere. If you do, you'll be on a plane back to Detroit, and you won't see *any* evidence in this case. Catch my drift?"

"Thanks, Chief."

Ten minutes later, Matt Jordan and the entire company arrived at the crime scene.

A heavyset, gruff woman approached them. She could have been Alexander's sister. *Buforda?* Micah thought, chuckling.

"May I help you?" she asked.

Zachary handed her a business card. "I'm Zachary Blake. I'm Captain Dylan's attorney. This is Micah Love and Matt Jordan. They're part of my team." Zack referred to his client as 'Captain' to remind the woman she was investigating a cop.

"Sheila Prince, Manistee Detective Squad. What can I do for you, gentlemen?"

"Jack Dylan is a good cop, Detective. He was working a case undercover when this happened. He wouldn't kill anyone unless his life or the lives of civilians were threatened. He certainly wouldn't blow a criminal up, especially when he was trying to investigate a larger crime or conspiracy."

"Noted," Prince replied flatly. "But that doesn't answer my question now, does it?"

"According to my client's previous statements, a known terrorist named Bart Breitner took out a grenade and blew himself and his boat up. You should find grenade residue, shrapnel, and other explosive materials lying in and around the water and the dock."

"That's not our working theory of the case. We believe the evidence shows your client blew up the boat and the victim and had a strong motive to do so. A private citizen can't take the law into his own hands no matter who the victim is." she replied. "Thanks for the information. We will take everything into account, and this investigation will be unbiased, by the book. In the end, if the evidence supports your version of the facts, then your version will be in my official report."

"Good to hear, Detective. Can you tell us anything, 'cop to cop?'" Shaheed asked. He was troubled by her reference to Jack as a 'citizen.' His unofficial status was going to be a significant factor in the investigation going forward.

"Nice try, Lieutenant . . ."

Matt interrupted. "Please, Detective, can you tell me whether you found any grenade fragments?"

"In the interest of 'cop to cop' relations, we've found a whole lot of bomb-making paraphernalia, lots of shattered boat and other fragments, and some small body fragments and blood. That's about it so far."

"May I ask for a favor?"

"Depends on what it is."

"Please make a special effort to collect all of the grenade parts you can. We need fingerprint evidence on the grenade pieces. We recently found the victim's prints in our system. If there are prints on the grenade pieces and they belong to the victim, that would support Dylan's theory Breitner pulled the pin and killed himself."

"We would do that anyway," she said. "Most of this stuff will be processed by the Michigan State Police Crime Lab or the Feds. They also have the latest and greatest equipment."

Zack was encouraged by her somewhat cooperative attitude. "Thanks," he said. "That's all we can ask. Matt and his team have some leading, state-of-the-art fingerprint technology and fingerprint experts at their disposal. No expense has been spared in acquiring it. Please, if there are any questions about evidence analysis, will you consider letting Matt and his team assist?"

"Maybe. We'll see where things go. We will consider the request if we feel it will help us get to the truth. Prepare to deal with the State or the Feds, though, because they will process the evidence. Now, if you gentlemen will excuse me, I have to get back to work."

Zack took the not-so-subtle hint. "We're out of here, Detective. Thanks."

# Chapter Nineteen

The following morning, Jack was arraigned in the 85th District Court on 3rd Street in downtown Manistee. The courtroom was built and decorated in grand old turn-of-the-twentieth-century style. Upon entry, one's gaze would first traverse up to the vaulted dome ceiling, outlined by ornate windows. The bench sat high on a pedestal, as judicial superiority and appropriate citizen reverence to the judge were the themes of the time.

A biblical quote, 'Justice, Justice, Shalt Thou Pursue,' was stenciled in gold behind the bench. There was a thirteen-seat jury box to the left of the bench. On this morning, the box was empty. The attorney and prisoner sections, on the other hand, were full, because there were multiple arraignments scheduled. A stenographer and an elderly court officer were present, awaiting a signal from the judge. The courtroom screamed: 'Serious legal business conducted here,' but in truth, district courts were smaller-case courts. District court judges handled criminal arraignments, traffic matters, lower-value civil matters, and small claims cases.

A door off to the right opened, and the court officer slammed a gavel. "All rise!" The spectators rose in unison. "Hear ye, hear ye, hear ye. District Court for the County of Manistee is now in session. The Honorable District Court Judge Joseph Abernathy presiding. You may be seated."

Judge Abernathy assumed his bench. He had thick silver hair combed straight back, a full black judicial robe, and a pair of reading glasses perched on the end of his nose. Specks of dandruff were visible on both shoulders. He scanned the spectators and the lawyer benches, observing a full house. He sighed. *This is going to be a long day.*

"For those of you who are new to my courtroom, my name is Judge Joseph Abernathy. I see we have a full house this morning. This is the time designated for us to do arraignments. Our schedule has been preset. Those of you with lawyers will go first so we can get those people who are being paid by the hour the hell out of here." He peered out over his reading glasses, looked to the attorney's bench, and smiled.

*Real funny,* thought Zack and virtually all the other lawyers. Courtroom decorum and tradition required them to humor the judge, so they chuckled, in deferential respect. Besides, most lawyers actually *do* appreciate judges who call represented clients' cases first and get the lawyers "the hell out of here."

"When the court officer calls your name, your attorney will approach the bench with you. Please do not approach the bench until your name is called. I seriously advise you to follow protocol and our court officer's orders, or you may be facing additional charges for contempt of court. Does everyone understand?" His Honor asked, peering over his reading glasses. He did not wait for a response before saying "Good."

The judge studied his docket, turned to Officer Helman, and said, "Call the case of *People v. Riley*, criminal trespass."

"Chad Riley, criminal trespass, please approach!" screamed Helman. As Riley, a middle-aged man, approached the bench, Helman shouted, "Chad Riley stands accused of entering onto the property of another, to wit, his ex-wife's, Karen Riley, without valid consent, even though he knew said entry was forbidden. Furthermore, when the victim advised Mr. Riley his presence was unwelcome and ordered him to vacate immediately, said defendant failed and/or refused to do so."

"Do you have counsel, Mr. Riley?"

"Lawyer filed an appearance, but I didn't pay him. I can't afford an attorney."

"That explains why your case was on the 'represented by counsel' list."

"I can't afford a lawyer because that bitch over there"—he pointed to a woman who was, presumably, his ex-wife—"took all of my money."

The gallery erupted in laughter, and the judge slammed his gavel. "That will be quite enough! I will clear this court!" The spectators were silent almost immediately. "Mr. Riley, you will refrain from these outbursts and the use of profanity in my courtroom."

"Ain't truth supposed to be a defense, Your Honor?"

That comment prompted chuckles and head nods from the attorney section. The judge glared at the attorneys and rolled his eyes.

"Mr. Riley, if you can't afford a lawyer, one will be appointed for you by the court. Meanwhile, we will enter a 'not guilty' plea on your behalf and release you on your own recognizance. Stay away from your ex-wife's property, or I will place you in jail until your trial. Do you understand me?"

"Yes, Your Honor, but it ain't her property, it's mine!"

"That issue was probably resolved in her favor in divorce court, Mr. Riley. If you have evidence to the contrary, please bring it with you to the trial. If you want to avoid a return to the city jail, you will follow my orders, understand?"

"Yes, Your Honor."

"Get Mr. Riley out of here, Officer Helman." Helman followed orders, and then he and Judge Abernathy continued through the list of counsel-represented cases. Finally, after a half-hour or so, the judge called the case everyone in the gallery was waiting on.

"Calling the next case," said the judge. "*People v. Dylan*. The charge is murder in the first degree. Appearances, please?"

"Jarrod Weaver, Manistee County Prosecutor, Your Honor, appearing for the State of Michigan."

"Zachary Blake, appearing for the defendant, Jack Dylan, Your Honor."

"The charge is murder in the first degree. What do we have, Officer Helman?"

"The defendant, Jack Dylan, is charged with first-degree murder, to wit, he willfully and premeditatedly committed the crime of murder against one Barton Breitner after planning and lying in wait to commit said murder."

"How does the defendant plead, Mr. Blake?"

"The defendant stands mute, Your Honor," replied Zachary.

"Very well. A not-guilty plea will be entered," said the judge. "People on bail?"

"This was a particularly vicious and gruesome crime, Your Honor. The defendant stalked the victim and exploded a grenade on his boat, killing him," said Weaver gravely. "The people suggest remand, Your Honor."

"Your Honor, Jack Dylan is a decorated police officer. Things are not as the prosecutor would have you believe, and the last time I checked, a man was still innocent until *proven* guilty in this country and this state," replied Zack forcefully. "Besides, Your Honor, the evidence would more appropriately support the alternate theory that Mr. Breitner, a terrorist wanted by the Dearborn Police on suspicion of attempting to commit mass murder, exploded the grenade himself, once he determined his arrest was inevitable. The police have not found a body. Rumor has it they may have found some parts of a hand and other tissue, but that's it. How can you charge someone with murder without a body? Captain Dylan has no criminal record of any kind. He has worked tirelessly to enforce the law and make his community safer. He is desperately needed by counsel to prepare a defense. He is willing to surrender his passport and credit cards to the court and wear a tether to monitor his whereabouts at all times."

Judge Abernathy glared long and hard at Jack Dylan. "*Mr.* Dylan," he finally said, "I am troubled by these allegations of vigilantism. You were and are no more than a private citizen in this jurisdiction. I am equally troubled investigators have not found a body." The judge paused again, gazed up at the dome above him as if to summon divine assistance then dropped his eyes and focused them squarely on Jack Dylan. "I'm going to release *Mr.* Dylan because he is a decorated police officer, has no prior record, and is needed by the defense to assist in resolving these important issues. Bail is set at five hundred thousand dollars, cash or bond. Officer Helman, call the next case."

Three hours later, bond was raised and posted, and Jack walked out of Manistee police headquarters, much to the chagrin of Chief Christopher Alexander. For now, at least, Jack Dylan was a free man.

# Chapter Twenty

Jack and his fellow Dearborn cops went for a drink to celebrate his release from jail. Zack stayed behind with Micah to discuss preliminary goals and assignments. Cops tend to think 'conviction,' while defense attorneys tend to think 'acquittal.' Zack wanted to discuss the case privately, away from the brotherhood in blue so they could take a fresh look at the situation from a defense only perspective.

"The first thing we need to do is canvas the area surrounding the crime scene and talk to all store managers, employees and any customers who we can identify. Maybe there were some regulars," Zachary said.

"We also need to ask Chief Alexander whether there were any traffic cameras or surveillance cameras in the area. Were there security cameras outside any of the waterfront stores? Did any of these cameras point to the scene of the explosion? Maybe someone saw or heard the explosion. Perhaps someone caught some cell phone video. Were there conversations of any kind leading up to the explosion? We have to check with hotels and motels along the waterfront. Can we obtain guest information from the date in question?"

"Micah, you and your people will canvas all beach houses and condos in the area. Let's see if anyone was on his or her porch and looking out at the lake at the time."

"We'll get on these things as soon as possible, probably as early as this afternoon, Zack," replied Micah. "Full cooperation from the local police would certainly help."

"I'll continue to work on getting them to cooperate, Micah," replied Zack. "In the meantime, I think we can make good use of the Dearborn squad. They are all brothers in blue."

"Good luck with that, Zack. The way these Manistee cops behave, this seems more like a betrayal in blue to me," replied Micah.

"They do seem to have very easily accepted the idea a cop could or would do something like this. Aside from that, the instrument of death makes no sense for a cop. Why would he need a grenade? He carries a gun," said Zack.

"Exactly," replied Micah.

"Let's have Reed Spencer and, perhaps, Noah Thompson investigate the electronic footprint in play here. While Jack said Breitner's use of technology was limited, we know for a fact Keith Blackwell, the Dearborn mosque bomber in the Blaine case, made use of technology and the internet. It makes no sense that Breitner and his men would not take advantage of twenty-first-century communications technology. Let's also examine Breitner and his habits. Did he live anywhere besides the boat? I'm told his group was headquartered in Lexington, Kentucky. If we find their meeting place, maybe we find the evidence we need. Maybe, if we dig deep enough, we find a link to the whole sarin conspiracy," Zack said.

"How was Breitner able to acquire a grenade? What were his plans? There must be an electronic paper trail of these activities. And let's talk to the FBI and state police. Maybe they aren't as willing to accept Jack's guilt as the local cops are. We could use their help."

"I'll talk to Reed and Noah right away and get that aspect of the investigation going. Maybe Shaheed can persuade Detective Prince to provide at least one contact at the state police. It is imperative that we work in a coordinated manner, all hands on deck. See if state and federal investigators are willing to work with us even if we can't persuade the locals to cooperate," said Micah, turning to his team. "Sounds like we have the beginnings of a plan. Let's roll."

\*\*\*

Clare Gibson and Ernest Cobb arrived in Manistee and met with Chief Christopher Alexander and Sheila Prince. The FBI had a vested interest in the Breitner investigation. They were angry with themselves over the Arlington mess, and Jack was a perfect scapegoat for their botched investigation and operation. They wanted the charges to stick and had an interest in seeing Jack Dylan spend the rest of his days in prison.

While Breitner's death was a blow to his cause, it was also a blow to law enforcement. Many of Bart's men were behind bars, but many of his disciples were still walking the streets. There was scant evidence of their identities and involvement in any of Breitner's mayhem. If Breitner was captured rather than killed, he might have turned on his men to save his own ass. Gibson's team would have to return to square one, re-interview Stone and confer with others who faced long prison sentences, then consider plea deals.

At issue was whether to continue Jack's prosecution in state court or move it to federal court. The Grand Rapids office of the U.S. Attorney for the Western District of Michigan serviced the city of Manistee. Thus, a federal trial would be conducted in Grand Rapids, one hundred twenty-five miles south of Manistee. The crime scene investigation and all the witnesses were in Manistee. Grand Rapids was logistically inconvenient, but Gibson, in particular, was very reluctant to cede jurisdiction to the local prosecutor on such a high profile case.

The locals, led by Chief Christopher Alexander and Manistee County Prosecutor Jarrod Weaver, argued the Coast Guard already handed off the case to Manistee and State and local crime scene investigations were underway. Jack Dylan was arraigned in state court and entered a plea. Weaver was a very experienced prosecutor. He filed an appearance and was directly involved in the investigation. He welcomed the FBI's *assistance* in the case but resisted a *takeover*.

In the end, the parties reached a compromise. The Feds would provide expertise, modern equipment and crime scene assistance to the locals. Gibson would stay on in Manistee and supervise the investigation, while the state and Weaver would prosecute the case. Alexander was not happy being relegated to a subordinate position, but there wasn't much he could do about it.

The Feds had the power to take over the whole case if they wanted. Secretly, Weaver was thrilled. The Feds had the tools to build a stronger case. Weaver did not like not guilty verdicts, especially in high-profile cases.

***

Zack and his team met with the Dearborn cops to discuss the preliminary investigative plan. Police officers have a different duty to law enforcement than attorneys and private citizens. Cops are required to disclose evidence even if that evidence is helpful to the person they are trying to convict, in this case, Jack Dylan. Private citizens (like Zack and Micah) have no such obligation. Zack had to be mindful of that difference in utilizing the services of the Dearborn cops.

Zack adjourned the meeting and asked to speak with Jack privately. The conversation he had in mind required the sanctity of attorney-client privilege.

"How are you holding up, Jack?"

"I'm fine, Zack. Thanks again for taking my case and for believing in me."

"Not too difficult in this instance, Jack. Am I supposed to believe you committed cold-blooded murder utilizing an explosive device as the murder weapon?"

"Why don't they see things that way?"

"Water over the dam. Maybe you pissed them off with your behavior and attitude, but, for now, let's work on proving them wrong."

"What can I do to help? I am a law-enforcement professional, Zack. Pick my brain."

"I fully intend to, Jack. You are a most valuable resource, the one cop I can trust absolutely in this investigation," Zack replied with a smile.

# Chapter Twenty-One

Reed Spencer arrived from Detroit and would take the lead on the defense cyberspace investigation. Noah Thompson was a cop and had the evidence reporting responsibilities of a cop, even if his findings were harmful to Jack. Reed's findings, because of his private retention by Zack and his team, would be protected by the attorney-client privilege.

Bart Breitner was allegedly backward. He'd often bragged he didn't own or carry a computer or a cell phone. After all, the technology could be traced while face-to-face communications could not. Reed was convinced, however, while Bart undoubtedly talked the talk, this was the twenty-first century, and it was much more difficult to walk the walk when one considered all the electronic communications tools at a terrorist's disposal.

Perhaps Breitner used a phone but kept ownership secret. Perhaps the same was true for a computer or tablet. He might have relied on others to perform legitimate internet or dark web searches for the group, maybe as a path to membership for some young computer geek with supremacist leanings. Perhaps Breitner and friends conducted searches on public servers, like those found in libraries or at internet cafés.

With these fresh ideas in mind, Reed's team began a multifaceted investigation. Micah and his team would research places where Breitner and company hung out. Reed would then investigate any digital footprint associated with Bart or the Free America Party. Private citizens had no Fourth Amendment obligations. Besides, they were not seeking to convict someone with the information. They were seeking to exonerate Jack. Law enforcement is never free to conduct warrantless searches, but private citizens were far less limited or restricted.

The more significant concern was the size of the "footprint." While Bart was a self-proclaimed anti-internet guy, Reed and Noah weren't buying it. He displayed a minimal, almost non-existent digital footprint. But if he *did* possess internet savvy or sophistication, he might have utilized anonymization tools and techniques that allowed him and others to conduct evil internet affairs in virtual secret. Fortunately, the investigators had appropriate knowledge and training to counter these techniques, and they were taking nothing for granted.

They pulled up the Free America Party's website, with its red, white, and blue colors and Old Glory electronically waving in the background. *Talk about your terrorist supremacist oxymoron,* thought Reed. The site boldly proclaimed the group's mission with a rambling, racist, anti-Semitic and anti-Islamic rant similar to the one penned by Keith Blackwell in his *Nomo Islam* manifesto.

The two men were not able to locate any cell phone or internet access accounts in Breitner's name or the name of the group, nor were they able to identify a cell phone or internet access account in either name. Other than their somewhat interactive website, there was very little social media activity. However, they were still very early in the process. They were confident they would find something eventually, especially on the dark web. No criminal could operate as effectively as Breitner did in planning the sarin attack without access to modern communications tools. The trick in these cases was to figure out how and where to find them. Reed made a mental note to do a reverse search to see whether others used Facebook or other social media tools to link with or "friend" Breitner, even if he was smart enough not to reciprocate.

Furthermore, there was a large variety of electronically stored information from which to choose. ESI, as it is known, is any information created, stored, or utilized via digital technology. Text messages, emails, voicemails, word-processing files, internet and social media searches, computer and cell phone storage, flash drives, and CDs are all examples of ESI. Reed hoped to find hard drives or flash drives because they weren't "live" and subject to change or removal, assuming he got to them before they could be wiped clean by someone from Breitner's world. Since the criminal in question was dead, there was a good chance of recovery, but time was of the essence.

Reed and Noah eyed each other. Silently, they agreed to talk out their strategy.

"Let's consider the possibilities," started Reed thoughtfully. "How many different ways might Breitner and company use technology to further their agenda?"

"And which ways are more likely than others?" Noah added. "He's a white supremacist or nationalist with a membership organization and a website. The number one use of technology would be for dispensing propaganda, incitement to violence, raising money, and recruiting members, no?"

"True. We can easily hack into his website and track visitors," replied Reed. "We can track videos on the site and YouTube. There might be cyber-ads on other white supremacist, alt-right, nationalist, or neo-Nazi sites. We need to research ideological messaging."

"I didn't hear you say 'hack,' did I? Remember, I'm an officer of the law."

"No, you didn't" replied Reed, slyly, still enthused by the prospect of hacking into Free America's site.

"And we need to follow the money. Financing terror isn't cheap. I suggest you investigate whether there is an electronic footprint for the group's fundraising."

"Will do," replied Reed, making a note of the suggestion. "The website might be a good place to begin that investigation, as well."

"PayPal, Venmo, or Skype are prime sites to search. If they go 'old school,' Western Union, ACHs, wire transfers, and credit card companies should be good places to look, as well."

"And there might be stolen credit cards or hacked bank accounts with large transfers at or near the time of the sarin gas incident," suggested Noah. "That's how I would have done it back in the day."

His former criminal juices were flowing. "Check out phony charities and philanthropic shell corporations. Look for those with patriotic or pro-Anglo-sounding names. Even those that look legit might have a transparent mission statement that reflects a white supremacist financier's hidden agenda."

"We should also check into Breitner's planning at or near the time of the attempted sarin heist. We have Breitner in Lexington, Howell, and Manistee. There must have been stops in between. How did Bart travel and was he alone? Where did he stay? Maybe he used a credit or debit card somewhere. Did he buy materials on the web and have them shipped somewhere? We need answers, fast."

"I would also not underestimate him, Reed."

"How do you mean, Noah?"

"Jack assumed Breitner wasn't internet savvy. However, we don't agree. I am assuming he was sophisticated at communicating anonymously on the web, especially when engaged in the planning of an attack and I would presume he used dead drops or code words in emails or texts. I would also presume he knows and utilizes encryption techniques."

"That's an excellent point, Noah."

"Jack is very important to me, Reed. He took a huge gamble on me, one that could have backfired big time, and I owe him. On top of that, he's a terrific boss and an all-around great guy."

"We'll see this through, Noah, and we'll get him out of this mess."

"Let's hope so. Any other thoughts?"

"Yeah. Again, looking at his dark web activity, coded searches, let's investigate public domains and see what pops up. He may have used aliases to search and purchase the materials or incidentals I mentioned before—travel and shipping sites too. These searches and purchases are probably disguised."

"We should also check whether there was any Voiceover IP activity. There would be subscriber invoices linked to his or his associates' internet accounts."

Reed paused, in deep thought for quite a while. Then he expelled a sigh of exhaustion.

"Okay," he said. "This is enough to stay busy for the rest of our lives. Let's divide things up. You take what you are comfortable taking, and I'll take the rest, especially stuff we don't want to disclose to the locals or the Feds."

"Agreed," said Noah. "Here's what I suggest…"

# Chapter Twenty-Two

Stewart Marshall was the Manistee County medical examiner. He was a courthouse veteran and testified in criminal cases on numerous occasions. However, he'd never examined the remains of bomb victims. *State v. Dylan* was his virgin bombing case. Manistee was a small, quiet lakefront community in Northern Michigan. These things didn't happen here. While it was unusual, even unique, for Marshall to examine parts of a body rather than an intact one, the issues presented, and the science utilized to present them was identical. Could a cause of death be determined, and if there was foul play, was there sufficient evidence to identify the perpetrator?

Marshall completed his autopsy on the limited body fragments retrieved from the crime scene. He published his findings to the court, and this required him to make himself available for questions. Almost immediately following Jack's arraignment, the case of *State v. Dylan* was transferred to the circuit court, the routine higher-level transfer for all Michigan felony cases.

The new circuit court judge was the Honorable Paul Shipley, a former prosecutor, and ten-year veteran on the circuit bench. According to local court-watchers, Shipley was considered a moderate and a good draw for a criminal defendant with a solid chance at an acquittal. Marshall, Weaver, Jack, and Zack were summoned to appear before Judge Shipley for a hearing. Clare Gibson and Chief Alexander were also in attendance, but only as observers.

Although Zack waived a preliminary examination, Judge Shipley decided to preserve Dr. Marshall's testimony by video deposition in case something happened to him before the trial. At least, that was His Honor's stated explanation for the day's hearing. If Marshall was available at the time of trial, no harm, no foul. Furthermore, his prior testimony would prevent him from straying too far from the truth. If he became unavailable, his testimony would be presented via the video. The judge obtained stipulations to this process from both attorneys, without objection.

Dr. Marshall was duly sworn and qualified as an expert in medical procedures, autopsies, and medical evidence collection.

"Good morning, Dr. Marshall. Good to see you again," said Judge Shipley.

"Good to see you, too, Your Honor."

"This deposition will be like one of those old coroner's inquests we used to have, understood?"

"Yes, Your Honor."

"Mr. Weaver? Is the State ready to proceed?"

"We are ready, Your Honor," replied Jarrod Weaver.

"Please proceed."

"Thank you, Your Honor," replied Weaver. He turned to Marshall, who was seated in the witness chair. "State your name and profession for the record, please?"

"Dr. Stewart Marshall. I'm a medical doctor and chief medical examiner for Manistee County."

"I won't go into your credentials, Doc. Mr. Blake here has stipulated to your qualifications."

"Thanks. That saves time."

"Now, in your official capacity, did you have occasion to examine one Barton Breitner?"

"Sort of, but there wasn't much left of him to examine, a couple of fingers is all that's been found so far."

"Your Honor," interrupted Zack. "The witness was asked a 'yes or no' question. Will you please instruct him to answer the question without editorializing? I would like his answer stricken from the record."

"It's only a deposition, Mr. Blake, but you're quite right. Doctor, please listen to the question and answer only the question without editorializing."

"I thought I did that, Judge, but I will try to be more careful."

"Per Mr. Blake's request, the answer will be stricken. Mr. Weaver, please ask the question again."

"Absolutely, Your Honor. Dr. Marshall, did you examine the body of Barton Breitner?"

"Yes." Dr. Marshall looked at Zachary with a sly grin.

"What was the date of the exam?"

"May 25th of this year."

"And what was the condition of the body?"

"Investigators have found only small pieces, parts of the ring and index fingers and other pieces of a right hand, fibers, blood and other tissue from a man who was last seen near an explosion. In my professional opinion, the body must have been obliterated by the explosion and other body parts floated out to sea." Marshall folded his arms and smiled, self-satisfied. Zack decided it was pointless to object. *Pick your battles…*

"You've examined many murder victims in your career, correct Dr. Marshall? Was there anything unusual about this one?"

"Yes. This was my first explosion case and, as I said, there was not much left of the body. The remains found were reduced to small pieces. The investigation is ongoing."

"Where did you discover these remains?"

"In the water, strewn about what was left of the boat, and on the dock. We searched a one-hundred-yard radius. In my opinion, the explosion caused the body to disintegrate. It was literally blown to bits. Other parts may have been carried out to sea. The body parts we *did* find were severely mangled and burned, but they were sufficient to identify the deceased and determine a cause of death."

"Your honor, I would appreciate it if you instructed the witness to stop editorializing, answer the question he is asked, and stop repeating, incessantly, that the body was 'blown to bits,' said Zack, standing at the defense table.

"Doctor Marshall. I have admonished you once on this issue, and I do not want to have to do it again. Listen to the question and answer the question without the histrionics. Understood?" Judge Shipley seemed perturbed.

"Yes, Your Honor. Sorry."

"Please continue, Mr. Weaver," the judge appeased.

"Thank you, Your Honor. Now, Dr. Marshall, in your professional opinion, why was there so little of the body left to evaluate and examine?"

Zachary Blake looked up, first at the doctor, then to the prosecutor, and finally to the judge. He rose, pondering an objection. This was a strange question, and he wondered why it was relevant. Judge Shipley stared intently at the witness, ignoring Zack.

"Because the explosion happened in direct proximity with his body."

"What do you mean?"

"Your Honor, I object," said Zachary, having never resumed his seat.

"On what grounds, Mr. Blake?"

"Your Honor, I stipulated to this witness's expertise as a medical examiner to establish the cause of death. If I correctly understand where this line of questioning is going, I believe the testimony Dr. Marshall is about to give will be beyond his expertise, especially considering this is his first bombing case and victim. In other words, the good doctor is about to engage in total speculation."

"Overruled. Let's see where this goes. It's only a deposition. If we have to, we can deal with anything that becomes problematic at a later date. How does that sound?" His Honor did not necessarily expect an answer, but he did want to create the appearance of fairness or professional deference to the lawyers and the defendant.

"Witness may answer," Judge Shipley continued.

Zack sat down and looked at Jack Dylan, who shrugged. He didn't understand the point Zack was trying to make.

As he rehearsed his testimony with the prosecutor, Dr. Marshall said, "Well, the lack of the body is consistent with the fact this bomb exploded in contact with the victim, as if someone threw the grenade directly at him. Disintegrated body parts could easily have floated out to sea."

"Objection, Your Honor! That is total speculation!" Zack shouted angrily.

"Overruled," said the judge.

"Overruled? Are you serious, Your Honor? The doctor is undoubtedly speculating about the direction and orientation of the bomb, its proximity to the victim, and the whereabouts and condition of other body parts!" Zack was livid.

"Be careful, Mr. Blake. I don't know how they do things in the big city, but here in Manistee, an attorney may place a formal exception to my ruling on the record, but he can't otherwise engage in excessive and offensive rhetoric simply because he disagrees with me. Do we understand each other, counselor?" Shipley glared at Zack.

"Understood, Your Honor. I apologize to the court," replied Zack.

"You may continue with your direct examination, Mr. Weaver," said the judge.

"Thank you, Your Honor. Doctor, were you able to determine the identity of the victim?" Weaver continued.

"Yes. As I stated earlier, we were able to retrieve two fingers and, eventually, other bits and pieces of a right hand. Mr. Breitner's prints were in the system, and we were able to get a positive identification from the print analysis."

"Did you determine whether there was foul play or not?"

"I did."

"Objection. Speculation, Your Honor."

"Overruled."

"And what was that determination?"

"Based upon the totality of the evidence, Mr. Breitner was the victim of a grenade blast thrown in his direction."

"Thank you, Doctor, no further questions. I tender the witness."

Zack rose and charged the stand. "Doctor, what conversations did you have with the prosecutor before your appearance today?"

"We discussed the case briefly."

"Did he tell you what he needed to hear to make his case?"

"No, I wouldn't say that. He asked me some of the questions he planned to ask today and what my answers might be."

"I see." Zack did not want to go any further than that. "And you concluded this might be murder because the bomb exploded in close proximity to Mr. Breitner?"

"Correct."

"Would the evidence you evaluated be consistent with the fact the victim was, in fact, holding the bomb? Would that explain the proximity?" Zack was setting a trap. A good attorney never asks a question unless he already knows its answer.

The doctor hesitated. "Well, yes. But he wasn't."

"And how do you know that, Doctor?" Marshall was falling into it.

"Because we found part of an intact hand. Two fingers were blown off, and some parts of a hand, although seriously damaged and burned. If he were holding it, his hand would have disintegrated like the rest of his body. His hand must have been out and away from the rest of his body, perhaps in the water, which slows the explosive trajectory."

"I'll get back to that in a second, Doctor. You said you identified the victim from a print card, correct?"

"Correct."

"The prints were in the system because the victim had a criminal record, correct?"

"Correct."

"Do you know whether the victim was right-handed or left-handed?"

"May I refer to my notes?"

"By all means," Zack said with a smirk.

"He was right-handed, according to his file."

"And, I know you've already testified to this, but I want the record to be absolutely clear here. Which hand was semi-intact for you to do fingerprint analysis, Doctor?"

"The left." The doctor recoiled, discomfited. He now understood where this was going, and he was helpless to stop it.

"If a right-handed man wanted to commit suicide by a bomb, which hand would most likely hold the bomb?"

"His right hand," replied Marshall helplessly.

That's all I have... Oh, one more question, Doctor. The crime scene technicians never found Mr. Breitner's right hand or arm, did they?"

"No, Mr. Blake, they did not."

"Thank you, Doctor. Nothing further."

"Mr. Weaver?" Judge Shipley asked. "Any redirect?"

Weaver rose, a question forming on his lips. Zack did damage. Weaver underestimated the big-city lawyer, a mistake he'd try not to repeat.

"Dr. Marshall, did Mr. Blake's cross-examination change your opinion on the cause of Mr. Breitner's death?"

"No, it did not."

"Nothing further, Your Honor."

The judge now glared at Dr. Marshall and Jarrod Weaver in disbelief. *If you want a conviction, your evidence must be a lot better than this.*

"Mr. Blake?" asked the judge.

"I have nothing further at this time, Your Honor. I do, however, reserve the right to cross-examine this witness at a later time."

"That's all for now, then. Court is adjourned. I will take a transcript, please."

"So will I," said Zack, staring down Dr. Marshall.

Zack walked outside the courtroom with Jack Dylan.

"That was incredible, Zack," said Jack.

"We are in this for the long haul, Jack. I doubt Weaver will make a mistake like that again. Still, this was a perfect start."

"Here's to a perfect start," replied Jack, holding up a fictional drink. "Lunch?"

"Sure. I'm buying."

"I wouldn't have it any other way."

# Chapter Twenty-Three

Micah, Shaheed, and Andy met with Alexander, Prince, and Gibson at police headquarters. Gibson and Alexander arranged the meeting as a gesture of 'professional courtesy' to the Dearborn contingent. They were willing to share, within limits, what their investigation revealed to date.

"I'm sure you're aware of Dr. Marshall's testimony," Alexander said.

"Yes, we are." Micah restrained himself from critical comment. While they were cooperative, he felt Marshall's testimony was a fabulous beginning, for the *defense*.

"Cause of death and criminality have been established," said a smug Alexander.

*Sure it has,* thought Micah.

"On behalf of the FBI, and to preserve the rights of the accused, I ordered a canvas of the entire area. We came up with three different video surveillance cameras offering three different viewpoints of the crime scene. Our techs are analyzing those as we speak," offered Gibson.

"May our techs be present during the review of these tapes?" Shaheed asked. "We have excellent people in that field."

"That shouldn't be a problem," replied Gibson, prompting a disgruntled grunt from Alexander.

*So much for professional courtesy,* thought Micah.

"Anything else?" Andy asked.

"Yeah. We might have a line on someone who was at an outdoor restaurant in the area and apparently videoing the band. Her iPhone might have caught the explosion. We are investigating," replied Alexander.

"What restaurant are we talking about?"

"More of a bar. It's called The Dirty Duck."

"What's the customer's name?"

"We will let you know when we're done with her unless the judge orders an earlier release of the evidence."

"But we can help with your investigation if you'll let us," replied Shaheed.

"Thanks, but we don't need the help right now. If things change, we'll be in touch," replied Alexander. Micah noticed Prince and Gibson look away. *They think Alexander's behavior is bullshit. Is this exploitable?*

"As soon as you're done?" Shaheed asked.

"Sure," replied Alexander.

"Anything else?"

"A witness will testify Dylan was obsessed with going out on the boat with Breitner. He may have overheard some conversations, as well."

"That's nothing new. Dylan *did* want to go out on the boat with Breitner. He was undercover. He wanted to infiltrate the organization," Andy said.

"Your Chief told me Dylan was on vacation. Dylan left word through another officer that he needed R & R," replied Gibson.

"He *was* on vacation, stalking the victim," said the sarcastic Alexander.

"Says who?" Micah asked.

"Says this witness," Alexander replied.

"We'd like to interview this witness."

"When the judge orders the evidence release," replied Alexander, enjoying himself. Gibson rolled her eyes again.

"Is that it?" Andy asked. "We can use anything we can get."

"Lots of witnesses who heard the explosion, not many who saw it," replied Prince.

*'Not many?'* Micah thought. *Was that deliberate?*

"We'll provide witness statements…" Alexander began.

"We know," said Andy, "when the time comes and the judge orders you to do so."

"You catch on fast, Toler."

Gibson rose, signaling an end to the meeting. "If you gentlemen don't mind, we have work to do."

*Assholes!*

# Chapter Twenty-Four

Judge Shipley invited Zack Blake and Jarrod Weaver to have a seat in his chambers. The court reporter sat to the left of the judge, facing the attorneys.

"This is the day and date set for pre-trial in the matter of *State v. Dylan*. How's everything going, gentlemen?"

Weaver started to say, 'fine,' but Zack usurped him.

"We are having difficulty getting information, Your Honor. The prosecution and the investigators are just going through the motions. I need a formal discovery order. I need subpoenas issued, and I need you to order the prosecution to turn over all evidence in its possession, not *some* of the evidence it *chooses* to turn over, but *all* of it. The prosecution is putting us at a considerable disadvantage. I can't build a defense without access to and an evaluation of the evidence."

"What evidence are you referring to, Mr. Blake?" Judge Shipley asked.

"*All* of it, Judge. They've given us *nothing*. For starters, the defense would like the coroner's report and supporting evidence turned over to our pathologist. There are multiple eyewitnesses. We need their names and contact information. The prosecution continues to 'analyze' surveillance video, which is code for 'we don't feel like turning it over yet.' And, Your Honor, the crime scene hasn't been released yet, and we need access."

"Mr. Blake, your points are well taken. Your request is granted. Mr. Weaver will have everything you have asked for within, what, Mr. Weaver, twenty-four hours?"

"Absolutely, Your Honor. That was going to happen anyway," replied Weaver, lying with a straight face.

"Witness list exchange in four weeks?" Judge Shipley framed this as a question, but it was an order.

"Yes, sir," replied the attorneys.

"Discovery cutoff in eight weeks?"

"Yes, Your Honor."

"And trial will commence the second week in August." No question this time. This was an absolute order.

"August 13th, gentlemen."

"Fine by me, Your Honor," replied Zack.

"Me as well," replied Weaver.

"If you don't get all of the evidence you are seeking, Mr. Blake, and I mean *all* of it, I want to know immediately," said Shipley, with an icy glare at Weaver. "Mr. Weaver here knows my policy on these things. He is intimately familiar with my non-compliance policies. I don't think you'll have a problem."

Weaver was visibly angry, but, to his credit, held his tongue.

"That's it, then. Let's go off the record," said Shipley.

The stenographer began to break down her equipment. The judge turned to Weaver.

"Get him what he needs, sooner rather than later, Jarrod."

"He should have the materials by this afternoon or early tomorrow at the latest, Judge. As I said, the release was already in the works."

"I'm sure it was," replied Judge Shipley.

"Asshole," exclaimed Weaver after they exited. "Always with the comments."

"What was that all about?"

"That prick put me in *jail* once. I've got a job to do, too. And I'm the one who deals with the cops. You guys have no idea."

"Oh, I get it, Jarrod. In the 'big city,' as you guys call it, no one gets more shit from the judges than the defense attorneys. It's part of the job. Shipley was right, though. We should have had this stuff long ago."

"Tell that to Alexander. He pulls this shit, and I'm the one who gets crapped on."

"A discovery order from the judge should make an impression. If he doesn't comply, maybe the judge locks his ass up this time."

"You'll have what you need. You have my word. Want to grab some lunch?"

"I've got some work to catch up on. Rain check?"

"You got it. See you soon, Zack."

"See ya, Jarrod. Thanks."

"For what?"

"Not being an asshole," replied Zack as he walked away.

# Chapter Twenty-Five

The Dylan defense team met in the Bay Shore conference room. The hotel catered the event, and a smorgasbord of food sat before them. Food, however, was not the priority. The team received the evidence dump and was especially focused on the eyewitness statements and videos. Having previously read the transcript of the medical examiner's testimony, the men knew it was weak and attackable, thus, not a priority. However, if a witness could be identified and located, or a camera picked up the encounter between Bart and Jack it might be 'game over' for the prosecution.

Computers and a small projection screen were set up in the middle of the conference table. Zack pulled out a flash drive and inserted it into the computer. The machine whirred and clicked, and rotating video images of the dock, boat and businesses filled the screen. The camera angle captured Breitner's boat from the back. It included images of Bart and Jack on the deck. There was no audio, but both men's lips were moving. Due to the camera angle, only heads and shoulders were visible. The conversation seemed to begin cordially but eventually morphed into a heated argument. Zack wondered whether an audio version was available or whether the video they were currently viewing could be enhanced to acquire sound.

As the argument became more hostile, Jack lunged forward. Both men disappeared from the camera's view. Shortly after that, Jack reappeared. He stood at the front of the boat. Still, only the head and shoulders were visible. Jack was glancing around and appeared to be looking for something or someone, presumably Breitner. Suddenly, with what the men interpreted to be a panicked look on his face, Jack turned and jumped into the water. The boat exploded, and billowing dark clouds of smoke filled the screen. Breitner's image never reappeared. Zack hit the remote and froze the image.

"Not much help," he declared. "Can you walk us through the details, Jack?"

"We were talking. I thought he bought my story. He seemed ready to take me in and teach me what I needed to know to become one of his guys. That's when I slipped up and inadvertently called him 'Bart' instead of 'Bert.' He became immediately suspicious and hostile, pulled a gun on me and said he knew who I was the whole time. *He* was playing *me,* he said, not the other way around. I continued to tell him I made an honest mistake and I didn't understand why he was so upset, but he wasn't buying it. He frisked me and found the wire Noah planted. And that's when I told him to give himself up. What you guys are looking at is me putting my arms out and saying something like, 'Whoa, fella, take it easy.' But the back of the boat is elevated, and that's why you can't see much."

"How did he react to finding the wire?" Zack asked.

"I didn't wait for him to react. I lunged at him and dislodged the gun. It slid across the deck. I dove and grabbed it. When I turned back to Breitner, he was gone. You can see me in the video, walking to the front of the boat. What you can't see is Breitner standing at the threshold of the cabin, brandishing that damn grenade. He said that he would die before he'd ever go to prison. Then he pulled the fucking grenade pin and threw it toward me. I jumped over the side of the boat seconds before it exploded, and all hell broke loose."

The men watched several videos. Each one varied in distance, range, and angles but none of them exposed the two men's lower-body movements, the gun, grenade or who pulled the pin.

"Micah," Zack said. "We need to find a witness who was out on the water that night. I prefer a witness with a cell phone video or *any* kind of video, but I'll take anyone or anything."

"On it, Zack."

"You don't have to reinvent the wheel. There are numerous witness statements in here, including names, addresses, and telephone numbers. Start with them. It's possible the cops didn't ask the right questions."

"You mean the kind of questions that might get Jack off the hook?"

"Yeah, *those* kinds of questions. And if you find any witnesses, ask them if they know any others. We need to see if the cops are doing this by the book. By the way, do you have a fingerprint guy, Micah? A guru?"

"*Of course* I have a guy. If he's not available, he'll know a guy."

"We need an expert up here, pronto, and we need a forensics guy to assist Eric. He's a cop, so there are limitations to our ability to use him. We need to scour the crime scene and find anything local, state or federal investigators might have missed. We need to find more body parts if possible, and we need divers and evidence retrieval specialists. You got those, too?"

"Just say the word, and they are yours, as the song goes."

"What song?"

"The Tom Jones song. 'Help Yourself.' Do you guys remember that one?"

"You're really old, Micah. How old is Tom Jones, anyway? Eighty?"

"I don't know. So what? Is it illegal to remember Tom Jones?" Micah turned his fist into a microphone, held it up to his mouth, and began to sing and circularly gyrate his lower torso, his best imitation of Tom Jones in his prime years.

"Now *there's* an image that will be impossible to erase from my mind," Zack said, looking repulsed.

The group laughed at the banter, enjoying the chemistry between the two men. The occasional break from the realities of a murder investigation was appreciated. A murder investigation was no laughing matter, even when there appeared to be no murder.

"How much is all of this going to cost? We've never really discussed fees and costs for all of this, Zack." Jack Dylan's voice cracked through the banter.

"I won't sugarcoat this for you, Jack. 'All of this' as you refer to it, is expensive," replied Zack. Instantly, gloom and doom regained momentum.

"I'm a small-town police captain on a salary and a government pension. Look at the size of this operation. If I lose, I'll spend the rest of my life in prison. If I win, I'll be paying you all for the rest of my life. It's the classic no-win scenario. I wouldn't be in this nightmare if I listened to Shaheed and left Breitner to the locals." He banged his fist down on the table and hung his head. "I'm a fucking idiot!"

"We'll get through this, Jack. When it's all over, and you're a free man, we'll sue the city of Manistee and the federal government for wrongful arrest and imprisonment. We'll make them pay your legal fees and then some," offered Zack.

"Yeah, how often do you think Dearborn gets sued because of that hot-headed captain guy? What's his name?" Andy joked.

Every man chuckled, except for Jack Dylan.

"If that's really possible, thanks, Zack," Jack said, tears forming in his eyes. He glanced at the others, sitting around the room. "And thanks to all of you guys, too." He rose and bolted from the room. He returned more composed, shortly after that. The men carried on as if he never left.

"Hey, Jack? Think back for a second. Did you see or hear a boat or any motor that evening, like immediately before the explosion?"

"I can't remember. I was too busy doing what my mother always told me to do."

"What was that?"

"Go jump in the lake."

Everyone laughed. "Let's take a dinner break, men," Zack suggested. He looked around the room at the men and the impressive tray laid out on the table. He winked, smiled and quipped: "If we win this thing, we can make the government pay for all of this food."

"Amen to that, Zack," said Shaheed. Soon, all of them were chatting, enjoying the food and each other's company. The looming murder investigation and trial could wait, but not for long.

# Chapter Twenty-Six

Crime scene preservation and recordation, witness statements, forensic reports, and crime scene photos are crucial for any investigation upon which a trial is pending. On the one hand, the results could indicate murder. On the other, Breitner's death could be classified or ruled as a suicide, and Jack would win an acquittal.

Following the evidence dump, Micah's forensics team descended upon the crime scene. The fact that so much relevant evidence was submerged in the lake was problematic for both sides. Unfortunately, the cops had their guy and far less interest in finding the proverbial "smoking gun" that would reveal the truth.

Micah was hoping there was evidence the police failed to look for or hadn't found. The most critical piece of this type of evidence, the Holy Grail so to speak, would be anything (shrapnel, the pin or part of the pin, etc.) that had Bart Breitner's fingerprint on it. Micah's suspicions were correct: there was plenty of "leftover" evidence found at the crime scene. Even so, was any of it the crucial link to freedom for Jack Dylan?

*** 

Divers were going in and out of the water all day long, recovering boat residuals, small body part pieces, body fluids, bomb materials, and engine components. They worked in teams of two. While one recovered, the other was an eyewitness and processor of that recovery.

The evidence retrieval specialists were surprised at the small amount of blood and fluid found floating around the perimeter. The police didn't retrieve much DNA evidence either. The divers were not surprised by the *government investigators'* minimal findings, because *those* investigators presumed Jack's guilt. An attorney of Zack

Blake's skill would have a field day poking holes at the forensic investigation at trial.

Micah's principal underwater forensic investigator was a man named Lyle Manor. Because of his stellar reputation in the scientific community as it related to underwater evidence recovery, it was Lyle, rather than Matt Jordan, who supervised the treasure hunt. To determine whether evidence literally floated away, Manor secured and dispatched a helicopter with a high-powered scope attached in order to survey a two-mile radius from where the explosion has occurred. Unfortunately, the search produced nothing more than a few boat and engine fragments.

Manor was concerned, but hopeful, about the quality and preservation of the evidence already collected. Processing underwater evidence is unique in that it must be dried out, kept separate from other pieces, and then repackaged. While Manor and his team were adept at the process, they could not be sure government investigators shared a similar skillset.

There were two crucial issues for which the evidence recovery and analysis team were to focus. The first was the sheer *volume* of evidence. They found so many pieces of evidence; Zack could persuasively argue the police's crime scene recovery techniques were lax and/or inadequate. Second, comparisons of defense-discovered evidence to police-discovered evidence might provide larger pieces of the puzzle. Larger pieces could prove more susceptible to the testing needed to exonerate Jack.

As in all of Micah's cases, evidence was handled correctly and sent to a laboratory owned by an affiliate of Love Investigations. The collections team knew lab protocols and followed them to the letter. The techs inspected, re-inspected and relabeled all the items, and each step in the process was legibly printed on the box or bag in which it arrived.

All chain-of-custody information was entered into the company's computer system and assigned a barcode for tracking purposes. This protocol was vital to the admissibility of evidence in court. It allowed the company to determine who handled each piece of evidence from the time collected through evidentiary hearings and trial, all the way to its final disposition.

Anyone who touched an item was required to sign his or her name and enter date and time. When each piece of evidence was returned, the lab manager signed for it and re-dated and time-stamped the receipt. When each piece was transported to the lab, the same procedures were followed. When the evidence was returned to and used in court, as long as packaging and seals were intact, the judge and the litigants knew the property's chain-of-custody integrity was maintained.

While this was going on, Micah and his investigators were going door to door along the dock, stopping at every residence, store, restaurant, or coffee shop within sight or earshot of the explosion. The investigators were relentless, leaving no stone unturned and no witness unquestioned. Unfortunately, no one interviewed saw or heard anything helpful in Jack's case. The investigators left business cards with everyone interviewed in case they remembered anything or spoke to anyone who remembered anything. The police had better luck. They found tourists who saw or heard the commotion and the explosion. Micah retained their contact information and planned to re-question them. The trial was looming closer, and the team was still struggling to find the evidence it needed to procure an acquittal. Jack Dylan's freedom and career hung in the balance.

# Chapter Twenty-Seven

The following day, the private lab received more evidence retrieved from the crime scene, as well as the samples that were the subject of the medical examiner's report. The lab, in this case, retained three units with unique and specialized heads. Technicians' efforts to prove Jack's innocence focused on confirming three things: the explosive device was a grenade, the deceased was Bart Breitner, and there were fingerprints on the grenade. After all, if fingerprints *were* found, Jack's innocence would be virtually assured if they were *not* his.

Dr. Werner Spellman once worked as a physical scientist with the explosives unit of the Federal Bureau of Investigation. While with the FBI, Spellman handled bombsite evidence and assisted in training post-explosion investigators. He received some specialized training in post-blast investigations at a United State Air Force base and was now a renowned freelance expert, for sale to the highest bidder. Clare Gibson contacted Spellman to discuss *State v. Dylan*, but, in the end, the highest bidder was Zachary Blake. Matt Jordan was Zack and Micah's usual choice for this type of investigation, but everyone knew, especially Matt, the case needed a more specialized expert. *This case required Werner Spellman.*

Spellman's assignment was to examine and test all physical evidence that passed through the lab. He would identify pieces of explosives and attempt to reassemble them. Then, he would determine, based upon markings and/or source, what type of explosive was used. Spellman was also tasked with determining the direction shrapnel traveled (in this case, from Jack's position or toward it), and the location of the explosive's origin.

For DNA sampling and testing, Micah turned to Dr. Stephanie Jacoby. She was a forensic scientist, formerly with the Michigan State Police Crime Laboratory, Crime Scene Response and Criminalists

Unit. It was her job to process samples for biological evidence, if any remained or, for some reason, wasn't processed earlier.

Charles Snyder was a former state trooper with the Michigan State Police. He had almost twenty years of experience in accidental death, homicide, and suicide investigations. His specialty was crime scene processing with particular emphasis on fingerprint and footwear impressions. Micah chose Snyder as the fourth member of this team of experts. Snyder had, perhaps, the most critical task of all. He could clear Jack Dylan simply by finding shrapnel that contained an identifiable print belonging to Bart Breitner.

The moment the additional evidence arrived at the lab, the experts and the tech assistants went to work on their respective samples. Each was well aware of the importance of their work to the case. Each was well qualified and well compensated, an excellent combination for the prospect of freedom for Jack Dylan.

***

Micah began re-interviewing some of the witnesses who previously spoke to Shaheed, Gibson or the local police. He started in Lansing at Capital Airport, where he tracked down Alan Berger. The interview was held in an airport conference room during Berger's mid-morning break. Micah arrived first and was asked to wait in a conference room. Berger was brought in about five minutes later, and introductions were exchanged.

"I'm Micah. May I call you Alan?"

"Sure. I can't believe this whole thing. I would never have put these guys together if I knew something like this was going to happen."

"I know you gave a statement to the police, but I haven't read it," Micah lied. "I'd like to start fresh. What do you mean, 'put these guys together?'"

"Well, I met Jack on the beach, and we got to talking. He said he was looking to go fishing but was unable to find someone good to take him out. I told him about Robert."

"What about him? What did you tell Jack?"

"I told him Robert—at least that's what he said his name was—was a great fisherman and the guys and I caught lots of fish with him. I also warned him about Robert's temper. On a prior trip, Robert was ranting about some deal he'd set up that went bad. I didn't think much of it at the time. Unless the subject was fishing, Robert wasn't especially talkative or friendly. In fact, most of the time he was angry, especially if the subject was politics. He'd tell you to shut up if he didn't agree with what you were saying."

"You told all this to Jack?"

"Yeah, I did. I may have been a little tipsy at the time. I told him where to find the boat. But I swear, Micah, I didn't know anything like this was going to happen."

"The police are suggesting Jack 'stalked' Robert. You know, like he was obsessed with him or something. Do you know where they would have gotten that idea?"

"No, I don't. Jack said he was there for a little R & R and wanted to go fishing. He *did* get a bit piqued when I told him the name of the boat."

"Which was?"

"*White Knight.*"

"What do you mean, 'piqued'?"

"I don't know, more *interested* once he heard the name or something. I didn't ask why."

"Did you say anything to the police that would have made them think that Jack was specifically looking to target Robert for some reason?"

"No! I liked Jack. He was a nice guy. I didn't see this coming at all, except, well, maybe…"

"Maybe what?"

"Maybe from Bert's side of things. As I said, he was an angry bastard. He'd get pissed if you looked at him the wrong way or touched something he didn't think you should be touching. The littlest thing could set him off. He was like a keg of dynamite waiting to blow. Sorry, I guess that's not a very appropriate analogy."

"Probably not. So, let me get this straight. Jack wanted to fish, and you knew a great fisherman. Maybe the guy's a hothead but stick to fishing and there are no major issues. So, you send Jack over there…"

"Well, no. I didn't send him. We all went fishing together the day after Jack and I met. I told him where the boat was, and apparently, he went out there on his own and met Robert that afternoon. The bombing happened the night after we all went fishing. By that time, my friends and I were long gone."

"Understood. Last question and I don't want to put words in your mouth."

"I wouldn't let you. I tell it like it is."

"Good, I'm glad to hear it. Between Jack and Robert, based on what little you know of the two men, who do you think would be more likely to start an altercation ending in death?"

"That's easy. Robert. But as you say, I didn't know either of these guys that well. I didn't know Jack was a cop, and I didn't know Robert was actually…well…what he was. But it all makes sense now."

"How do you mean?"

"Robert, or Bart, was a bad dude, and he was wanted by the cops. Jack was a cop, duh-uh…"

"Point taken. That's all I have. Oh, by the way, would you be willing to testify in court for the defense?"

"I've already been asked to do that by the prosecution."

"And what you told them was the same as what you told me today?"

"Yeah, except for the part where Jack hung back and talked to Robert alone after we returned from the fishing trip."

"Huh?"

"Originally, I left them alone, but I forgot something and came back. They were alone on the boat, chatting. They didn't see me, and I decided to keep it that way."

"Did you hear anything about what they discussed?"

"It was something about organizing."

"Organizing what?"

"Robert liked President John. He wanted to help, you know, 'Make America Pure Again' and shit."

"And you would testify to that?"

"Sure."

"Anything else you can think of?"

Alan lowered his head, deep in thought. Suddenly, he lifted his head and shouted, "Oh yeah, I forgot about the money!"

"What does that mean, Alan?"

"Jack offered to pay me for including him on the fishing trip. He paid the whole three hundred buck charge for my group's day of fishing on the *White Knight*."

"Why would he do that?"

"I don't know, because he was grateful?"

"Good answer. Stick with that. Don't let the cops or anyone else suggest otherwise."

"I won't. I tell it like it is."

"Right, I forgot. Thanks, Alan."

***

"That's the whole thing. What do you think?" Micah turned off the recorder after playing the entire interview for Zack.

"It depends on who's listening," replied Zack, reflecting.

"Yeah, that's kind of how I felt. It can go both ways. Jack might be a cop doing his job, or he might be a vigilante throwing money around for a chance to be alone with this guy."

"Exactly. If I'm being objective, though, and we both know I'm not, I read this as more favorable to cop than to terrorist."

"I'm far more objective than you are, and I see the same."

"At best, I can say this is another positive development. Keep up the good work. What's next?"

"I'm going into hostile waters to track down some witnesses."

"Hostile waters?"

"Lexington, Kentucky."

"I see. Bring along some muscle. What do you hope to get there?"

"The truth, the whole truth, and nothing but the truth."

"We are counting on you, Micah. Don't let us down. Oh, and Micah?"

"Yeah?"

"Do this quickly. We're running out of time."

# Chapter Twenty-Eight

Micah landed at Blue Grass Airport in Lexington. His destination was a small boarding house operation on the outskirts of the city. He was hoping to sweet-talk the caretaker into letting him into what turned out to be Breitner's two-room flat.

Micah rented a car, hopped on I-75 South, and drove a short distance to his exit. He found the boarding house, located directly across from the northbound exit back onto I-75 North. The property backed up to the freeway. Micah could hear heavy traffic as he ascended the office steps. *How can anyone live here with all this noise?"*

The boarding house was at some time, long ago, a one-story motel. There were ten names listed on the entry door, with corresponding numbers for each of the ten rooms. One of the names listed was "Robert Bright." Micah retreated down the stairs, walked out toward the highway, and faced the building. He counted ten doors, with five of them positioned somewhat close to each other and five more spread out over a distance roughly twice the size of the other side. Again, looking at the old rectangular structure with private entrances, Micah guessed it was a once a fifteen-room motel converted into a boarding house. Ten rooms were turned into two-room flats, while the other five remained in their original one-room, studio type configuration.

Micah returned to the office entry door and knocked loudly. An elderly woman answered, and Micah flashed his credentials and a gold badge. He introduced himself as 'Special Agent Love of the Kentucky Bureau of Investigation.' The old woman was wide-eyed with enthusiasm.

"Yes, sir, officer, sir. What can I do for you? What did you say your name was again?"

"Love, ma'am. Special Agent Love," he replied in his best Joe Friday *Dragnet* imitation—*just the facts, ma'am, just the facts.*

"We are conducting an important investigation, and I was wondering whether you have a Robert Bright living here?"

"Sure do, but he doesn't hang around here much. What's he done now?"

"Huh?"

"Wouldn't surprise me if he'd done something. He's a pistol, that one."

"What do you mean?"

"He's a rabble-rouser. And I mean that seriously. He talks a lot about the Confederacy, the south will rise again and all that stuff. Even hosts meetings about it down on our porch over there. He scared a few prospective tenants away, and I put a stop to it. I've always wondered whether he's one of those white power guys or something."

"Well, actually that's why I'm here. By the way, have any other law enforcement officials been here?"

"No, sir."

"That's interesting. Any chance I can see his room?"

"I would have to call him for permission."

"He has a phone?"

"He has a cell phone, one of those old model iPhone jobs, an original, I think."

"I'm surprised he still has a phone. My office tried to reach him several times on the number we have for him, and he never answers." Micah never minded lying to get the information he needed.

"I've seen him use it from time to time, plus he got drunk one night and dropped it in the dirt. I found it, and when I returned it to him, he got all hot and bothered, like I stole it or something. He's a pistol, that one."

"Yeah, you told me. What's your name, by the way, if you don't mind my asking?"

The woman began to fuss with her hair and brush off her dress. She fluttered her eyelashes and smiled, displaying a couple of missing teeth. "Name's Betty, *Special* Agent Love," she said in a flirtatious manner.

"Do you have a last name, Betty?"

"Sure, it's Olderman, Betty Olderman. I own this establishment. Inherited it from my daddy, may he rest in peace."

Micah crossed himself.

"Would you mind giving Robert a call, please? I left my notes with his old number back at the office. What number do you have for him, by the way?"

"I've got to go look it up."

"I'll wait right here."

She went into the office and returned with her own iPhone, a large iPhone 6 or 7. Micah had difficulty keeping up with the model changes. "I got all my tenant numbers stored in my phone. Here's Robert's."

Micah made a note of the number. This was a significant development. "Call it, please." She dialed the number, and both of them heard a phone ringing in the room behind them.

"That's coming from Robert's room," she said. "He must have left it there."

"Ma'am, would you mind calling the Kentucky State Police and asking them to get down here right away? I have to make another call. Will you call them, please?"

"Sure, Special Agent Love."

"I'm sorry to disappoint you, Betty, but I am not a special agent. I'm a private investigator."

"So?" Betty didn't understand the difference.

"So, when the State Police get here, I would sure appreciate it if you told them I was a private eye and not a cop."

"You mean like *Magnum PI*?" Betty asked, referring to the old Tom Selleck television show.

"Yes, exactly like that."

"Well, why didn't you say so?" Micah's deception hurt Betty.

"Some people won't talk to me unless I tell them I'm a cop," replied Micah.

"You aren't a very good judge of character, *Mr.* Love. Robert is kind of a jerk, and if he did something wrong, I want to know it. That goes for all my tenants. I don't tolerate that kind of crap around here."

"Please call the State Police, Betty. I'm sorry for my little white lie. By the way, you need to put a 'flat for lease' sign out front.

"Why?"

"Because Robert Bright is dead."

"Oh shit," replied Betty, promptly covering her mouth with her hand.

***

Micah called Zack and told him about his conversation with Betty and the discovery of the older-model iPhone. Zack called Gibson. He had a hunch he'd receive better cooperation from her rather than Alexander. His intuition was rewarded. When the Kentucky State Police arrived at the boarding house, the deputies in charge already had a conversation with their captain, who instructed them to share all evidence and information with the private investigator, a Mr. Love, who was present at the scene. Zack phoned Jarrod Weaver and filled him in. Together, they conferenced in Judge Shipley and filled him in on the developments. Shipley granted a search warrant and dispatched it electronically to the Kentucky state troopers. The operation was a go.

Betty brought them the master key so they could enter Robert's flat. It was, as Micah expected, a two-motel-room conversion. The first room was virtually intact as a standard motel living room. The door that would typically lead to an adjoining room was removed. The second room was converted into a large master bedroom with a small office and private bath.

Micah was dying to conduct the search and get his hands on the iPhone, but he knew not to interfere. The Kentucky cops found the phone in the office. One of them bagged and tagged it.

"Is there anything else you're interested in, Mr.?"

"Love, officer. Micah Love."

"I'm Trooper Patterson. This is Trooper Hutchner."

"Nice to know you guys. Yes, 'Robert Bright' was the local pseudonym for the late Bart Breitner, a known white supremacist and overall bad dude. He's the guy that planned and almost carried out that sarin heist in Arlington a few months ago. I'm sure you've heard about it."

"Shit, this is *that* guy?"

"Yeah, *that* guy."

"Please continue."

"Anyway, some Michigan and Federal authorities believe Breitner was murdered when his charter boat blew up with him aboard. A good cop is being charged with the murder, but the defense believes Breitner blew himself up to avoid capture."

"Why would they think a cop was responsible?"

*Because they're fucking idiots!*

"Because Jack Dylan, the cop being accused here, is a Dearborn Police captain who, obviously, has a particular interest in bringing this guy down. But the Feds were also tracking Breitner, and they wanted to usurp the investigation. So, Jack and the Feds have been cracking heads over this investigation for a while. I don't know if you've heard this or not, but Dearborn cracked the case, and the Feds took it away right before the catch and capture operation.

"Unfortunately, the Feds kind of botched the operation and let Breitner escape. Jack was undeniably pissed off and decided to track the guy undercover, without telling the Feds or the locals what he was doing. So, all these guys have their panties in a bunch because Jack acted without authority. When Jack had Breitner cornered, Breitner set off the bomb and killed himself. That's when the Feds and the locals decided Jack was the bad guy. They've accused him of stalking and killing Breitner, most likely because they needed a scapegoat."

"Can't honestly blame them for being pissed," said Hutchner with attitude. "Matter of fact, it's the same thing you almost did."

"Being pissed and charging a good cop when the evidence could easily be interpreted another way are two very different things."

"So, why were the Feds so cooperative this time?" Trooper Patterson asked.

"Which Feds?"

"One in particular. I think she said her name was Gibson."

"Because, finally, there may be some people involved in this case who want to see justice done."

"Okay. So, what are we looking for?" Patterson asked.

"A computer, a manifesto like the one the Unabomber wrote, names and addresses of any racist buddies, anything that might lead us to someone who was nearby that night and saw or heard something. Also, look for bomb-making instructions, grenades, purchase orders for grenades or other explosives, internet access accounts, wireless passwords, Google searches, any electronic footprint that suggests what this guy was up to."

"Well, that's good enough for me," replied Hutchner. "Let's toss this place."

"Whoa, whoa!" exclaimed Betty. "Gently, boys. Gently, please? I've got a flat to rent."

# Chapter Twenty-Nine

After recovering a treasure trove of pro-Caucasian, anti-everyone else garbage, multiple internet accounts, and a list of names from the search of Robert Bright's flat, Micah flew back to Manistee. Taking Zack's private jet meant he would avoid any airport delays or layovers. *Nice perk*!

He was returning empty-handed, but the troopers allowed him to photograph and catalog all the confiscated items. The original evidence was properly handled and shipped to Clare Gibson in Manistee. She was grateful for the new evidence and promised the defense team an opportunity to review everything independently.

Zack focused his review of the Lexington materials on three items: the computer, iPhone, and the names list. The following day, the evidence arrived and was promptly delivered to the crime lab. Zack, Noah, Reed, Matt, Shaheed, and Micah all converged on the lab, running into Gibson, Prince and a roadblock in Chief Alexander.

"What brings you gentlemen here today?" Alexander asked, dripping with condescension.

"Nice to see you, too, Chief," Micah replied.

"I invited them to observe and assist if needed," said Gibson. Alexander glared at Gibson, who glared right back.

"She doesn't have that authority, gentlemen. Only I can authorize that, and I authorize you to leave, now!"

"Chief, the FBI is in charge of this investigation. That was our agreement. I invited them, and as far as I am concerned, they can stay," challenged Gibson.

"This is a search for the truth, Chief," said Andy. "Isn't that what everyone wants? The truth? We would like to work with you."

"Like Dylan wanted to work with us when he decided to deal with Breitner on his own?"

"Look. We can all agree to disagree on Jack's behavior. If he had a do-over on some of the decisions he made, I'm sure he would do things differently. However, he is still a brother police officer, and he is entitled to the benefit of our best efforts to get at the truth, isn't he?"

"Evidence is the property of the prosecution, and after our review, we will make it available per the judge's order."

Zack was fed up. "How about this, then, Chief? How about I call Jarrod Weaver and Judge Shipley, and I tell them how cooperative you're being in processing evidence *we* obtained for you, or how you're impeding access to evidence the judge *ordered* you to release to the defense? How do you think *that* will go over with Shipley?"

"Call the judge. I don't believe we have to provide access to evidence the people have yet to review."

"Have it your way, Chief. I'll call the judge." Zack had no doubt how the judge would rule. The only issue was whether it would cost Alexander money or jail time. Micah bet on jail. Zack did not wish to see anyone go to jail and promised to go easy on Alexander when speaking with the judge. "One caveat though—please refrain from processing the evidence until we receive Shipley's ruling."

Alexander, Prince, and Gibson did not move or respond. Gibson smiled at Zack's bravado. The three appeared frozen in place. *I bet they'll be standing in that exact spot when I return with a court order.* Zack smiled to himself.

Fifteen minutes later, Zack and his team returned with a court order signed by Shipley permitting them complete access to the evidence. Alexander, Prince, and Gibson were standing in the lobby. Zack wasn't sure if they were occupying the exact same spots or not, but it was a close call. He walked up to Alexander and handed him the order.

"The judge would like to see you, Chief. I told him you were being cautious and wanted the cover of an order. I believe I diffused any penalty that might have come your way." *Although, being on the wrong side of a pissing contest with a judge is never a good thing.*

Alexander stormed off without so much as a 'thank you,' while the rest of the group was buzzed into the lab. It was far more impressive and modernized than Zack expected. This was the twenty-first century, state of the art.

Zack's entourage was introduced to Ian Miller, the crime lab's supervisor. Miller had superintending control of the process of cataloging all the evidence and observing all chain of custody protocol. He appreciated and welcomed the support of Micah's team, and Zack was grateful for his enthusiastic cooperation.

Miller divided everything and everyone into three groups: technology, document review and interpretation, and DNA/fingerprint processing and recovery. Noah and Reed were assigned to work with the Miller-assigned technology group. A second group, which included Micah and Andy, was assigned to verifying, testing, and interpreting the documents found in Breitner's flat. The third group, which included Matt Jordan, Eric Burns and Shaheed Ali, was responsible for fingerprint and/or DNA analysis on all the evidence.

The computer search bore immediate fruit, including many original documents and a contact list with the names and addresses of 'Midwest Members' in Michigan, Indiana, Illinois, Ohio, and Northern Kentucky. A search through the iPhone produced phone number matches to many of these contacts. Micah decided the best way to properly interrogate these men was to conduct surprise visits. He and Andy hopped the jet for a return flight to Detroit.

Over the next few days, the two men visited with several of Breitner's computer and iPhone contacts as far north as Bay City and as far south as Cincinnati. Some refused to talk. Others insisted the group was all talk and no action. "We would never actually hurt anyone." Beyond the expected white supremacist playbook, no one could provide any unique insight into the mind or motives of Bart Breitner. They claimed the group was only interested in exercising First Amendment rights, deporting all illegal immigrants, and

'Making America Pure Again.' Micah and Andy were extremely frustrated.

They were driving south on I-75, returning from a visit to Flint, seventy miles north of Detroit, and heading for Auburn Hills, a small, predominately blue-collar town, one that offered Breitner an opportunity to recruit new members. They were looking for the apartment home of the next person on their list, one Martin Sumner.

The two men arrived at a modest apartment complex and knocked on the door of apartment 3A. A tall, thin man in khakis and a sports shirt answered the door.

"May I help you?" the man asked.

"I hope so," said Micah. "My name is Micah Love, and this is Officer Andy Toler." Toler flashed his badge and Sumner was now aware this was 'official police business.'

"What can I do for you?"

"Are you Martin Sumner?"

"Maybe."

"We'll take that as a yes. We are investigating the death of Barton Breitner, and your name came up in the investigation," said Micah.

"Oh? In what context, may I ask?"

"We did a sweep of Breitner's flat in Kentucky and found a computer and an iPhone which featured a membership list that contained your name and address."

"Asshole!"

"Excuse me?"

"Oh, sorry. Not you... Bart. *Bart* is the asshole. He tells us to keep to the dark web and encrypt everything. 'Leave no footprint,' he says, and here he is using a fucking computer."

"And an iPhone."

"Seriously, man? What a dick! So, what do you guys want from me? I've done nothing wrong-First Amendment, baby. I market, march, lecture, attend meetings, that sort of thing."

"Ever attend a meeting about attacking citizens with sarin gas?"

"No, I must have missed that one. Besides, I'm opposed to violence of any kind."

"But you heard about such a meeting, didn't you?"

"Maybe. Might have heard something at a later meeting."

"Ever been to Manistee, Michigan?"

"To fish maybe, why?"

"Cut the shit, Sumner. The 'later meeting' you refer to was in Manistee, wasn't it?"

"Maybe."

"And you were there."

"Maybe."

"Why would you go if you don't agree with the violent actions the group was planning?"

"Because I still believe in the group's First Amendment core values and I didn't think Bart would resort to *violence*."

"You know Bart died in Manistee, shortly after your meeting, right?"

Sumner was suddenly defensive. "I left Manistee well before that happened."

"So, you were there? Well, we aren't accusing you of anything. We simply want to know what you know."

"Depends on what you want to know."

"We know several of your members got together in Manistee. Do you know why?"

"Bart wanted to meet. He called me personally and asked me to come."

"Were you in Virginia, too?"

"No. I already told you I wasn't there."

"So why agree to go to Manistee?"

"To tell you the truth, I was deathly afraid of Bart. After Virginia went wrong, he went kind of nuts. I was afraid if I didn't go, he'd go nuts on me if you know what I mean."

"We know exactly what you mean," replied Andy, speaking for the first time.

"What was discussed in Manistee?" Micah continued.

"I want immunity."

"But you said you didn't do anything wrong."

"I didn't."

"Then why do you need immunity?"

"Maybe because of what we discussed in Manistee."

"I'm not following."

"If Bart was planning something and I was there, hypothetically speaking, I could be charged with conspiracy, right?"

"I suppose it's possible, but that would depend on what was discussed. Besides, I don't have the authority to grant anyone immunity. I'd have to know what you have to offer to the investigation and whether the information is valuable. Then, the request would have to go through proper channels."

"Then I have nothing to say."

"Well, that is certainly your right. But this is extremely important. Is there any *guidance* you could give us?" Micah asked with a suggestive expression. "We'd like to get the ball rolling on an immunity deal. Help us out here man. What are we missing?"

"Nothing. It seems you already knew about Arlington and Manistee."

"True, but suppose Breitner's previous meetings and actions dictated his future ones? I would presume whatever he was planning was discussed in Manistee."

Micah was close to asking Sumner to incriminate himself without an immunity deal in place. Martin knew the same but was trying to bolster his case for immunity by cooperating.

"Look, Martin, we know all about Howell, Arlington, and the plot to steal sarin and release it in Dearborn. What we need to know is how that played into whatever he was planning in Manistee."

"Whatever plan Breitner had and wherever he had it failed. I wasn't a part of planning any type of attack. I told you. I exercise my First Amendment rights and nothing more."

"But we can assume some kind of explosive device was discussed in Manistee, right?"

"Well, that's how he died, right? You told me that."

"No, actually, I *didn't* tell you that. But, now that you mention it, it was a grenade."

"Interesting."

"Interesting-why?"

Martin hesitated. Was he about to clam up? He was perilously close to incriminating himself before he had an immunity deal. Andy was beginning to understand where the conversation needed to go.

"It appears Bart has a certain fondness for different kinds of explosive devices." Andy offered.

Martin smiled. "I wouldn't know."

"Do you know if any members had *access* to explosives or explosive devices?"

"No, at least not any *current* members I know of."

"Would you have met any new members if they attended a meeting or even the same Manistee meeting you attended?"

"Sure."

"And did you meet anyone new?"

"I may have. I'd have to think about that one." *Marty is smarter than I gave him credit.*

"So, let's go back to that Manistee meeting where you *possibly* met some new guys. Could Bart have wanted to discuss anything beyond the ordinary exercise of free speech?" *Will he answer this time?*

Marty smiled and began tapping his chin, trying to frame a 'hypothetical' response. *This idiot is enjoying himself,* Micah mused.

"Bart might have wanted to get together to discuss what went wrong in Virginia and how we might still exact our revenge."

"But the sarin gas was seized by the Feds. How would he have gotten his revenge?"

"Well, I'm only guessing here because none of this was ever discussed while I was there, but *perhaps* he might have gotten a line on some back on some other types of explosives from one of these *newcomers* you guys are talking about."

"Could he have disclosed the types of explosives he had in mind?"

"He could have."

"Could grenades have been involved?"

"That question is way above my pay grade. I'm a low-level guy who only asserts his constitutional right to free speech and assembly every now and then. Though, it's *possible* I know something . . ."

"Could you elaborate, please? I'm not sure I follow."

"Immunity."

"But we are speaking in hypotheticals."

"Sounds to me like we aren't anymore."

*He's a quick study.* "I have one more question, and then I'll go and try to get you that deal. You don't have to answer if you don't want to."

"I don't do *shit* unless I want to and I'm getting damned tired of this. In fact, I'm getting kind of dizzy." His smile disappeared.

"I'll need to get in touch to advise about the immunity deal. Can I reach you at this number?" Micah showed him an iPhone screen with Martin's telephone number on it.

"Where the fuck did you get that?"

"From Breitner's cell phone."

"Asshole. Hope he rots."

# Chapter Thirty

Trial in the case of *State v. Dylan* was looming, a mere two weeks away. Micah and Andy returned from their journey with one promising lead. Zack's task was to convince Clare Gibson or Dan Wolfe to grant testimonial immunity to Martin Sumner. Since the feds thought Jack was guilty, this would be a hard sell.

Meanwhile, the DNA and fingerprint team were hard at work on the new material. Human remains from the area surrounding the boat were conclusively identified as belonging to Bart Breitner, no surprise there. Bomb fragments and shrapnel were placed on a table, and various technicians attempted to "reassemble" the bomb. Smudges were found on multiple parts. Maybe these were fingerprints. So far, the results were inconclusive.

Security video was reviewed again. They tried running the video, freezing it, looking at different angles. At best, all video evidence was inconclusive. Zack wanted footage conclusively demonstrating Breitner, and not Jack, exploded the bomb. Failing that, Zack was confident video evidence would not assist the prosecution in proving Jack's guilt "beyond a reasonable doubt."

"We're missing something," said Zack.

"What are we missing, Zack? There's nothing there. We don't have the angle we need. Every video displays the dock view, front to back," replied Micah.

Zack continued to study videos and stills. Maybe he could *will* the images to suddenly morph into a full-body image of Breitner exploding the grenade. He froze the footage again and invited everyone to look at the frozen image. The men looked at the frozen image of the demolished boat, the debris floating in the black waters, boats docked nearby, and the dark waters of Lake Michigan beyond. Everyone drew blanks.

"Get Jack in here."

Andy left the room and returned with his captain in tow.

"Jack," said Zack. "Take a look at this still photograph and tell me what you see."

"The crime scene. The demolished boat." Jack pointed to a small round object in the water. "That's my head, I think."

"I didn't notice that before. Did you guys?"

Everyone shook their heads.

"That's my whole point. Maybe there's something else we're missing."

"Obsessing over it will not make it suddenly appear," said Shaheed. "Why don't we call it a night and reconvene in the morning?"

"Yeah, I guess that's a good idea," he replied, never taking his eyes off the screen.

"Shall I turn it off now, Zack?" Micah asked with his hand on the on/off button. Zack was still staring at the screen.

Zack blinked, looked away, and nodded his head. Micah turned off the projector. After everyone was gone, Zack and Micah walked back to the hotel together.

"A fingerprint on a bomb fragment would be wonderful, but without it, the key to this case is somewhere in the video and still photographic evidence."

"I know that's how you feel, Zack, but be realistic. I canvassed the area. I talked to everyone in proximity to the blast, and I reviewed every piece of video, and they all depict the same images. You cannot see who set off the bomb. What more can we do?"

"Well, they have the same video evidence, and they can't prove it was Jack. It's *their* fucking burden. I need reasonable doubt, not proof of innocence and these videos are the very *definition* of reasonable doubt."

They reached the hotel and went to their separate rooms. Trial was now less than two weeks away. Zack kept reminding himself he didn't have to prove Jack's innocence. Still, he was virtually obsessed with the idea of doing just that. He aimed to prove Jack's innocence, without a doubt. It was the only way Jack returned to Dearborn as the hero cop, rather than a rogue one who'd been convicted of murder or who was only found not guilty because the government couldn't *prove* his guilt. Not guilty under *those* circumstances would create a life-long cloud over his career and reputation.

***

With a week to go before the trial, Dr. Werner Spellman, Charles Snyder, and their teams were hard at work with bomb shrapnel and other residuals provided by Lyle Manor and his team. Spellman, Snyder and their men were sifting through bomb fragments and explosive residue, hoping to find Breitner's fingerprints on some piece of bomb material.

Snyder conducted a color test on the residue, applying solutions that contained reagents that changed color in response to certain explosives. If that test was promising, it could be confirmed with chromatography and mass spectrometry.

The most crucial test in this instance, though, was the Cyanoacrylate Fuming Method, more commonly known as the Super-Glue fuming test. With this test, the bomb specialist heats Super-Glue in a closed container with a piece of shrapnel or bomb residue. If a fingerprint is present, Super-Glue will gather around it, highlight and preserve it. This technique was developed because scientists discovered Super-Glue bonds exceptionally well with sweat and other residues on human fingers. This is also why a person's fingers stick together when using Super-Glue. Because fingerprints can burn off explosives when they ignite, the investigators were also looking for 'touch DNA,' where, perhaps, Breitner might have left dead skin cells behind.

The average twenty-first-century grenade is baseball sized and fourteen ounces in weight. It uses a pre-segmented body to cause the shrapnel to spread evenly, thus more lethally. The waffle or pineapple pattern most of us are familiar with creates weak points in the shell.

Those weak points break first when a grenade detonates. Since the average grenade has forty such bumps, that grenade will shoot the equivalent of forty bullets in all different directions. With an average kill radius of 16.4 feet (5 meters), Jack and Bart were both within blast range at the time of detonation. Jack saved himself by diving into the water. Scientific testing confirms water pressure against grenade projectiles actually causes them to disintegrate before they hit an underwater target.

The team focused on the largest pieces, including, apparently, a part of the pin. They meticulously applied Super-Glue and waited. The career, indeed the very freedom, of Jack Dylan hung in the balance.

***

Noah and Reed were searching through the computer and iPhone for encrypted, compressed, and password-protected materials related to Breitner's past and potential terrorist activities. For a self-proclaimed anti-technology white supremacist, they found his technical skills at a frustratingly high level. They searched for financial sources, as Jack instructed them to "follow the money." They searched for evidence of conspiracy, emails or websites devoted to recruiting people for illegal purposes or, better yet, specific terrorist events like the sarin gas episode.

In baseball terminology, the team was getting hits, but, to date, no one hit a home run. Someone located a couple of incendiary recruitment videos, but true to what Martin Sumner told Micah, and these were far more like First Amendment exercises than terrorist acts. Perhaps they were warm-up videos. Breitner might have recruited people for the rough stuff *after* they were trusted members of the tribe.

The techs were careful to establish the integrity of the digital evidence. This was essential to its admissibility in court and its persuasive value. Again, adherence to the strict chain of custody protocols for the computer, iPhone, and hard drive and other data storage units involved, was crucial to its admissibility in court. They also followed strict procedures in securing the data, and if they deviated from procedures, the reason and the results of that deviation were documented. They kept careful track of who handled and/or who had access to the evidence as soon as they obtained custody of it and when, how, and from where the evidence was collected.

Thankfully, everyone involved in this aspect of the investigation was a specially trained forensic expert. This was especially important when dealing with the recovery of deleted, defective, or complicated codes and encryptions. One could not rush this type of analysis, even though Zack checked in often and angrily demanded "some damned action for a change."

Suddenly, the quiet room erupted when Noah shouted, "Yes!"

Reed and the others rushed to his side and peered at two side-by-side computer screens. One, labeled 'Internet Café,' contained data from a café located near Breitner's boat dock. The second, labeled "Breitner Drive," contained data from the computer recovered from Breitner's flat. Noah began scrolling the screen entitled "Internet Café." In front of them was an email exchange from Breitner's address (as verified from the computer recovered in Kentucky) to a supplier. There was an order for arms, ammunition, and explosives two months before the Manistee explosion. Among the explosives ordered was an ample supply of M67 fragmentation grenades, an exact match to the type that exploded in Manistee. There were also numerous emails back and forth discussing the training of operatives to commit acts of terror using these grenades and other types of explosives, arms, and ammunition.

"Wow! This is fantastic!" Reed shouted.

Noah was the voice of reason and caution. "It's certainly all we could hope for. We can now prove in court Breitner purchased the grenade that blew up the boat. Still, we can't prove who detonated it."

"Maybe not to the cops, but it is solid evidence to a jury Breitner detonated the grenade and not Jack."

"True. Let's get Zack and Micah and show them what we found."

Finally, in a sea of uncertainty, there was a bright ray of hope for Jack Dylan.

# PART THREE—TRIAL

# Chapter Thirty-One

The *State v. Dylan* trial was a major news event. The jury was assembled and charged. The trial began and the state's attorney, Jarrod Weaver, was completing his opening statement.

"The State acknowledges and thanks Jack Dylan for his years as a decorated veteran police officer in his home city of Dearborn. He has performed some heroic and lifesaving acts. We cannot get inside his head to determine why he betrayed his oath to protect and serve. The Fifth Amendment of the Constitution prevents prosecutors from forcing defendants to testify in a criminal case. Unless Captain Dylan and his attorney decide to put him on the witness stand, the State will be unable to ask him that question. We may never know why he murdered Mr. Breitner. But the defendant's actions immediately before the explosion provide us with an excellent glimpse into his psyche at the time.

"The evidence will prove Barton Breitner was a known terrorist who plotted to use sarin gas in the City of Dearborn. SWAT and the FBI organized a mission to prevent the attack, and it succeeded except for one crucial item. While the team secured the sarin and made numerous arrests, Mr. Breitner escaped.

"Mr. Breitner's criminal history or status is not relevant to this case. A criminal defendant, even a terrorist like Bart Breitner, is entitled to due process. Police officers do not get to act as judges or jurors. They certainly don't get to act as executioners. In this case, the defendant wasn't even operating in his official capacity as an officer of the law. Still, the defendant decided to take the law into his own hands, and behind his own chief's back, the defendant chose to go after Mr. Breitner. In fact, the evidence will show the defendant was *obsessed* with finding Mr. Breitner.

"The defendant left a message for his boss, saying he needed R & R and was taking a leave of absence. He traveled to Manistee and took a room at the Bay Shore. He did not contact the FBI, which was leading the Breitner investigation, nor did he ask for local police assistance in identifying and arresting the victim. Only his own subordinates knew he was in Manistee. So, why did he keep the operation a secret? It was because he wanted to extract his own justice. The defense will claim the defendant was operating undercover, but, upon whose authority? This was a rogue investigation, authorized by no one other than the defendant himself. Yet, this claim of undercover authority is a major theme of the defendant's case. It is also its major flaw because Jack Dylan was nothing more than a vigilante who happened to possess an 'out of service' police badge.

"The defendant befriended some tourists who arranged a fishing trip on the victim's boat. One will testify the defendant was so intent on going on this trip he paid the cost for the entire group, which clearly demonstrates the defendant's obsession with finding and terminating Barton Breitner.

"The defendant, you will hear, arranged multiple meetings with the deceased apart from the rest of the group. At these meetings, the defendant made efforts to befriend the victim, using deception, and waiting for his chance to act. Their final conversation became heated and subsequently violent. You will hear testimony to that effect.

"Jack Dylan determined Bart Breitner was a terrorist. With malice aforethought, Dylan decided to become Breitner's executioner. The evidence will show Dylan threw a live grenade at the victim and jumped into the water to avoid impact and injury. This was a *strategy*, ladies and gentlemen. It required planning and precision timing. In the defendant's mind, these actions were necessary to silence a criminal while simultaneously protecting himself from harm. The law does not permit the defendant to make this judgment. By our laws, Mr. Breitner was an innocent man, and the defendant is a murderer. While a police officer has the right to pursue and apprehend a suspected criminal, the defendant was not acting with police authority in this case.

"The evidence of the defendant's guilt is overwhelming, and when we finish presenting it to you, we have no doubt you will find him guilty of murder in the second degree. Jack Dylan will receive a fair trial before Judge Shipley and you, ladies and gentlemen, a jury of his peers. Bart Breitner was denied this same constitutional privilege when the defendant decided to take the law into his own hands and murder Mr. Breitner. Please take your responsibility seriously, listen to all of the evidence, and find the defendant, Jack Dylan, guilty of murder in the second degree."

Weaver thanked the jury and the judge, looked at Zack, smiled, and sat down, exhausted. The judge thanked Weaver and then invited Zachary Blake to give his opening statement. Zack approached the jury box.

"Ladies and gentlemen of the jury. This is one of two times I will have to address you personally. What Mr. Weaver has just told you is not evidence. Nothing we lawyers say is evidence. Evidence comes from the witness chair and the exhibits admitted by Judge Shipley. Hopefully, you listened to the promises made by Mr. Weaver. Please listen to my promises, as well. Attorneys *must* keep their promises at trial. Use your own common sense when you see and hear the evidence presented. Jack Dylan and I will leave it to *you* and your sound discretion, to determine the value and validity of the evidence.

"Some of what Mr. Weaver told you is true. Jack Dylan *is* a decorated, experienced police officer. He achieved the rank of captain by being excellent at what he does. Jack *did* follow Bart Breitner, a white supremacist and terrorist, the mastermind of a plot to release sarin gas in the City of Dearborn. Mr. Breitner's stated goal was to kill cops and Dearborn citizens of foreign origin. He also sought to exact revenge for the capture and conviction of his 'friend,' convicted terrorist and bomber, Benjamin Blaine. Mr. Blaine, you will hear, is currently serving a life sentence for multiple counts of murder. These are the kind of friends Barton Breitner, hung around.

"Jack Dylan made some poor decisions, ladies and gentlemen, but questionable decision making does not equate with being a murderer.

Let's examine the chain of events. Jack pursued a terrorist without telling his boss or his fellow officers what he was doing and where he was going. He went undercover without consulting with local authorities here in Manistee. Maybe, this was poor judgment on his part. But it was exercised to protect and serve the citizens of Dearborn.

"Jack Dylan *did* go on that fishing trip, and he *did* try to befriend the terrorist. He sought to infiltrate a terrorist's organization. Video evidence will show he did not seek to kill, but to *arrest* the man. The evidence is confusing at this point. Additional video segments show an altercation, a boat explosion, and Jack diving into the water. What the video *fails* to show, however, is even more important. You won't see Jack Dylan detonating the explosive. You won't even see him in *possession* of any explosive. The prosecution, with no evidence whatsoever, leaps to that conclusion in its haste to justify an arrest of my client. This is extremely important, because, as Judge Shipley will instruct, the *State* must prove these things beyond a reasonable doubt. Jack Dylan doesn't have to prove a thing.

"When you watch the video footage, it will be impossible to determine how the explosive ignited. To convict my client, the State must prove my client was the bomber, and it cannot meet that burden. Let's suppose you decide to try to prove what the State cannot. Here are four important factors for you to consider: First, as I have already mentioned, the burden of proof belongs to the *State*. This alone compels you to find the defendant not guilty. Second, the proofs will establish the deceased was, indeed, plotting terrorist activity. There will be testimony that Mr. Breitner was looking to purchase or in the process of purchasing explosives and other weapons for future acts of terror. Third, the judge will instruct you to use your common sense. Who was more likely to explode a bomb under these circumstances? Was it the decorated cop who may have made some poor decisions, or was it the terrorist, the man who purchased explosives and was about to be arrested? Finally, Captain Dylan had a service revolver. Again, use your common sense. Why would he need to detonate an explosive? Why not simply shoot the bad guy?"

Zachary completed his opening statement. He told the jury it was their *duty* to find Jack not guilty. He called specific attention to perceived inadequacies of the State's case and promised to spend the rest of the trial saying, '*I told you so.*' Jack marveled at Zack's ability to connect with the jury, to humanize Jack and demonize Breitner. Jack was 'decorated,' 'experienced' and a 'hero.' Bart was a 'terrorist,' a 'bomber' and a 'revenge seeker.'

Jack was angry with himself. He should have done things by the book, sought his chief's permission to go undercover and allowed the chief to liaise with the FBI and local authorities. He shouldn't have allowed himself to be alone with the terrorist, but his obsession with capturing him clouded his judgment. Now, he faced the ultimate irony. Here in this place, at this time, he stood accused of being a criminal, the type of person that he spent his career bringing to justice.

Zack took his seat. Drained of energy, he looked at Jack, smiled, and patted him on the leg. Jack Dylan was not a religious man, but he thanked God that Zack was a more talented lawyer than he, Jack, was a police officer. *Zachary Blake is a master. He will never mimic my carelessness. Somehow, he will persuade the jury to find me not guilty.*

Jack never thought this case would reach this point. He assumed the FBI and the Manistee police would drop the charges, apologize and he would return to Dearborn a hero. But, here he was, a criminal defendant, on trial for murder. Jack's freedom was in the hands of Zachary Blake and twelve strangers. He hoped and prayed Zack did his job better than Jack had done his. *My career is over, guilty or not.* Poor judgment in Manistee would haunt him for the rest of his life because he was the only person left alive who knew, for certain, that he was innocent.

# Chapter Thirty-Two

"Good morning."

"Good morning."

"Please tell the jury your name, where you work, and what you do."

The first full day of trial started. Jarrod Weaver called his first witness, FBI Special Agent Clare Gibson.

"My name is Clare Gibson. I'm a special agent of the FBI's anti-terrorism task force."

"And what is the FBI's interest in this case, Agent Gibson?"

"The FBI has been monitoring the movements and activities of Barton Breitner for quite some time. I am a supervisory agent, in charge of that investigation."

"Under whose authority?"

"Ernest Cobb, Special Agent in Charge of the Detroit office of the FBI."

"Please tell the jury how long you have been an FBI agent."

"Seventeen years."

"Please tell the jury about your training and expertise."

Zack interrupted the answer. "Your Honor, the defense will stipulate to this witness' expertise as an FBI agent, terrorist task force supervisor and criminal investigator." This was a strategic legal move. While Gibson's credentials may have bored the jury to tears, they might have also given jurors an inflated glimpse of her background and talents. Impressive résumés or curriculum vitae tended to do that, and Zack did not want the jury to inflate her stature.

"Mr. Weaver?"

"We thank the defense for saving us the time it would take to properly qualify the witness as an expert," replied Weaver. "Now, Agent Gibson, did anything unusual happen to you this past spring?"

"Yes, it did."

"Please tell the jury what happened."

"We received credible information a man named Barton Breitner, who was on our terrorist watch list, was about to obtain a supply of sarin gas in Arlington, VA and release it in the city of Dearborn."

"What did you do?"

"We conferred with Dearborn P.D. and decision makers from both units concluded the FBI would take the lead in investigating and, hopefully, stopping the plot."

"Was that decision welcomed by Captain Dylan?"

"No, quite the contrary, Captain Dylan was distraught."

"Why was he upset, if you know?"

"He wanted Dearborn to take the lead. He wanted to bring Breitner down himself. He seemed obsessed with the idea."

"Objection, Your Honor. Perhaps I should withdraw my offer to waive Agent Gibson's curriculum vitae. I wasn't aware she was a psychiatrist."

"What is the legal basis for your objection, Mr. Blake?" Judge Shipley would not tolerate a smart-ass.

"The witness lacks the expertise to render an opinion about the defendant's mental state. Furthermore, unless she heard these supposed words directly from Captain Dylan, they are hearsay."

"Sustained. The jury will disregard."

"I'll move on, Your Honor," said Weaver. "Agent Gibson, after the little 'turf battle' you had with Captain Dylan, did he become a team player?"

"Not really, but, in fairness, there wasn't a team. Dearborn was not investigating Breitner in Arlington, the FBI was. Dylan and his team weren't needed and weren't invited to participate."

"How did Dylan feel about being left out?"

"I thought he was okay with it, but, apparently, I was mistaken."

"Anything in particular cause you to feel that way?"

"Well, a plot to release sarin gas was discovered. The gas was stored in Arlington, but the target was Dearborn. We investigated, cultivated an insider/eyewitness and eventually discovered the plot.

The witness identified Breitner as its chief architect. Dearborn wanted to see the investigation through, but the FBI usurped it, conducted its own investigation and thwarted the plot before the perpetrators could do any harm."

Jack rolled his eyes and let out an audible sigh at this distortion. It was *Dearborn cops* who cultivated Jonathan Stone and the information leading to Arlington and any chance to 'thwart' the sarin plot.

"What happened, exactly?"

"We prevented the theft and caught everyone involved except Breitner."

"Why except Breitner?"

"Because he, alone, escaped our dragnet."

"That was an unfortunate development."

"The fact that Breitner escaped? Yes, that was a *very* unfortunate development."

"Did there come a time when the defendant became aware the Arlington mission failed to capture and confine Bart Breitner?"

"Yes, I believe I informed Captain Dylan myself."

"What was his reaction?"

"He was outraged. He felt we botched the job. He said Dearborn wouldn't have allowed Bart to escape."

"Was that true?"

"Well, it was true we lost Breitner, but, as I said, we stopped the attack and caught all of the perpetrators except Bart. I think the mission was *very* successful."

"What happened next?"

"We began the process of organizing a team to search for and find Breitner."

"And how did that go?"

"Well, it didn't."

"Why not?"

"Because someone beat us to it."

"I'm not sure I follow."

"Breitner was found and eliminated, but not by us."

"Who found him and eliminated him?"

"Objection, Your Honor. Foundation. There has been no evidence Bart Breitner has ever been found, much less eliminated. There is no foundation."

"Sustained."

"I'll ask the question another way, Agent. Following the Arlington operation, did you attempt to locate Bart Breitner?"

"Yes."

"But you didn't find him, did you?"

"No."

"Who did?"

"Captain Dylan."

"Where did he find him?"

"Here in Manistee."

"And since you were the lead investigator, Dylan contacted you immediately, is that correct?"

"No, it is not correct."

"Well, what happened?"

"Dylan did not inform the FBI he had a lead on Breitner. He lied to his immediate superior officer, Chief Acker, and swore his men to secrecy. He traveled to Manistee, without color of authority, conducted a rogue search and capture operation, and it appears he murdered Bart Breitner."

"Objection!" Zack shrieked. "There has been no evidence of any kind to even remotely suggest Captain Dylan killed anyone, Your Honor."

"Sustained. The witness will refrain from assuming facts not in evidence."

"Mr. Breitner has disappeared, has he not, Agent Gibson?"

"He has."

"What leads you to the conclusion he's dead?"

"Because some of his body parts have been found floating in the lake."

"Did you investigate what happened to Mr. Breitner?"

"Yes, Mr. Breitner's presumed death prompted a criminal investigation, and I was placed in charge."

"And what were the results of this investigation?"

"The evidence demonstrated the defendant, Jack Dylan murdered Barton Breitner. After the two men got into an argument, Dylan tossed a grenade directly at Breitner. Seconds later, the grenade exploded, killing Mr. Breitner."

"And the defendant? What happened to him?"

"He jumped into the water, seconds before the explosion. He emerged from the water with no more than a scratch."

"Did that lead you to any conclusion?"

"Yes, we concluded the defendant threw the grenade. Only the person who tossed it could know where it was going and how to escape serious injury or death."

"How so, Agent Gibson?"

"Water significantly impedes the force of a grenade blast. A trained criminal investigator like the defendant would surely know that."

"Thank you, Agent Gibson. I have no further questions."

Zack was out of his seat before Judge Shipley could say "You may cross-examine, Mr. Blake."

"Agent Gibson. Isn't it true the Manistee Police already decided Captain Dylan was guilty before you came to town?"

"Well…yes…but I reviewed the evidence and came to the same conclusion."

"You interviewed every so-called eye-witness on this list, true?" Zack held up a piece of paper. Observers could not determine if it was an actual list of names.

"Or read and reviewed statements already taken."

"Did any witness say he or she saw Jack Dylan throw or explode that grenade?"

"Well… we…"

"Yes or no, Agent?"

"No, but . . ."

Zack interrupted her. "Thank you, Agent Gibson. You've answered my question. Investigators found bomb fragments, did they not?"

"Yes, they did."

"Does anything found on, in or around the debris or anything else at the crime scene link Jack Dylan to the death of Bart Breitner?"

"Taken together with the witness…"

"Your Honor. Please instruct the witness to answer only my question."

"Objection, Your Honor. Mr. Blake keeps interrupting Agent Gibson's answers," Weaver said. "Let her speak."

"Overruled. Agent Gibson, listen to the question and answer only the question, please. The reporter will please read back the question," replied Shipley.

The court reporter read back the question, word for word.

"Other than fingerprints and eye-witness statements confirming the defendant's presence, and an argument with the victim at the crime scene, at the time of the blast, no, Mr. Blake, there wasn't," Gibson finally replied.

"When I ask you a 'yes or no' question, please limit your answer to 'yes or no.' Is it fair to say the Dearborn Police and the FBI discovered the sarin plot simultaneously?"

"I'm not exactly sure."

"I'll put it another way. The Dearborn Police already knew about the plot when you came to tell them about it, correct?"

"I didn't know it at the time, but, yes, they knew about it."

"Despite Breitner being on the FBI's radar, as you said, Dearborn uncovered this plot, as well?"

"Yes."

"And when Dearborn shared its information with the FBI, you and your associates pulled the rug out from under Dearborn's anti-terrorism task force so the FBI could have the glory from Bart's capture, isn't that true, Agent Gibson?"

"Well, I wouldn't put it that way…"

"Yes or no, Agent?"

"Yes."

"If another agency pulled a case you worked and solved, right at the moment agents were preparing to foil the plot and capture the criminals, how would you feel about it?"

"Objection, Your Honor. How Agent Gibson would have felt is irrelevant and speculative."

"Maybe so, but I'd like to hear her answer," replied Shipley. "Overruled."

"I would not have been happy."

"Angry?"

"Yes."

"Mad as hell…"

"Your Honor…" Weaver stood and began to object.

"We get the point, Mr. Blake, move it along," replied Shipley.

"No further questions at this time, Your Honor, but the defense reserves the right to recall this witness."

"Granted. Let's take a break."

When the combatants returned, the state called Chief Christopher Alexander to the witness stand. After the same preliminary process used to qualify Gibson, Weaver began his direct examination.

"How did you first discover there was possible criminal activity involving Mr. Breitner's boat?"

"We received a 9-1-1 call about an altercation involving firearms on board a fishing vessel at the harbor across from Shirley's Bar & Grill."

"How did you respond?"

"I put out an 'all-hands-on-deck' alert and four officers, and I headed to the scene."

"What did you do when you got there?"

"As we exited our vehicles, the vessel in question suddenly exploded. We were knocked to the ground by the force of the blast.

After recovering my faculties, I ran up to the area where the boat was docked. My first instinct was to determine whether anyone was injured and needed medical attention. I peered into the lake and saw a man treading water. My officers and I helped him out."

Jack chuckled to himself. He didn't remember it this way. Alexander trained a gun on him and ordered him out of the water. He penned a quick note to Zack: '*He's lying.*' Zack pushed the note away. *The truth continues to be unimportant in this case.*

"What happened next?" Weaver continued.

"I asked the man what happened. He said Barton Breitner, a man he called a terrorist, tossed a grenade in his direction, and when he saw it, he immediately jumped into the water to avoid impact."

"Would you recognize that man today if you saw him?"

"Yes."

"Is he in the courtroom?"

"Yes, that's him over there." Alexander pointed to Jack Dylan, seated at the defense table.

"Let the record reflect the witness has identified the defendant, Jack Dylan," said Weaver.

"Did you believe his story?"

"Honestly, no. It takes skill to avoid a grenade blast, especially one you have no idea is coming."

"How do you know that?"

"Because I had previous bomb squad training and worked with the State Police bomb squad before coming to Manistee."

"What years were those?"

"I was trained in 1995, and I worked on the bomb squad as a commander from 1996 until 2000."

"What did you do?"

"I led a team that responded to suspicious package or explosive device calls all across the State of Michigan. We also handled calls like this one, where an explosive already detonated. We did protective and dignitary sweeps. I trained and supervised an explosive detection canine unit."

"Dogs?"

"Dogs."

"Got it. So, Chief Alexander, what did you do next in *this* case?"

"Three men came up to the scene and identified themselves as Dearborn Police officers and told me the man in the water was their captain. I told them to stand back and not interfere, or they would be arrested. Then I instructed my officers to seal off the crime scene. There would be no one in or out. We called the State Police crime lab and asked them to send crime scene investigation personnel. Once the crime scene was secure, I questioned the man we pulled from the water."

"What, if anything, did he tell you?"

"He confirmed he was Captain Jack Dylan from the Dearborn police force, which kind of aggravated me."

"Aggravated you why?"

"Because four policemen from another city came into my city and conducted a rogue operation without permission or even notification. This is against standard police protocol and etiquette. The Manistee Police knew nothing of this case until I got that 9-1-1 call."

"Back to the night in question. What did you do next?"

"I waited for the crime scene techs to arrive, at which time, I gave them some ground rules. Then I took Captain Dylan down to the station and allowed his men to follow. Once there, we sought to take a preliminary statement from Dylan."

"Did he, in fact, give you a statement?"

"Yes. Dylan told us he was working undercover. He said that he befriended the deceased to take down what he referred to as the deceased's 'terrorist' organization. Before we could question him further, his men informed me his lawyer was on his way. At that point, I terminated the interrogation. Sometime later, I spoke to his chief, Acker was his name, and he informed me there was no such undercover operation. I asked the three officers who accompanied Dylan to headquarters whether they were aware of an undercover operation. Lieutenant Shaheed told me, he and his men were fully aware that Captain Dylan was conducting an unofficial, off-the-books operation.

"We continued to collect evidence about Captain Dylan's obsession with Mr. Breitner, and we determined Captain Dylan carefully planned his trip, deliberately concealed it from his superiors, and came to Manistee without color of authority.

"Captain Dylan stalked the deceased, gained his trust, and killed him at his first opportunity. We felt we had an excellent case of first-degree murder because of his careful planning of the operation, but you decided to charge him with second-degree murder instead." Weaver winced at the subtle dig.

"Anything else to add, Chief Alexander?"

"The crime scene guys collected a significant amount of evidence. It was all bagged, tagged, and analyzed…"

"Objection, Your Honor. Hearsay."

"Well, hold on, Mr. Blake," replied the judge. He turned to Alexander and said, "Chief, did you supervise this evidence collection process?"

"Not personally, Your Honor, but—"

"Objection is sustained," Judge Shipley ruled, interrupting Alexander mid-sentence. "If you want this evidence discussed and/or admitted, please call to the witness stand the crime scene tech people who processed that evidence."

"Yes, Your Honor," conceded Weaver. "No further questions."

"May I approach the witness, Your Honor?" Zack asked.

"You may."

Zack walked up to the witness box, faced the jury, and said, "You don't like the defendant much, do you, Chief?"

"He's a murderer."

"Objection, Your Honor. Defense moves to strike," replied Zack. "In fact, the defense moves for a mistrial because the answer is a legal conclusion and the jurors have been prejudiced because they heard that pronouncement from the Manistee Chief of Police." Zack was livid.

"The objection is sustained. The answer will be stricken from the record, and the jury will disregard," ruled the judge.

"And my motion, Your Honor?"

"Seriously, Mr. Blake?"

"Seriously, Your Honor."

"Ladies and gentlemen of the jury, does the Chief of Police's pre-determination of the defendant's guilt sway you in any way to the same conclusion? In other words, as I will *instruct* you formally, after the evidentiary portion of the trial, there *must* be evidence of guilt beyond a reasonable doubt. If the state has not met its burden, you *must* find the defendant not guilty. And this is true, regardless of Chief Alexander beliefs or testimony, understood?"

Every juror nodded in the affirmative.

"Your Honor—"

"Proceed, Mr. Blake."

"Yes, Your Honor." Zack relented, but he was still angry. He decided to take it out on Alexander. "Chief Alexander, isn't it true you were angry with the defendant for sneaking around behind your back? Yes or no only, please?"

"Yes."

"And yes or no, weren't you angry with the defendant because you felt he was a big-city snob cop who thought he could do the job better than you and your cops?"

"Yes."

"Objection, Your Honor," said Weaver.

"Grounds?"

"Big-city snob cop? Really? Your Honor, that's inflammatory."

"Overruled. The witness has answered, and I think the jury understands the issue."

Zack did not wait for Weaver to interrupt him again. "And yes or no, Chief Alexander, didn't you determine Jack Dylan's guilt the minute you found out who he was?"

Alexander hesitated and replied, "No, absolutely not."

"No? Please tell these nice ladies and gentlemen of the jury, how soon after Captain Dylan was brought to the station did you decide to charge him with murder in the first?"

"Maybe a couple of days later."

"And when did the crime scene evidence get analyzed, with results reported to your office?"

"I'd have to refer to my notes," replied Alexander. He paused, flipping pages, buying time. He knew where this was going.

"We'll wait," snarled Zack.

"Exactly three weeks later," Alexander muttered.

"Pardon me? I didn't hear you," Zack pounced. "Louder, please?"

"Three weeks later," Alexander huffed.

"And that evidence includes videos of an altercation between the defendant and the deceased shortly before the explosion, true or false?"

"True."

"The jury will see multiple videos of the altercation and the explosion, and they can decide for themselves. However, Chief Alexander, considering what an expert you are at policing and investigating, is it fair to say these videos do not confirm one way or the other who pulled the pin on the grenade and set off the blast?"

"The videos are not the only evidence . . ."

"Chief, a man's life is at stake. Do these videos, by themselves, definitively determine the defendant threw the grenade, yes or no?"

"Well, not exactly, but the other evidence—"

"Yes or no?" Zack demanded.

"By themselves, no."

"And isn't it true you determined that this decorated police officer was guilty and then made sure the evidence backed up your determination? Tell the damned truth, Chief Alexander!"

Jarrod Weaver leaped to his feet. "Objection, Your Honor. Badgering,"

"Withdrawn," Zack sneered, eyes on the jury. "No further questions at this time, Your Honor. Reserve the right to call this witness on direct or rebuttal."

"Noted," the judge chuckled. *This big-city boy is good. I'm going to enjoy this trial.*

# Chapter Thirty-Three

"Call your next witness, Mr. Weaver," ordered Judge Shipley.

"The State calls State Police Trooper Jordan Ring."

Trooper Ring rose. He was dressed in full uniform to properly impress the jury. He was sworn in and seated by the deputy.

"You may proceed, Mr. Weaver," said the judge.

"State your name for the record, please?"

"Jordan Ring."

"And what do you do, sir?"

"I'm a State Trooper."

"It's obvious, isn't it, ladies and gentlemen?" Zack said, interrupting Weaver. The courtroom erupted in laughter, and the judge pounded his gavel for quiet.

"Your Honor?" Weaver was not happy.

"Mr. Blake, address your comments and objections to the court, not the jury. And please observe proper etiquette and decorum in my courtroom," Judge Shipley admonished.

"Sorry, Your Honor," replied Zack, winking at some smiling jurors.

"Continue, Mr. Weaver. Mr. Blake will behave himself," said the judge, glaring at Zachary Blake.

"What is your current assignment with the State Police?"

"I am a crime scene investigator and technician."

"What does that mean?"

"We respond to crime scenes when asked to. We begin an investigation, take photographs, gather evidence, videotape, process fingerprints and DNA, and the like. We are first responders after the crime scene is secured."

"How long have you been doing this, Trooper Ring?"

"Eight years."

"Were you involved in the Breitner murder investigation?"

"Objection, Your Honor," cried Zack, rising to his feet.

The judge was not pleased. "What is it this time, Mr. Blake?"

"There has been no evidence Mr. Breitner was murdered, Your Honor. The defense contends his death was a suicide."

The judge smiled to himself. *He has a point.* "The objection is sustained. Rephrase your question, Mr. Weaver."

"Were you involved in the Breitner *death* investigation, trooper?" Weaver asked, frustrated anger rising in his tone.

"Objection, Your Honor," said Zack, forcefully, rising as he spoke.

"What is it this time, Mr. Blake? Judge Shipley asked, impatiently.

"There has been no evidence of a death, Your Honor," Zack replied.

Shipley paused, rethinking previous testimony. *Again, the man has a valid point.*

"The objection is sustained. Find a different question based on the evidence produced thus far, Mr. Weaver."

"Your Honor..." Weaver protested.

"Move along, Mr. Weaver. The judge waved his hand at Weaver gesturing him to move on.

"Were you involved in the investigation of the explosion on Barton Breitner's boat? Weaver asked in frustration.

"Yes, I was."

"How was it you got involved in this investigation?"

"We were called in by Special Agent Clare Gibson of the FBI and Chief Christopher Alexander of the Manistee Police." *A compromise choice* thought Zack.

"Where was this crime scene located?"

"On the dock directly in front of Shirley's Bar & Grill."

"Over on Bay Shore Drive?"

"Yes."

"May we please have Exhibit One?" The court officer walked to the middle of the courtroom and turned on an overhead projector. A photograph of the crime scene appeared on a screen set up at the front of the courtroom.

"Trooper Ring, what are we looking at here?"

"That is one of the pictures I took of the crime scene upon my arrival."

"And is it an accurate depiction of the scene you described earlier?"

"It is."

"Move to admit Exhibit One, Your Honor."

"No objection," said Zack, half rising from his seat.

"The exhibit is admitted," ordered the judge.

"When you arrived at the scene, Trooper, was there anything specific you were looking for?"

"Yes. The lead investigators asked me specifically to evaluate whether or not a crime was committed and whether there was evidence of murder."

"And did you investigate those things?"

"We did."

"Who's 'we?'"

"My team and I."

"How many people?"

"Five people including me."

"Were the other four supervised by you?"

"Yes."

"And what, if anything, did you find?"

"We found a demolished boat. In the water, we located floating body parts, boat debris, grenade fragments, and blood. We also processed some wood pieces on which fingerprints were discovered. On the dock, we found more body fragments, blood and boat debris."

"Did you process the blood and body fragments for a DNA match?"

"We did."

"To whom did the blood and body fragments belong?"

"The deceased, Barton Breitner."

"And the fingerprints?"

"The deceased, the defendant, and many others we could not identify."

"And what did you conclude from your review of the evidence?"

"That someone, probably Mr. Dylan, exploded the boat." Zack decided to let this bit of speculation go for the time being.

"What led you to that conclusion?"

"The debris and body parts we discovered led us to the conclusion someone died. The DNA match determined the dead person was Mr. Breitner. Interviews with various witnesses who were at or near the crime scene immediately before the explosion assisted us in concluding Jack Dylan exploded the boat."

"And what were the sum and substance of those interviews?"

"The decedent and the defendant had a violent argument immediately preceding the explosion. One of the witnesses stated the defendant had a particularly keen interest in meeting the decedent."

"Objection, Your Honor. All of this is hearsay," Zack argued.

"Your Honor, this is background. All of these witnesses will be called to testify. We are not using their statements to prove the truth of them, only to explain to the jury why the trooper came to the conclusion that he did."

"Objection is overruled. Please continue," ruled the judge.

This was probably the correct ruling, and Zack decided to let it go. He would call or cross-examine every one of these witnesses, including Alan Berger.

"To sum up, Trooper Ring, boat and bomb parts, blood and body parts belonging to the deceased, and fingerprint evidence belonging to the defendant, were all discovered at the scene. On top of that, you had witnesses who stated the defendant was arguing with the deceased moments before the explosion, is that correct?"

"Objection, Your Honor. This is also leading."

"Withdrawn," said Weaver.

Weaver handheld the witness through rather graphic testimony. After identifying various exhibits and photographs, Ring painted a gruesome picture of a deliberate murder committed by Captain Jack Dylan. The judge admitted a sizable number of exhibits into evidence. They were passed around the jury box, and the jurors viewed them in horror. The most gruesome were several photographs of small body parts, probably pieces of a hand, floating in the water. Zachary Blake did not object to any of the exhibits or testimony. He appeared bored throughout the trooper's testimony. When Weaver asked his last question and admitted the last of several crime scene exhibits, he passed the witness. Judge Shipley invited Zachary to cross-examine Trooper Jordan Ring.

"Trooper Ring, did you go to the crime scene with a preconceived notion Jack Dylan murdered Barton Breitner?"

"I don't know what you mean. I go to every crime scene with an open mind."

"Chief Alexander was one of the people who asked you to investigate what he called a murder, did he not?"

"He did."

"So, you had a preconceived notion there was a murder, right?"

"I guess so."

"Did you consider anything else?"

"I don't understand. Like what?"

"Like an accident or a suicide, for instance?"

"No, I guess I didn't."

"You indicated you found the defendant's and the deceased's fingerprints at the scene, correct?"

"Correct."

"And you said you found others?"

"Yes."

"Whose?"

"Unidentified."

"How many different prints?"

"Several."

"More than three?"
"Yes."
"More than five?"
"Yes."
"More than ten?"
"Yes."
"Did you consider any of those people to be possible suspects?"
"No one else argued with the deceased."
"Did you consider the deceased a suspect?"
"That's ridiculous."
"Oh? Why?"
"You can't murder yourself."
"Isn't that what suicide is?"
"I suppose,"
"You are aware suicide is a crime, are you not?"
"I am."
"Trooper Ring, I am going to ask you a question that calls for a 'yes or no' response, and I only want you to answer yes or no. Do you understand?"
"Yes, no problem."
"Does your evaluation of the physical evidence at the scene rule out the possibility the decedent committed suicide by setting off the bomb himself?"
Ring paused, thinking, trying to evaluate the evidence in his head. "No, I guess it does not rule out that possibility."
"Did the witnesses state they saw the defendant jump into the water at the time of the explosion?"
"Yes, a couple of them did."
"And you interpreted their statements as evidence Captain Dylan set off a bomb and jumped in the water to avoid the effects of the explosion, correct?"
"Correct."
"Again, sir, same rules, yes or no only. Could Jack Dylan's dive into the water be explained by the deceased holding a grenade,

deciding to commit suicide, pulling the pin, and Dylan realizing he was going to die or be seriously injured if he didn't jump into the water?"

Ring paused, giving the theory serious consideration. "Yes, I suppose it could," he finally responded.

"And other than this 'argument' the deceased and the defendant supposedly engaged in, not a single shred of evidence you collected is more suggestive of murder than it is of suicide, correct?"

"Other than the argument? No."

"Thank you, Trooper Ring. I have nothing further."

"Trooper Ring, you may step down, sir. Mr. Weaver? Next witness, please?" Judge Shipley demanded.

"The State calls Terrance Phillips, Your Honor."

Terrance Phillips rose, walked to the witness box, and was sworn in as a witness for the State. He was qualified, with no objection from Zachary Blake, as a bomb tech expert.

"On the night of Mr. Breitner's untimely death, Mr. Phillips, you were called to the crime scene, true?"

"True."

"Who called you?"

"State Trooper Jordan Ring."

"What were your instructions?"

"I was instructed to go to the dock over by Shirley's."

"Did Trooper Ring tell you why he needed you to come?"

"He said there was an explosion and he wanted me to collect and subsequently examine bomb fragments."

"Where did you travel from and how long did it take you to get to the crime scene?"

"Objection, Your Honor."

"On what grounds, Mr. Blake?"

"I object to the continued use of the words 'crime scene' to describe the dock where Mr. Breitner met his untimely demise. The defense contends no crime was committed unless your honor wishes to instruct the jury that suicide is a crime." Zack continued to hammer the notion into the jurors' heads that there was no murder, but the suicide of an evil, dangerous man who, when cornered by Captain Jack Dylan, decided to take his own life rather than spend what was left of it in prison.

"Your objection is sustained, Mr. Blake. Please refrain from using the words 'crime' and/or 'crime scene,' Mr. Weaver. These terms call for a legal conclusion the evidence has not established."

Zack almost laughed out loud at Judge Shipley's ruling on his objection. The jury just heard the *trial judge* say there was insufficient evidence offered, thus far, to establish a *crime*, let alone a *murder*. Weaver was seething.

"Yes, Your Honor," replied Weaver with disdain. "Mr. Phillips, where were you at the time of the call, and how long did it take you to arrive at the scene of the explosion?"

"I live in Cadillac. It takes maybe an hour or so to get to Manistee."

"What did you do when you got to the scene?"

"My techs and I put on diving gear, went into the water, and commenced with the deliberate process of collecting all of the grenade fragments we could find."

"Where were these fragments located?"

"In the water, near the dock, directly in front of Shirley's Bar & Grill."

"How deep was the water?"

"Seven to eight feet."

"Was the residue floating, or did you have to search under the water?"

"May I refer to my notes?"

"By all means."

Phillips opened a file and began to flip through pages, reading as he went along.

"Here it is," he said, finding the entry in his notes. "All of the bomb fragments we collected were found floating in the water. There was no underwater search."

"Did you test the material?"

"Yes, we bagged it, tagged it, followed strict COC procedures, and brought it back to our Cadillac lab for testing."

"What is COC?"

"Sorry. It means chain of custody. We keep track of where evidence is and who is handling it at each and every step in the process."

"What did your tests reveal?"

"We determined the explosive involved was an M67 fragmentation grenade."

"And did you find any residue on any of the pieces?"

"Yes, we found bits of blood and tissue on the grenade fragments."

"And were these samples tested for a DNA match to anyone involved in this case?"

"Yes, they matched the deceased, Barton Breitner."

"What did this tell you?"

"That Mr. Breitner was killed in the explosion."

"How many explosion cases have you investigated, Mr. Phillips?"

"I'm not sure, certainly in the hundreds."

"And how many of those involved a deliberate act by the person with the explosive?"

"Most of them. There were a couple of accidents."

"If two people were present when a grenade exploded and one of those people lost his life, which of the two would be more likely to have exploded the grenade, the one who lived or the one who died?"

"The one who lived, of course."

"And why do you say, 'of course?'"

"To put this into lay terminology, the one who pulls the pin and throws the grenade has the element of surprise, knows which way he's going to throw the grenade and approximately how long he has to get the hell out of there."

The jurors, the gallery, and even Zachary and the judge laughed at that one.

"Did you come to any conclusions from your analysis of the fragments?"

"Yes, we concluded a grenade explosion killed Mr. Breitner."

"No further questions. Pass the witness."

"Mr. Blake?" Judge Shipley asked with somewhat palpable anticipation. "Your witness."

"Thank you, Your Honor. May I approach the witness?" Zach liked to get up close and personal with a hostile witness.

"Within reason, Mr. Blake."

"Mr. Phillips," Zachary began. "It's true, is it not, you did not find the defendant's fingerprints or DNA on any piece of bomb fragment found?"

"No, we didn't, but…"

"Yes or no, Mr. Phillips?"

"No."

"In fact, other than the witness statements, you couldn't find any forensic evidence the defendant was even present at the scene on the night of the explosion, could you?"

"That's not true. We found his fingerprints on various boat fragments."

"But that only proves he was once on the boat. He admits to going fishing on Mr. Breitner's boat. Wouldn't that fact account for the presence of his fingerprints?"

"Yes, it certainly would. However, in addition to that, Chief Alexander and others found Captain Dylan treading water at the scene, immediately following the explosion. That is quite powerful evidence he was there at the time, sir."

"Point taken," Zack confessed.

"Now, about the cause of death. Isn't a scenario that Mr. Breitner meant to commit suicide by a grenade as plausible as the prosecution's murder theory?"

"Statistics say no, Mr. Blake."

"Forget statistics. I am asking you about tests and physical evidence."

"Yes, the tests and the physical evidence would support that theory, although it is unlikely."

"Move to strike the last part of the witness's answer as non-responsive, Your Honor."

"Sustained. The jury will disregard."

"In fact, Mr. Phillips, the evidence supports another explanation, too, does it not?"

"I'm not sure what you're getting at, Mr. Blake."

"It could have been an accident, no? He might have pulled the pin and held on to the grenade for too long, or he might have tripped and fallen with it in his hand. Possible?"

"There are all sorts of possible occurrences, Mr. Blake, but only one logical one: Mr. Breitner was murdered."

"Objection. Move to strike, Your Honor," said Zack smugly.

"Overruled."

"What?" Zack was incredulous at the ruling.

"Careful, Mr. Blake. You are close to contempt of court."

"It was a 'yes or no' question, Your Honor."

"No, it wasn't, Mr. Blake. It was a 'what's possible under all possibilities' question, and he answered the question posed to him. Move on."

"Just so we're clear, Mr. Phillips, the other scenarios are possible, too, yes or no?"

"That, Mr. Phillips, is the 'yes or no' version of the last question. Please answer yes or no," ordered the judge.

"Yes, those other scenarios are possible."

"Did you conduct a color test on the residue, Mr. Phillips?"

"No, we didn't."

"Did you perform a Super-Glue fuming test?"

"No."

"The kill radius of an M67 fragmentation grenade is about five meters, is it not?"

"Yes."

"If the person is holding the grenade at the time it explodes, that same person is well within the kill radius, is he not?"

"Objection, Your Honor. Calls for speculation." Weaver, again, fell into Zack's trap.

"Exactly, ladies and gentlemen, the whole case rests on speculation. No further questions, Your Honor."

Weaver, dumbfounded, glared at Zack. *Stupid, stupid, stupid,* he chastised himself. He opened his mouth to speak but then wisely said nothing.

"Redirect, Mr. Weaver?" Judge Shipley asked.

Weaver gathered himself. "One question, Your Honor."

"Proceed."

"Based upon the witness statements you reviewed, and the testimony expected from those witnesses, the defendant and the deceased were both within the 'kill radius' of each other when they were arguing, correct?"

"Correct."

"Nothing further, Your Honor."

"Let's call it a day," said the judge. He pounded the gavel. "Court is in recess."

## Chapter Thirty-Four

"The point is, Your Honor, the evidence techs failed to administer many of the most important evidentiary tests on the samples."

Weaver and Zack were back in front of Judge Paul Shipley the following morning. The two men were arguing an emergency motion outside the presence of the jury. Following yesterday's cross-examination of Jordan Ring and the other crime scene witnesses, it was apparent to Zack the prosecution's crime scene experts found numerous fingerprints at the scene, but none of them performed sufficient fingerprint analysis on the *bomb fragment samples*. Charles Snyder, Werner Spellman, and their teams tested the limited quantity of samples they received, and all tests were negative for fingerprints. Zack wanted the rest of the samples released to Snyder and Spellman so they could "clean up the sloppy mess of an investigation that was conducted by careless police department personnel, who have already made up their minds about how the death occurred and who was responsible for it."

"Your Honor, we object. If untested samples are to be tested, they should be tested by techs representing the interests of the state, not the interests of the defendant," argued Weaver.

"I disagree, Mr. Weaver. Don't get me wrong. I'm not deciding yet who should do the testing, but I don't believe it is a question of which litigant's interests the test should serve. I believe the test should be conducted in the interest of justice, don't you? I believe the test should be a search for the truth, right?" With over twenty years on the circuit court bench and a neutral position with no skin in the game, Judge Paul Shipley was the wisest man in the room.

"I agree with you one hundred percent, Your Honor. The State's had the samples for weeks and failed to test them for the simplest evidence of all-fingerprints. Mr. Weaver and his team had their chances with the samples. I'm sticking my neck out and saying I believe so strongly in my client's innocence I am willing to have Mr. Snyder and Dr. Spellman test the samples and report their findings to you rather than to my team and me. Snyder is a world-renowned expert in fingerprint lifting and analysis. You cannot find anyone more qualified," Zack argued.

"Mr. Weaver? What do you say to that?"

"One moment, Your Honor." He turned to Chief Alexander and Clare Gibson, seated behind him. He motioned them over. Whispering, the three engaged in vigorous debate causing the entire courtroom to endure a delay. The least-patient man in any courtroom is always the judge. Judge Paul Shipley gave them ample time to chat before interrupting the confab.

"Mr. Weaver?"

"Yes, Your Honor. After speaking with Chief Alexander and Agent Gibson, on the premise the testing will be done independently by Mr. Snyder and released directly to Your Honor, the state is willing to stipulate to the additional testing in the interest of justice and a search for the truth," Weaver consented.

"Your Honor, those were my terms in the first instance," Zack grumbled. *Brown-nosing kiss ass! I don't give a shit. I'm about to get exactly what I want.*

"Perfect," Judge Shipley chirped, satisfied. "Let's continue with scheduled testimony today and allow the testing to be done. Is Mr. Snyder present in the courtroom?"

A tall, rugged, middle-aged, bearded man rose. "I am, Your Honor."

"Mr. Snyder, your reputation precedes you. Thank you for being here. It is my understanding you are willing to test the samples counsel here is referring to. Is that correct?"

"That is correct, Your Honor," Snyder replied.

"Perfect. How long will the testing take, Mr. Snyder?"

"No more than a day if I can get started this morning. I will need to confer with Dr. Spellman and make sure we secure samples appropriate for our testing."

"Gentlemen, may we excuse Mr. Snyder? I'd like to have a court officer escort him over to the lab, make sure he gets all of the testing materials he needs, and have him back here as soon as possible to report his findings."

"Yes, Your Honor," replied Zack, deliberately chiming in before Weaver.

"We have no objection," replied Weaver with a sideways glance at Zack.

"I'm sure you've been kicked out of better places than this one, Mr. Snyder. Please go do what you do," said the judge, smiling at his own joke. The gallery was less enthusiastic about his attempt at levity, but the judge didn't seem to notice or care.

"Thank you, Your Honor."

"Bailiff, would you please summon another court officer to escort Mr. Snyder to the lab? This officer is to stand guard until he or she completes his or her shift and another officer relieves. I want a guard posted at the lab with the samples until the completion of the testing. Is that clear?"

"Crystal," said the officer. He pointed to the exit and escorted Charles Snyder out of the courtroom.

"Let's take a ten-minute break. I'll see counsel in chambers," said the judge. With the court officer out in the hall, there was no one to announce the judge's departure, so he slammed the gavel, said, 'We're adjourned,' and exited the courtroom without the usual pomp and circumstance. The two attorneys followed him out the private door and into his chambers.

"Have a seat, gentlemen." The judge motioned for them to sit in comfortable side chairs that flanked a rather plain-looking hardwood desk. The office was huge, and the men found themselves completely encased in wood shelves lined with hundreds of law books. These were primarily for show. Research, these days, was done by others and by computer. But the look was impressive, as was the view overlooking Lake Michigan.

"So? What do you think?"

"About what, Your Honor?" Weaver asked politely.

"How do you think the trial's going so far?"

"As well as can be expected," Weaver responded.

"I agree with that assessment," offered Zack, wondering where this was going.

"I have to say, Jarrod, they didn't hand you the most solid case in history. Even if this cop is guilty, our big-city visitor is poking huge holes in your case. You will have to plug them if you hope for a conviction," said the judge sincerely.

"Are you prejudging this case, Your Honor?" Weaver asked, getting fidgety and annoyed.

"Not at all," replied the judge. "I'm evaluating the evidence I have heard up to this moment. What do you think, Mr. Blake? Are you happy with the way things are going?"

"I'm rather pleased so far, Your Honor, but we have a long way to go. Jarrod is a fine lawyer and a worthy adversary."

"That he is, but he is not a miracle worker. Of course, the jury might be seeing things completely differently. An outsider defendant with his outsider hot-shot lawyer, who knows?"

"Judge, if I may ask, not to be disrespectful of course, but what is the purpose of this meeting?" Weaver was very uncomfortable.

"I wanted to shoot the breeze and get to know you gentlemen better. Also, I wanted to ask: what is the prosecution going to do if Spellman's fingerprint analysis is positive and the deceased's fingerprints are found on the bomb fragments?"

"That's not a fair question, Your Honor," replied Weaver sharply. "In your so-called search for the truth, are you considering what the defense will do if fingerprints are identified and belong to the defendant?"

"Sorry, Jarrod, you are quite correct. I meant it only in terms of the length of the trial. Do you intend to dismiss the charges if the deceased's fingerprints are found on the fragments? I suppose I could ask Zack if his client will cop a plea if we find the defendant's prints instead, but I think we both know the answer to that one."

"We'll have to cross that bridge when or if we come to it, Your Honor. Anything else? I have a case to try," Weaver said, rising, dismissing the judge.

Judge Shipley smiled. He admired Weaver's advocacy. "That's it, boys. Let's take twenty. I'll see you out there in a bit."

The attorneys re-entered the courtroom through the judge's private doors. It was empty except for the attorneys and cops on both sides of the case.

"What was that all about?" Jarrod Weaver glared at Zack Blake.

"Apparently, Judge Shipley believes the city and the Feds could have brought you a better case. I would have to agree with him."

"That has never happened to me before. Do you think I should report this?"

"To whom?"

"The Judicial Tenure Commission." The commission reviewed complaints against judges when citizens or lawyers accused them of improper conduct.

"Whoa, Jarrod. His comments fall way short of that. Why don't you take them as constructive criticism? Why not take some time to determine whether it is wise to pursue a case against a cop with no prior record of wrongdoing simply on *this* evidence?"

"You're right, Blake. I should drop the case because Dylan's *unbiased* defense attorney thinks it's the right thing to do," Weaver snarled.

"No, I'm not suggesting that at all. I *am* suggesting as an officer of the court, you should always be certain all your ducks are in a row before trying a case against a decorated cop or accusing a judge of misconduct over an off the cuff comment. If either guy were actually guilty of something, we'd be having a different conversation. I'm a realist."

"I'll take your suggestion under advisement. Please excuse me. I have to talk to some people." Weaver turned and walked out of the courtroom, followed by the Manistee contingent of cops.

"What's his problem, Zack?" Micah asked as he, Jack, and the others approached.

"Oh, he's just pissed the judge told him that he is losing so far."

"The judge actually *said* he's losing?" Jack beamed.

"In so many words," Zack reported. "It's a good sign that a judge with Shipley's experience sees things our way, but it doesn't matter much."

"Why not?" Andy queried.

"Because a determination of guilty or not guilty in this case belongs to the jury, not to the judge."

# Chapter Thirty-Five

The trial continued, with Weaver parading in a series of eyewitness bar/restaurant and ice cream parlor patrons. Most of the witnesses heard some sort of commotion, described a heated argument, and/or saw Jack jump out of the boat. They'd been unable to see the man Jack was arguing with. He was blocked from view. Some opined Jack knew the bomb was about to explode, which explained why he jumped. Zack cross-examined each witness, poking holes, coaxing alternate theories. Nevertheless, the sum and substance of the eyewitness testimony described a violent argument, which was quite damaging to the defense.

Zack attempted to personalize the events for the witnesses. An attorney cannot ask members of a *jury* to place themselves in the shoes of the defendant, but when he cross-examines a *witness*, he is permitted to do so. Zack asked several witnesses to assume they were Jack, standing on the deck, and to further imagine they were arguing with another person.

"If that person suddenly pulled out a grenade and pulled the pin, what would you do?" Zack asked.

Every witness admitted, one way or the other, some in colorful language, he or she would "jump into the water." However, it was clear that each witness believed Jack caused or contributed to the death of the person he was arguing with. If these witnesses could believe this scenario, the jury could too. Zack's job, over the balance of the trial, would be to impugn Bart's character further and make it virtually impossible for the jury to believe Jack exploded a grenade rather than Bart. Still, eyewitness testimony was causing both Jack and Zack many sleepless nights.

\*\*\*

A few miles away, in the basement lab of a government building, Charles Snyder and Werner Spellman unsealed an evidence bag that contained the bomb fragment samples. They were somewhat anxious, as both met and liked Jack Dylan. They were hopeful that they could find something that would exonerate him. At the end of the day, however, these men were scientists. People lie, cheat, steal, even commit murder. Science, contrarily, always tells the truth.

The previous tests of various pieces of evidence confirmed that the device was a grenade and that both Breitner and Dylan left fingerprints at the scene. Dr. Spellman identified qualifying samples of the new grenade fragments. Snyder repeated the tests and came to the same conclusion. Their primary goal, however, was to locate a sample with an identifiable fingerprint, even a partial print, which they privately hoped would tend to prove Breitner, not Jack, ignited the explosion. They would follow the evidence, and Snyder would report their findings as to the trained scientists they were. But they discussed the case and the victim and did not like men like Bart Breitner.

Snyder didn't need to perform the color tests he performed on the previous samples. Those tests confirmed what type of material he was dealing with. In the case of these samples, he knew he was dealing with an M67 grenade. Thus, chromatography and mass spectrometry confirmations were not necessary.

The vital test with these samples would be the Super-Glue fuming test. Snyder heated Super-Glue in multiple closed containers. Each container housed a piece of shrapnel, bomb fragment, or bomb residue. He began pacing back and forth, from one sample to the next. If there was a fingerprint, the Super-Glue would gather around it, highlight it and preserve it. Snyder was also looking for touch DNA or dead skin cells of anyone who'd come into contact with the bomb. The blast did not injure Jack, so touch DNA, if any was identified, belonged to someone else. That "someone else" could only be Breitner.

Dr. Spellman made a rather surprising discovery in sorting through and identifying samples for Snyder's testing. As he was lining up the fragments for Snyder, he noticed one of the new fragments was a partner to the piece of grenade pin Snyder tested previously. The two fit together like a partial puzzle piece. The previous piece contained no fingerprint or DNA residue. What, if anything, would Snyder find on the second piece? He glanced at his watch, growing impatient. The clock was ticking. Soon the two men would be the first to know whether some form of identification was present on any of these samples.

***

The trial continued the following day, and as Zack expected, another endless parade of witnesses entered the courtroom and testified they sat in front of this bar or that coffee shop and saw the whole thing. Some embellished the events, enjoying their fifteen minutes of fame. One witness even suggested she "might have seen" multiple bodies or body parts fly overboard on the opposite side of the boat. She recanted on cross-examination when presented with diagrams that demonstrated that her vantage point made it virtually impossible to see the opposite side of the boat. She was confident Jack Dylan jumped off into the water on her side of the boat and equally confident she saw something else, perhaps debris, fly off the other side.

Before the lunch recess, Judge Shipley dismissed the jury and called the lab to check on Snyder's progress. The scientist was hard at work seeking to extract what he thought could be touch DNA on the second piece of pin. The judge asked for his timetable, and Snyder advised he 'should' have something by the end of the day.

Weaver was hoping Snyder was having difficulties with the new samples. He was still angry about the judge's comments in chambers, especially that Shipley made them in front of Blake, the arrogant outsider. He liked Zack. He now understood why the big city lawyer was so successful. He was doing a terrific job for his client. But Weaver resented Zack's arrogance, his expensive suit, and private jet lifestyle, as well as his arsenal of retained investigators. Blake had substantial money to spend on this case and the power that goes with fame and fortune.

By contrast, Jarrod Weaver was a career prosecutor, destined to spend the balance of his career in Manistee. When this trial was over, Zachary Blake and entourage would hop into their fancy jet and fly back to posh Bloomfield Hills with another large payday. Win or lose, Zachary Blake lived in luxury and basked in fame. If Zack lost *State v Dylan,* he would suffer no serious consequences.

Weaver smiled as he remembered, word-for-word, his criminal procedure professor's 'three rules' lecture for criminal defense lawyers: 'One, get the money up front. Two, the client does time, not you. And three, get the money up front.' Zachary Blake was a guy who *always* got paid, one way or another.

Weaver didn't really care whether Jack Dylan was guilty or not. He wanted to beat Zachary Blake. Only Weaver would face the consequences if he failed to win. Losing was out of the question.

Weaver was very pleased with the eyewitness testimony. Although it was somewhat monotonous for the jury to hear witness after witness testify to the same basic scenario, their testimonial consistency was remarkable. Two men were talking, alone on a snazzy boat. Their conversation became heated and morphed into a violent bomb explosion, leaving one combatant alive and unhurt, and the other, literally, blown to bits.

Zack, despite remarkable cross-examination skills, could do nothing to dissuade these witnesses from concluding that a conversation became an argument and the argument resulted in an explosion. No eyewitness testified he or she saw Jack pull the pin or throw the grenade, but each was convinced he did.

The veteran prosecutor also knew this testimony was worthless if Charles Snyder found Breitner's fingerprints on a vital grenade fragment. It was the *fingerprints or DNA* that would acquit or convict

Jack Dylan. For Jarrod, a dismissal based on either of those was far better than a jury's not-guilty verdict. Fault for a fingerprint or DNA dismissal would rest squarely with Alexander, the FBI and Alexander's rush to judgment.

If the jury acquitted Jack, their verdict would brand Weaver as the loser of the most prominent case in Manistee history. The community would remember. Local judges, defense lawyers, and fellow prosecutors would remember. Weaver would be that prosecutor who couldn't convict the bombing guy.

Weaver wished these career-defining efforts weren't wasted on someone unworthy of his efforts. Breitner was a criminal and a *terrorist*. Weaver knew the criminal element quite well. He'd sent several people to prison and despised hatred and bigotry. His parents raised him to be colorblind in a country that couldn't seem to get over its differences. His dad despised what he used to call 'hate for the sake of hate.' However, Manistee was not this way. His parents chose to live in Manistee because its people seemed to share their views. Guys like Bart Breitner deserved their fates, and if Dylan killed Bart, then, good for Dylan. Jack's mistake, if he was guilty, was doing the deed in Jarrod Weaver's district. *Nobody* got away with murder in Jarrod Weaver's district.

***

Late that afternoon, after another slew of eyewitnesses testified to the same set of circumstances, Judge Shipley was about to recess for the evening. Charles Snyder entered the courtroom, accompanied by a court officer.

Judge Shipley addressed the jury: "Ladies and gentlemen, that's it for the day. You are excused until tomorrow morning. The court has some housekeeping issues to deal with this evening, so you folks have a nice evening. Please remember not to associate with any of the parties, witnesses, or any of the attorneys or their employees. And please do not discuss the case with anyone, including your fellow jurors. If anyone approaches you or tries to influence you in any way, please report that incident to me personally. Do not make up your mind about the case until you have heard all the evidence and have received my instructions at the end. Do not contact anyone or read anything to gain a greater understanding of the case, and please, do not visit the scene where the alleged events occurred. Does everyone understand?"

The jurors all nodded affirmatively. They were tired of hearing the same speech at the end of each night. They could recite most of it by heart. The judge dismissed the jurors, and the court officer led them out of the courtroom.

After the jury was gone, Shipley addressed Snyder and asked him and the attorneys to approach.

"Mr. Snyder, do you have any news for us?"

"I do Your Honor."

"Your Honor?" Zack asked.

"Yes, Mr. Blake?"

"I suggest we swear Mr. Snyder in as a witness outside the presence of the jury for the purpose of creating a record. We can re-swear him for the jury if his testimony is necessary.

"I like it," replied the judge. "Mr. Weaver?"

"No objection, Your Honor. Before Mr. Snyder presents, however, I'd like Chief Alexander and Agent Gibson present in the courtroom to hear his testimony," replied Weaver.

"Make your phone call, Mr. Weaver. We'll take a ten-minute recess."

Judge Shipley pounded his gavel and left the courtroom. Snyder approached Zack to give him the news, but Zack waved him away. Zack wanted no conversation with or presentation by Snyder unless the judge and the entire prosecution team were present.

Fifteen minutes later, the judge returned to the courtroom with little fanfare and resumed his seat on the bench without the usual pomp and circumstance. Chief Alexander, Sheila Prince, Clare

Gibson, and Pete Westmore were present, as was Zack's entire investigative team.

"We are back on the record, and the court recalls the case of *State v. Dylan*. I understand, by stipulation of the attorneys, we are going to take some testimony from Mr. Charles Snyder outside the presence of the jury. If this evidence is not dispositive of the case, but either side wishes to present it to the jury, we will reconvene tomorrow to present the testimony, either live or by video. Have I presented the situation to everyone's satisfaction?" Judge Shipley orated.

"Yes, Your Honor," Weaver concurred, finally beating Zack to the punch.

"Yes, Your Honor," Zack repeated.

"Bailiff, swear the witness." Snyder stepped forward, was sworn in, and assumed the witness chair. "Who's going to take this witness's testimony?"

Both attorneys stood simultaneously and said, "I will, Your Honor."

"It is part of my case in chief, Your Honor," argued Weaver.

"How about this? Shipley interjected. "I'll question the witness. You guys will fill in any blanks, okay? If additional testimony is necessary, Mr. Weaver will go first." The attorneys assented although Weaver thought it was a distinction without a difference. This was still *his* case.

"Mr. Snyder, you have been sworn in, and you are under oath, understood?" Shipley stated.

"Yes, sir."

"Do you gentlemen want the witness qualified or shall we stipulate to his qualifications as an expert witness in the field of fingerprint recovery and analysis?"

Weaver and Zack looked at each other then back to the judge. They nodded for the judge to proceed.

"Let the record reflect that prosecution and defense counsel have silently nodded assent," said Shipley.

"Sorry, Your Honor, I assent," said Weaver, standing.

"As do I, Your Honor," added Zack.

"Very well. Mr. Snyder, as an expert in fingerprint recovery and analysis, did you have occasion to examine certain samples of bomb debris and fragments from the boat and incident that is the genesis of this trial?" Judge Shipley asked.

"Yes, Your Honor. Two different sets were prepared for me by the renowned bomb residue expert Dr. Werner Spellman."

"The first set, examined as part of your retention by the defense, was done a few weeks ago, correct?"

"Correct, Your Honor."

"You have not yet presented on that evidence, but I am led to believe those tests were negative. Is that true?"

"Yes, it is."

"In other words, no DNA or fingerprints were identified in that initial review?"

"This is correct."

"Let's talk about this second batch of fragments. Did you conduct the same tests as those performed with the first?"

"I did, Your Honor. Although I did not perform rigorous color testing because we knew we were dealing with an M67 grenade. Thus, the same level of testing was not necessary."

"Can you briefly, for the record, tell the court what tests you performed the second time around?"

"Yes, Your Honor. With confirmation from Dr. Spellman, the explosive was an M67. We performed comparative analysis testing to determine whether these new samples were consistent with previous samples. Afterward, we tested to determine whether they came from the *same* M67."

"The result?"

"Same M67, Your Honor."

"How did you do that, sir?"

"While it is normally difficult, it was not in this case for two reasons. First, crime scene investigators collected all the evidence available. Following chain-of-custody protocols, as I know they did, it is easy to conclude the evidence came from the same bomb."

"Agreed, Mr. Snyder. That's one reason. You said there were two. What was the other?"

"A pin fragment from the second batch was a match with a fragment from the first batch. In layman's terms, we matched one puzzle piece to another. The two pieces comprised most of the M67's pin. This confirms both pieces came from the same grenade."

"Does that matter?"

"By itself, no. But together with the other tests, it does assure us the samples came from the same bomb."

"We already knew that, though. Why does that matter?"

"Because I was able to extract touch DNA sample from the second piece."

There was a collective gasp from the professionals in the courtroom.

"Quiet, please," ordered the judge. When it became quiet, he continued. "For the record, Mr. Snyder, please tell us what touch DNA is."

"Touch DNA is essentially the dead skin cells of anyone who came into contact with the bomb. In this case, a fingerprint, with dead skin cells and all, was literally burned into the pin fragment because of the intense heat of the bomb."

"And were you able to identify whose fingerprint and touch DNA was found on the pin?"

"I was, Your Honor."

"How were you able to do that?"

"The Super-Glue fuming test is the definitive, scientifically reliable test for DNA and fingerprints."

"For the record, sir, will you please tell the court how this test is conducted?"

"Sure. This test is performed with the glue product all of us use around our houses, which causes our fingers to stick together. In the case of fingerprints or touch DNA, we scientists have found if you heat Super-Glue in a closed container with the object you are seeking fingerprints or DNA from, the glue will gather and bond with human residue. In this case, I performed this test with each sample. While all the others were negative, one sample, the one extracted from the second piece of the grenade pin, was positive."

"So the record is complete, you also tested to see whose fingerprints or touch DNA was a match for the test sample, right?"

"Yes, I did."

"How did you do that?"

"By comparing them to samples of fingerprints and DNA already on file from the deceased and the defendant."

"Please tell the court who they belonged to."

Charles Snyder took a long breath in and looked directly at Jack Dylan, the only other person in the room who knew, without question, what his answer would be. The two men enjoyed a moment of mutual recognition.

"The prints and the DNA belonged to the deceased, Barton Breitner."

The defense team and the Dearborn police officers pumped their fists and shouted for joy. Pandemonium erupted. Weaver, Westmore, Alexander, and Gibson huddled together to discuss the serious ramifications of this finding.

"Order in the court. Quiet, please," ordered Judge Shipley. "Mr. Snyder, do you have an expert opinion as to how the prints and DNA got on that part of the pin?"

"I do, Your Honor."

"Please publish your opinion for the record."

"It is my expert opinion Mr. Breitner was the person who pulled the pin from the grenade. Based on the evidence, it is my further opinion his finger was in contact with the pin when the grenade exploded."

"Let me get this straight, Mr. Snyder. He probably threw the grenade, and was holding the pin at the time of the explosion?"

"Correct."

"Now, I've heard of something called 'blast radius.' Can you tell us what that is?"

"Yes, Your Honor. Blast radius measures the approximate distance in which a bomb blast is most deadly or effective."

"In the case of an M67, what is that radius?"

"About five meters or fifteen feet."

"For this pin to look like it does and for it to have the deceased's touch DNA and fingerprint burned into it as it does, what does that tell you about the blast radius in this case?"

*I need to make Judge Shipley a partner in my firm. He should be a defense attorney!* Zack mused. He glanced at Jack. He had a stunned smirk on his face. *Two minutes ago, his career was hanging by a thread. Look at him now!* Zack turned to Weaver, huddled and conversing with Clare Gibson and Chris Alexander. *What are they going to do?*

"The victim's hand would have to have been a very short distance from the bomb when it exploded for fingerprints to be burned into the pin in this manner."

"Based upon the evidence you reviewed, sir, do you have an opinion based on reasonable scientific certainty whether Jack Dylan was responsible for the death of Barton Breitner?"

"I do, Your Honor."

"And what is that opinion?"

"That he was not responsible, Your Honor. Based upon sound and reasonable scientific evidence and principles, Barton Breitner was killed after he tossed a live grenade, but failed to get far enough away to avoid the blast."

"And Jack Dylan?"

"Again, based upon my review of the evidence and scientific principles, Captain Dylan faced certain death if the grenade exploded in his vicinity, so he took evasive action. He jumped into the lake, probably knowing this was his only move if he wanted to stay alive."

"Do either of the attorneys have any questions?"

"No, Your Honor," Zack grinned, silently thanking the judge.

"Mr. Weaver?"

Weaver continued to converse rather heatedly with Alexander and Gibson. Those who witnessed the exchange were unable to determine the content of the conversation or perspective of each participant. Suddenly, Weaver stood and walked away from the two cops. One person in attendance would later tell the press he'd heard Weaver utter something that sounded like "stubborn asshole."

Weaver approached the prosecutor's podium, avoiding a return to the prosecution table, where Gibson and Alexander sat.

"Can we confer in chambers, Your Honor?"

"Absolutely. Court is in recess."

Zack and Jack headed for the back door. Gibson and Alexander followed toward the same exit. Judge Shipley and Weaver made eye contact. Shipley immediately understood the circumstances.

"Attorneys only," the judge ordered in deference to Weaver. Jack turned to Zack in protest. "Don't worry about it," Zack said with a smile. "I'll explain later."

"Your Honor?" Alexander stood in protest. He wanted in. "The Manistee Police Department and the FBI have vested interests here. We demand attendance at this meeting."

"The sign on the door says, 'Courtroom of Circuit Court Judge Paul E. Shipley.' This is my courtroom, and I determine who I will meet with and when. You, sir, are dangerously close to contempt," replied an indignant Judge Shipley.

Alexander did the smart thing for a change. He sat down and shut up. Zack motioned for Jack to sit as well. Zack followed Weaver and the judge into chambers, nodding his grateful acknowledgment to Snyder, who shrugged, indifferently. All he did was report the science. Unlike human beings, science always tells the truth.

***

Shipley, Blake, and Weaver retired to the judge's chambers.

The judge hand gestured for the attorneys to be seated. "Wow, that was rather shocking," said Shipley.

"I'll say," replied Zack.

"Jarrod? What does the state intend to do with this evidence?"

"Your Honor?" Weaver replied, still reeling from Snyder's testimony and his heated conversation with Gibson and Alexander.

"As an officer of the court. You are duty-bound to pursue the truth. It appears the truth, in this case, is that Mr. Breitner, not Captain Dylan, is responsible," the judge suggested.

"You made sure of that, Your Honor," Weaver grumbled.

"How so?"

"You've been pimping for Dylan's innocence throughout this trial."

"*Excuse* me, Jarrod?"

*Oh shit!* Zack gasped. *'Pimping?' Did the Manistee Prosecuting Attorney just accuse the presiding judge of 'pimping?'*

Weaver doubled down. "You heard me, Judge Shipley. Federal and city officials have instructed me to bring charges against you before the Judicial Tenure Commission."

"Take a moment, Mr. Weaver. Order a transcript of these proceedings thus far. I don't think you'll find a single ruling or even a comment that would warrant your outrageous accusation."

"We move for a mistrial, Your Honor. We request you recuse yourself and order a new trial in front of a new judge."

"That is not going to happen, Jarrod. Mr. Snyder has all but exonerated Captain Dylan, who, may I remind you, is still a Michigan police officer. The state, the city, and the FBI should be jumping for joy the terrorist is guilty and the cop is innocent. Mr. Snyder testified by stipulation so how do the consequences of his testimony fall on me?"

"Chief Alexander feels your questioning displayed a bias toward the defense."

"Even if Alexander's feelings were accurate, how do they change the outcome? A world-renowned expert concluded Mr. Breitner is responsible. That's the science speaking, not the judge. I could have asked nothing other than 'Mr. Snyder, please publish your findings in the case,' and the results would have been precisely the same."

"I am unable to persuade them to dismiss, Your Honor."

And *this* was the bottom line. When the prosecution is confronted with concrete evidence of a defendant's innocence during a trial or investigation, or even after a jury renders an erroneous guilty verdict, that prosecutor must come forward, as an officer of the court, to make sure justice is done. Defense attorneys have no such obligation, even when they know their clients are guilty.

"Okay, Jarrod. Let's put aside the fact you accused me of pimping…"

"I apologize, Judge Shipley. Truly, I do." Weaver bowed his head in genuine shame. "I lost my temper. I'm in a tough spot."

"I accept your apology. Do you agree the defendant is innocent, Jarrod? Yes or no?"

Weaver paused. "Yes," he finally said.

"Good. I am glad to hear it."

"So am I," said Zack, only to remind the two of them he was still there and they were discussing *his* client.

"Kind of forgot about you, Blake." The judge smiled and turned back to Weaver. "Jarrod, do you want me to take the decision to dismiss away from you?"

"What do you mean, Judge?"

"We go back out into the courtroom. Zack makes a motion to dismiss all charges based upon this newly discovered fingerprint and DNA evidence. You put forth a vigorous argument demanding we continue with the trial. Argue there is other evidence to consider that suggests Dylan is guilty and we should let the jury weigh *all* of the evidence and decide its relative value. Demand to cross-examine the witness in front of the jury. I will rule against you, and you can go out kicking and screaming about me being a crappy judge who pimps for guilty defendants—"

"I offered a sincere apology, Your Honor…" Weaver replied, interrupting. He could not afford for this to become a festering sore.

He would be appearing in front of Shipley on many more cases in the future.

"I was joking, Weaver. I *know* you're sorry, and I *know* you will never say anything like that to me ever again." The judge smiled. "Anyway, your clients will demand an appeal. Maybe they'll want to bring my conduct before the JTC, but that's where Zachary Blake and Jack Dylan come in."

"Huh?" Weaver was confused.

Zack said, "Tell us what you have in mind, Judge Shipley, and I will run it by my client."

"All I can ask for, Mr. Blake."

"Please call me Zack, Your Honor. We're becoming very good friends . . ."

"Zack, the pursuit of these charges on this evidence was bullshit from the very beginning, and when Jarrod calms down and reads the transcript, he'll come to the same conclusion."

"Go on..." said Zack, with keen interest.

"I am quite certain that you and your client, have reached the same conclusion. This was a bad arrest and prosecution, and you guys plan to sue everyone in sight, the city, county, state, and Feds. Am I right, Zack?"

"If you dismiss the case, Your Honor, absolutely, I am duty-bound to recommend any, and all, civil remedies to my client, and to pursue those remedies vigorously," replied Zack. *I love this guy! Can we move him to Detroit?*

"Were I in your shoes, Zack, that's exactly what I would do. So, here's what I propose: The various government entities do not appeal my ruling to dismiss all charges. There would be no JTC complaint, although this is not a condition of the agreement. I would never use my judicial leverage to avoid the consequences of my own misconduct. If you decide to proceed, though, you better be damn sure the charges are proven.

"Dylan and Blake agree to settle all claims for wrongful arrest and imprisonment as well as malicious prosecution in exchange for the various governments reimbursing Dylan for all legal and investigative fees and expenses as well as back salary for his time off work. There will be no admission of liability and no public acknowledgment a civil suit was considered or resolved. The parties will sign a complete non-disclosure and confidentiality agreement. Jack Dylan walks out of here a free man, absolved of all legal and financial burdens resulting from this prosecution. That's the whole deal. What do you guys think?"

The two attorneys faced each other, shrugged, and nodded.

"This will be a tough sell for me, Your Honor," said Weaver.

"I have faith in you, Jarrod," replied the judge. "Zack?"

Zack was elated. Jack was free. The financial burden crushing Jack would be alleviated entirely, and Zack would receive a handsome fee, including reimbursement of all case and business expenses. Jack would be ecstatic, but Zack needed to confirm his acceptance of the deal. This was his obligation to his client. "I will do my best to persuade my client to accept the deal or something very close to it, Your Honor," he replied.

"I know you will, Zack. Shall we put this on the record?

"Why don't we wait until everyone has agreed to the terms? Let's sleep on it and get everyone on the same page." Zack wanted the dismissal, but he also wanted to confer with Jack. Besides, he was confident Snyder's testimony, for all practical purposes, ended the case. He wasn't risking much in asking for a slight delay.

"This will also give the prosecution team time to digest the agreement, run things up the flagpole and obtain their necessary approvals. I like that idea, Your Honor," said Weaver.

"Then we have the basis for an agreement. I will see both of you bright and early tomorrow morning. I expect to have the confidential paperwork resolving the civil case handed to me first thing in the morning. Are we good to go?"

Again, the two attorneys faced each other and nodded. "Good to go, Your Honor," replied Zack.

"I'm good, Your Honor. Thanks for your understanding. Again, I'm truly sorry for my abhorrent behavior," said Weaver.

"What behavior?" Judge Shipley replied with a wink. "We're adjourned; get it done, gentlemen."

# Chapter Thirty-Six

Team Dylan met in the Bay Shore conference room. Zack wanted every person involved in the case to hear and opine on the terms of the fabulous deal. The attorney-client privilege protected the discussion for the investigative team but *not* for the Dearborn cop contingent. To assure confidentiality, Zack required everyone in the room to execute a confidentiality agreement. A tray of food was brought in -- this time from Shirley's Bar & Grill. The Bay Shore and the Manistee restaurant community would miss these guys.

Zack recited the entire agreement to the group. There were cheers and high fives all around when he disclosed the agreement required all charges against Jack be dismissed. When Jack heard he was giving up his right to sue the bastards, he was not happy.

"No, Zack. This kind of lawsuit is right in your wheelhouse, a meat and potatoes case. I remember reading about your case against a Farmington church. You didn't give those bastards an inch, fought hard and kicked their butts. Governments have lots of insurance, probably an umbrella policy and/or a self-insurance fund, and I want this to hurt. These jack-asses put me through hell. Besides, I don't need to give up the civil suit. This judge likes me, and he hates them. He's going to dismiss this case anyway."

"You may be right, but this was the judge's idea. He may not like you as much as you think he does, and if you turn down *his* deal, who knows how he will react? If we don't throw the city and county a bone, they are going to appeal Judge Shipley's ruling. They might try to re-file the charges, and we could be doing this all over again," Zack advised. He *planned* for Jack's resistance.

"Well, I don't care. Fuck these assholes. If this is how they treat a brother in blue, let them re-charge me. In fact, I fucking dare them. I *will* sue them, and when I'm finished with them, I'll own the whole damn town. They will be changing their name to 'Dylanistee.'"

Zack and the others chuckled.

"Come on, Jack, please be reasonable," said Zack. "You do not want this hanging over your head. They're going to pay all of your legal and investigatory expenses. They're going to pay for all the time you missed from work. You will not be a dime out of pocket. I am all for maximizing recoveries, but you have a career to consider. Not only will you miss more time from work, but you'll also be suing other cops and refusing to let go. Isn't that every bit as much of a 'betrayal in blue?' You would be no different than them. How is that going to help you?"

Jack began to soften. "These bastards shouldn't get away with this. They could have ruined me."

"But they didn't, Jack. And now they're paying dearly for going forward with this. We have a favorable judge who may not be there the next time around. Exoneration, freedom, and being made completely whole sound great to me. Anybody else want to chime in?" Zack was searching the room, looking for support. Shaheed Ali provided it for him.

"Jack, I know you're pissed. I can't blame you. But think about people like Arya who let go of their anger and came out stronger and better on the other side. The law enforcement community will appreciate this. It is not only the right thing to do, but it is also the smart thing to do—unless you want to retire to Florida or something."

"You're not getting rid of me that easily, Ali," Jack grumbled. "Florida? Are you kidding? I hate golf, and it's too fucking hot down there. They have *hurricanes*, for Christ's sake. I'm not ready to retire."

"Take the deal, Jack," said Noah. "There is still the possibility they could convict you on re-trial. Have you considered that? A cop can't risk that."

"Hadn't thought of that. Does everyone think I should take the deal? This whole thing feels like such a betrayal. Would we treat a visiting officer like this? Can you imagine Dearborn choosing a terrorist over a cop? That would never happen, that's for damn sure."

"I hear you, Jack, loud and clear. We all do. But this deal is in your best interest and the best interest of our community and our police force," replied Shaheed.

"Do all of you feel this way?"

Everyone in the room expressed a 'yes' in one form or another.

Jack hesitated, deeply contemplative. He started to speak a couple of times and then paused again, staring into space, collecting his thoughts. Finally, he said, "Okay, Zack, I'll do it, but if these bastards don't end this thing immediately, all bets are off. We will sue the hell out of them and own this town. Agreed?"

"Agreed, Jack," replied Zack. "I wouldn't mind owning a share of the Great Lakes. I may even move to Dylanistee."

The room erupted in laughter. Even the sulking Jack Dylan started to laugh. This long nightmare was almost over.

\*\*\*

"That smug bastard is guilty. Why should I permit an obviously biased judge to let him off the hook?" Christopher Alexander was irrational. He would not let the Dylan case go without a fight.

"Dylan is not smug nor is he guilty, Chris. He's already won the case. If we make him finish this and the jury acquits, or the judge dismisses, we will be on the hook for millions," replied Weaver.

"Over my dead body," said Alexander.

"If you don't accept this deal and Dylan walks anyway, you will *wish* you were dead because the mayor and the commissioner will be all over your ass," offered Prince.

"And that damned shyster, Blake, he's another smug, arrogant son-of-a-bitch," said Alexander.

Clare Gibson was silent until this moment, but she had enough. "He may be smug and arrogant, but we now know he has the truth on his side. I thought Dylan was guilty. That's why I pursued this case. Part of me didn't like pursuing a cop, especially when his victim was a terrorist, but I tried my hardest to find enough evidence to convict. In the end, the evidence proved him *innocent*, Chris. I will not be a party to prosecuting an innocent man, especially an innocent *cop*. Your stubborn insistence on continuing the trial is going to cost all of us, and not only money. You have to let this go."

Alexander placed his elbows on the conference table. He put his head in both hands, closed his eyes, and started rubbing his temples. "I'll agree to the dismissal, but not the legal fees and wages, okay?"

"No Chris, not okay," said Weaver. "If we take the deal, we all walk away. Maybe we'll take some heat for a while. But, if we turn this down and Dylan is acquitted, he *will* sue everyone in sight, and he will have one of the best lawyers in the State handling the case. Gibson is absolutely correct. Maybe at first when we thought he was guilty, we figured we could put away a bad cop in a big case and, perhaps, make names for ourselves. But we didn't call 'time out' when we began to question his guilt. Instead, we tried to jam the evidence into our version of the facts, even though we could sense it didn't quite fit. If we look at things objectively, this case was always a square peg in a round hole."

Weaver deliberately used 'we.' Silently, he blamed Alexander, but to get Alexander to sign off, he had to be diplomatic. So, he accepted blame to get Alexander to at least accept a share. It was time to do the right thing, time to move on. "What was that Johnny Cochran line?" Weaver asked.

"If it doesn't fit, you must acquit," replied Gibson.

"If it doesn't fit, you must acquit," Weaver repeated.

"Shit! No admission of guilt or liability?" Alexander asked.

"None."

"Legal and investigatory fees and wage loss only?"

"No tort recovery, no punitive damages."

"Damn! Okay, I'll do it. I'm not very happy about it, but I'll do it."

"Good choice, Chris. I'll call Blake and the judge."

\*\*\*

The parties met in Judge Shipley's chambers and hammered out the paperwork for the confidential agreement. When they were finished, and the agreement was executed, everyone went back into the courtroom and put the case dismissal on the record. Weaver made quite a show of defiance for the press.

Zack filed a motion to dismiss based upon the testimony of Charles Snyder. The scientific evidence has proven beyond a reasonable doubt, Jack Dylan is innocent of all charges. He did not kill Bart Breitner. Jack was probably guilty of impeding a federal investigation, but that small issue seemed to have been forgotten in everyone's quest to put *State v. Dylan* in the rear-view mirror.

Weaver ranted something about Snyder and Spellman being bought and paid for *defense* experts, making their credibility suspect. He claimed other 'renowned' experts might easily reach very different conclusions, especially if *they* were well paid for *their* contrary opinions. He cynically argued expert testimony is always about which side is paying for the opinion.

He lobbied for the opportunity to re-test the evidence with a different expert, one retained by the government. He recounted all of the lay witness testimony suggesting this case was about an argument turned deadly and a rogue cop who became a murderer.

Jack was livid. *How much more of this shit do I have to take from these people?* He wanted to call off the agreement. "How can an attorney who knows I'm innocent stand there and continue to call me a murderer?" he whispered. Zack reminded him a vigorous argument was a necessary part of the agreement. "It's almost over, Jack," Zack soothed.

The judge listened to the arguments of counsel and called for a recess to deliberate. It was terrific theatre, and the press and the public ate it up.

Fifteen minutes later, Judge Shipley returned. He called Charles Snyder's testimony compelling. He appreciated the many witnesses who came forward to testify and said citizens should never hesitate to do their duty. The scientific evidence was clear, however, and it exonerated Jack Dylan.

"I hereby direct a verdict of not guilty. After court is recessed, I'll visit the jury room and notify the jury the case is over. They may go home to their families with the thanks and respect of this court," the judge advised.

"This court, the prosecutor's office, Manistee law enforcement, and the FBI offer our profound apologies to Captain Dylan, who is, by order of this court, an innocent man. With this ruling, he is also now a free man. Captain Dylan? Good luck to you, sir. This case is hereby dismissed, and your bond is discharged. Court is adjourned."

Pandemonium erupted as Judge Shipley left the bench. The press stormed the litigants on both sides, desperately trying to be the first to get each party's reaction to the judge's ruling. All parties were peppered with questions until there were no questions left.

Zack Blake and Jarrod Weaver shook hands. Each congratulated the other and Weaver said he hoped never to see Zack again. Jack and Chris Alexander avoided each other. Alexander exited the courtroom followed by a trail of local reporters seeking to get a few choice quotes. Clare Gibson approached Jack, shook his hand, and offered an apology, which Jack grudgingly accepted. The trial was suddenly over, and these former adversaries would return to their previous lives.

The entire Dearborn police contingent checked out of the Bay Shore. Shaheed, Andy, and Noah had a four-plus hour drive ahead of them. Zack, Jack, and Micah boarded Zack's jet for the plane ride home. The plane took off over Lake Michigan, looped back around toward Michigan's western coast, and headed southeast. Jack looked out the window and saw the boardwalk and a still empty boat slot, marking the spot where Breitner's boat exploded.

*What a nightmare!* Jack thought. *Maybe someday, I'll wake up.* Amidst the celebratory atmosphere and the noise of the plane, Jack Dylan reclined his seat, lowered his Detroit Tigers baseball cap over his eyes, and fell into a deep sleep.

# PART FOUR—AFTERMATH

# Chapter Thirty-Seven

The limousine pulled into the driveway of Zack and Jennifer Blake's Bloomfield Hills mansion at three in the morning. Zack called Jennifer immediately after the trial to deliver the good news. He provided an *ETA* and made her promise neither she nor the boys would wait up.

He grabbed his suitcase and briefcase, thanked and generously tipped the driver, and told him to get a good night's sleep. As the limo rolled down the circular drive, Zack turned and ogled his impressive home. His 'new' life was still hard to fathom. Much happened over the past few years. Fame, family, and fortune replaced frustration, solitude, and poverty. This beautiful home was a symbol of the transformation. However, the true blessings of the new and improved Zachary Blake were sleeping inside.

Zack climbed the front steps, put the key into the lock and pushed the front door open. An alarm began to chirp quietly. He walked to a keypad and entered the code. The alarm fell silent. A small table lamp dimly lit the foyer. Zack started up the winding staircase. Suddenly, every light in the house came on. Music began to blast over the intercom, and a huge 'Welcome Home, Dad' sign unfurled over the staircase. Jennifer and the boys came running down the stairs, screaming 'surprise,' throwing confetti and blowing New Year's Eve-type celebration horns. The family met and embraced midway, and Jake and Kenny dragged Zack into the kitchen, where a pot of coffee and a 'Welcome home' Sanders' Carmel Cake, Zack's favorite, awaited him. The family spent quality family time celebrating, eating cake, drinking coffee or milk, and discussing '*Jack and Zack's Excellent Manistee Adventure*,' as Jake labeled it. Zack forgot he was utterly exhausted.

Two hours later, the boys began to rub their eyes. They said goodnight, hugged their mother and the man who'd become their father before returning to their separate bedrooms. Zack and Jennifer were alone in the kitchen. They glanced at each other, and Jennifer jumped into his arms and kissed him.

"I'm so proud of you, sweetheart. Are you okay? We really missed you!"

"I missed you guys, too, more than you know. Thank you for this terrific greeting; what a nice surprise!" Tears welled in his eyes. His family made everything worthwhile.

"And how is Jack?" Jenny asked. "He must be on cloud nine!"

"Well, I don't know about cloud nine, but he's very relieved and grateful. We not only proved his innocence, but we persuaded the city to pay all his legal and investigative expenses. These expenses were weighing heavily on his shoulders. He's not a wealthy man."

"You would have given him a break. I know you, Zack Blake. Under that macho super-lawyer persona lays a compassionate wimp." She tweaked his cheeks and kissed him.

"Yeah, well, don't tell anyone. It would ruin my image," Zack said, gazing into her eyes, with his arms around her waist and his hands locked behind her. "Besides, now I don't have to be a compassionate wimp. I can be a passionate wimp. Has anyone ever told you you're gorgeous?" He scooped Jennifer up into his arms and kissed her again, long and hard. They started up the stairs.

"Eeww, gross," said Jake, seated at the top of the stairs.

"You guys are disgusting," said Kenny, seated next to him.

Jennifer and Zack looked at each other and started laughing. They raced up the stairs, going after the two boys. Jake and Kenny jumped to their feet and dashed into their bedrooms with their parents close behind. The two boys shrieked as they ran. When they reached their rooms, they literally slammed the doors in the faces of their parents. Zack and Jennifer were laughing like teenagers at a slumber party. The ruckus felt terrific after the daily grind and constant pressure of a murder trial. Only a trial lawyer could understand the stark contrast in emotions.

"Go to bed, you guys!" Jennifer yelled, feigning anger.

"Yeah!" Zack managed, trying and failing to suppress his laughter.

"Oh, big help you are, Mr. Big-Shot Wimp."

"Sorry."

The two of them walked to the bedroom, arm in arm. It felt like they were apart for years, not a couple of months. Zack looked into the eyes of the woman he loved with all his heart.

"I really missed you, Zachary Blake. I love you so much." She squeezed him tightly like she'd never let go.

"I love you, too."

"I love you more."

"I love you less."

"I love you the most."

***

The following morning, after a late breakfast with his exhausted family, Zack left the house to spend a few hours of office catch-up time. The reunion with his wife and kids was wonderful, especially after the boys went to bed, but it was time to return to reality.

Zachary Blake was a busy trial lawyer. The problem with being retained to handle a lengthy murder trial is the lawyer's other cases, or business goes virtually unattended while he's away. There are other firm lawyers, usually associates, to make court appearances, with paralegals and legal secretaries to help pick up some of the slack, but the work continues to pile up while the senior partner is gone. These clients were *his* personal clients, the files were *his* files, his *babies,* and they required *his* personal touch.

Zack walked into his office. The place looked like the home of a hoarder. Stacks of files lined his massive, ornate hardwood desk. Very little surface space was exposed. His phone messages were stacked up and sorted by date, and when he tried to sit down, he noticed his mail was stacked high on the seat of his ergonomic executive chair.

He reached for his office intercom and buzzed his legal secretary, legal assistant, and primary associate to enlist their support in plowing through the backlog. The few hours he planned to spend at the office almost turned into a full day, but he could finally see a glimpse of light at the end of a long, dark tunnel. There was still much to be done before a substantial dent was made in his massive workload. As morning turned to afternoon, Zack found himself missing his wife and children. He made a snap executive decision. He would call it a day and first thing in the morning he would call for additional office support.

*Isn't that why they call these people 'support staff?' I can't do everything myself, right? I'm only human. Even a parent calls in a babysitter once in a while.* Zack was a dedicated professional. His cases and his clients meant the world to him, and he was struggling to assuage his guilt. On the other hand, he *was* the boss, and bosses have the power to delegate, even though Jennifer was correct to call him a wimp.

As he started out the door, he eyed his briefcase and two '*State v Dylan'* file boxes he brought back from Manistee. *Was that this morning or last night? Same thing, I guess. Seems like a week ago.*

The boxes sat atop some files piled high on a side chair. Inside were some of the more important exhibits from the Dylan case. He picked up the briefcase, opened it, and pulled out the picture that haunted him throughout his time in Manistee.

He studied the picture. *We were definitely missing something. What was it? There's something important here. But, if so, how could all of us view the same images repeatedly and not find it? Perhaps the non-stop viewing exercise caused us to see the same thing each time. Maybe the fact that I haven't looked at it in a while will give me a fresh perspective.*

He turned the picture upside down and then sideways. Zack studied the one feature or image in the photograph he and everyone else failed to notice. Jack noticed it and pointed it out to everyone: it was Jack's own head. It popped out of the water as he emerged from his frantic dive and began to tread water. According to the testimony, the cops focused on him and ordered him out of the water.

Zack's eyes wandered over to the other side of the boat, toward the bow or front. *What is that? Not sure I noticed it before…is it what we saw before or…? Is it the same image or something similar? Kind of looks like the other… shit! It can't be, can it? I've got to reach Jack!*

# Chapter Thirty-Eight

A year ago, Jack Dylan stood before a large crowd to accept the Public Safety Officer Medal of Valor for his heroic work in bringing down Benjamin Blaine and saving Arya Khan. He was now returning to work, trying to catch up on cases and other odds and ends that were neglected during his long absence. He took some time to visit with Chief Acker, who made it a point to chastise and berate him for his stupidity, stubbornness, deception, and disobedience. Privately, the chief was relieved to see him back where he belonged, at police headquarters. Publicly, he advised Jack he was not welcome, an inquiry would have to evaluate his insubordinate conduct, and an appropriate penalty would be meted out before clearing him for duty. "I don't want to see you around here, Dylan. Don't finish the day. That's an order."

The chief next addressed Jack's assistant, Mary Lewis. "Mary," he commanded, "you are to see to it Jack Dylan leaves here in short order and has no contact with this office, not by phone, not by email, and certainly not in person until he is cleared for duty, understood?" The chief turned, winked at Mary and smiled.

Turning back to Jack, he said. "Captain Dylan, you are hereby suspended…*with pay*," he added softly, "until you are cleared for duty. Dismissed." He saluted, and Jack saluted back, shooting the chief a nasty look, which Acker returned in kind. Jack returned to his office to retrieve his backpack. Acker's 'penalty' was a paid vacation, but Jack was too angry to realize his good fortune.

Before he departed, Jack decided to have a quick meeting with Shaheed, Andy, and Noah. The men grabbed some stale coffee and donuts and moved to the conference room.

\*\*\*

Meanwhile, on the first floor, a man entered the building wearing a uniform identifying him as an elevator repairman. He reported to the sergeant's desk.

"I'm here about the elevator malfunction," he said.

"Nobody said anything to me. Do you have a work order?" The desk sergeant asked.

"Damn! Must have left it in the van. I'll be right back," replied the seemingly frustrated repairman.

A moment after the man walked out the front door, a mass of cops and citizens stormed into the lobby. Apparently, a demonstration of civil disobedience got out of hand, and numerous arrests were made. Noticing the desk sergeant was having difficulty dealing with the chaos and was devoting full attention to the protestors, the repairman returned and breezed by the desk. He held up what appeared to be a work order while the frazzled sergeant eyed him, then shooed him toward the elevators.

The man entered the first elevator to arrive and pressed '2.' As the elevator rose, he pushed the emergency stop button. He had exactly one minute to release the button before an alarm sounded. He reached into his large toolbox and pulled out a vest packed with an explosive device and detonator. The vest was also loaded with ball bearings, nails, screws, and bolts. He unzipped and removed his jacket. Thirty seconds. He placed the vest flat against his stomach and fingered the straps. He had difficulty grasping the straps behind his back because he was having some trouble with his right hand. Despite the initial struggle, the man got a firm hold of the straps, reversed the vest to his back and secured the straps. Then, he carefully reversed the vest back to his stomach and pulled the straps as tight as he could.

He'd read somewhere tight constraints would channel the explosive energy outward, toward the person or persons standing in front of him. And he fully expected Jack Dylan, hero cop, would be standing in front of him. Ten seconds. He reversed his jacket, put it back on and zipped it, covering the vest and hiding the repairman logo. He knew he would have limited time to get ready, and the trouble he was having with his hand made things difficult. Because of his steadfast determination, he'd practiced these maneuvers for months. He pressed the button with a second to spare.

*Damn government couldn't get the job done. No surprise there. Dylan should be in Jackson or Ionia Prison or some fucking prison somewhere, locked up with people he put away. Fitting justice, a cop locked up with a bunch of guys who hate his guts. Load up on the Vaseline, buddy boy! You're about to be someone's bitch!*

*The evidence was overwhelming. Jack Dylan was a murderer, but he was still free. Shit, he wasn't even injured, not a scratch on him. Many mourned the loss of his victim, while others cheered his death. A beautiful boat was obliterated, body parts floating in the lake. Yet, that asshole judge wanted more. Can't convict a cop without more. Today, Jack Dylan, hero cop, will face justice. Today will be his day of reckoning.*

The man opened an electrical panel, cut all the wires, stepped off the elevator and approached the detectives' desk.

"Captain Jack Dylan, please?"

"Who's calling?" Mary asked.

"Zachary Blake," replied the stranger.

"Oh, Mr. Blake! It is so nice to meet you! Thank you so much for everything you did for the boss. I'll ring him for you right away. I think he's in the conference room."

"Thank you, Mary," the man said, politely reading her name off her badge.

"Please have a seat." She pointed him to a waiting room with chairs lining its back wall. *Perfect, he can't get behind me.* He entered and sat down. Facing the room's entrance, he waited.

Mary buzzed Jack in the conference room to advise Zachary Blake was waiting to see him. Jack excused himself. He was pleased. He needed an excuse to stay at headquarters. What was he going to do at home, even with pay? He was absent for too long already. Bureaucrats like Acker would never understand. Jack rose, exited the room and walked down a long hallway to the waiting room.

"Son-of-a-bitch, Zack Blake! Slumming it in Dearborn!" Jack yelled. He rounded the corner, walked into the waiting room and eyed his visitor. *No! It can't be!* Jack was completely shocked to find not Zack Blake, but the ghost of Bart Breitner seated in his waiting area. Breitner was holding a detonator and unzipped his jacket to reveal his explosive suicide vest. On instinct, Jack pulled his service revolver and yelled, "Freeze, asshole!" which caused several cops in the immediate vicinity to come running.

"Clear the building!" Jack yelled to anyone within earshot. Breitner remained silent and seated. Jack continued to train his weapon on him.

"Hey, Jack," Breitner finally said. "Surprised to see me?"

"Move a muscle, and you're dead asshole!"

"If I die, you die," Breitner replied. "And if you don't do exactly as I say, we will take a shitload of people with us."

"What do you want, Breitner?"

"I want you, Jack. I want you to have a seat. I want you to tell dear Mary and these officers you rescind your order to clear the building and they are to lock all the doors leading to the second floor. *I've* disabled the elevators."

Jack did exactly what he was told.

"Now I want you to call Zachary Blake. Tell him that you have an emergency and need him to come to police headquarters immediately."

"I won't do that, Bart. I won't put a citizen in harm's way. This is between you and me…"

"Then, I'll just press this little red button here…"

"No, don't. Don't do that! I'm calling him, man. I'm calling him. Stay calm!"

"That's a good boy. I don't care what you tell him, but whatever it is, make sure it gets him down here."

"Bart, by now, everyone in the building knows there's a guy in here with a bomb. They're mobilizing forces as we speak. They have a playbook, and they will run it. When Zack gets here, he won't be able to get into the building. And you're not getting out of here alive."

"Neither are you, but that's kind of the point. I missed when I tried to kill you the first time, and I won't make that same mistake today. After that last try, I had to listen to you and that kike bastard, Blake, call me vile names and slander me in that courtroom. And I still want revenge for Blaine and his men. I can kill two birds with one stone. You make me sick, and I want you dead. Because I'm a swell guy, though, I'm giving you a choice. Me, you, and Blake can take a walk, and only three people die. Or, I set off the bomb here and anyone who is still on the second floor will die with us. Which do you prefer?"

"You're the boss, Bart." Jack kept his weapon pointed at Breitner's head. *A moment's distraction...*

"I like the sound of that. Say it again."

"You're the boss, Bart. See, look, I'm calling him." He held up his iPhone for Breitner to see him dial Zack's number.

"Zachary Blake & Associates. May I help you?"

"Zack Blake, please."

"Who's calling?"

"Jack Dylan."

"Oh! Congratulations, Mr. Dylan. Your case is the talk of the office. I'll buzz Zack."

"Thank you."

Jack was placed on hold. Music played in the background. The music stopped as Zack picked up the extension.

"Jack! Thank God you called! I was just going to call you! I think Breitner is alive...Do you hear me, Jack? Breitner is alive! Remember that picture? I knew we were missing something! I took another look. If you look closely, it isn't *you* in the water. It's *Bart*. You can barely make him out, but it's Bart." Silence greeted this news. "Jack, did you hear what I said? Breitner is alive!"

"Zack, there is an emergency, and I need you to come down to police headquarters in Dearborn right away."

Zack was upset Jack was so calm after hearing the shocking news. His reaction was perplexing.

"I'm up to my eyeballs in work this morning, Jack. I'm backed up from the trial. Can it wait until this afternoon? What's it all about, anyway? Besides, you need to drop everything, rally the troops, and go after Breitner right now. Don't you agree?"

"Zack, there is an emergency, and I need you to come down to police headquarters in Dearborn right away," Jack repeated.

"What's going on, Jack? Come on, man, talk to me."

Jack held the phone away from his ear and shrugged at Breitner, who motioned him over and asked for the phone. Jack walked over and handed it to him. He kept the gun trained on Breitner's forehead the entire time.

"Zack, buddy. It's me, your old pal!" Zack could not place the voice.

"To whom am I speaking?" Zack asked the caller.

"To whom am I speaking?" Breitner repeated. "So fancy, Mr. Hot-Shot Barrister. You've been talking shit about me in court for weeks. It's time we met, on *my* terms."

"Breitner?" Zack was dumbfounded. He had no idea what to do or how to react. *Shit! What do I do? What do I do?* "How is this possible?" He finally managed.

"Simple. Jack threw that damn grenade, and we both jumped in the water. I knew water would protect me, and I couldn't exactly let this asshole live and I die, now could I? Unfortunately, I didn't get my hand under fast enough, and the bomb caught part of it. Hurt like a son-of-a-bitch. Your buddy Jack was floating around the lake, waving at his buddies. The cops were devoting all their attention to him, so I dove underwater and swam to the other side of the dock. No one even noticed."

"Which explains why they only found two fingers and parts of your hand."

"Exactly. Now, you may think that your buddy is innocent of murder, but that doesn't make him, or you, innocent. Ben Blaine is still in prison, and my plans for revenge went all to hell. I lost my beautiful boat and *part of my fucking hand!* Someone has to pay!"

"What do you want, Bart?"

"I want to reminisce, just the three of us, over drinks, perhaps. I want to discuss old times, good times. *What the hell do you think I want?* I want you to get your ass over here, *now*."

"Why should I do that?"

"Because if you don't get here within thirty minutes, I'm going to huff and puff and blow this place down. Get my drift?"

"Put Dylan back on."

"I give the orders around here, asshole. Now, if you ask me nicely…"

"Please put Dylan back on."

"Hold, please. To whom am I speaking?" Breitner replied, mimicking Zack's receptionist, enjoying himself.

"Please put him on, Bart."

Breitner handed the phone to Jack. Jack shrugged, and Breitner nodded permission for Jack to tell him what was going on.

"I don't know how the bastard got in here, but he's here, and he's got a suicide vest attached to his chest. He's threatening to level the whole place with a whole bunch of people still inside."

"What do you want me to do?"

"He says if he can meet with you and me alone, he'll let everyone else go. It's suicide, Zack."

"It's murder if he doesn't show. He has a chance to save all of these '*innocent*' people," said Breitner.

"Put Breitner back on, Jack."

"No."

"Put him back on, Jack. Now!"

Jack handed the phone over to Bart. "What?" Bart asked.

"I'm on my way. It takes longer than thirty minutes to get from Bloomfield Hills to Dearborn. I need forty-five."

"You have forty," replied Breitner, only to be the 'in charge' asshole.

"Don't do anything stupid, Bart."
"Too late," replied Breitner.

# Chapter Thirty-Nine

Zack Blake dashed out of his office, dialing his phone. His first call was to Shaheed Ali, who answered on the first ring.

"Shaheed, what the fuck, man?"

"What are you talking about, Zack?"

"Are you at work?"

"Yes, I'm in the conference room, meeting with Andy and Noah, why?"

"You're going to get a 9-1-1 alert at any moment because I just called them," said Zack, hopping in the car and starting the engine.

"Huh?"

"Bart Breitner is alive! He's at Dearborn Police headquarters, right now, and he's holding Jack and others hostage. He's wearing a suicide vest."

Shaheed was stunned, speechless.

"Shaheed?"

"Yeah, I'm here, Zack. Sorry. This is too much…Breitner? *Alive?* Let me think… Who else knows about this?"

"If I had to guess, everyone but you. I'm sure all police forces in the area are mobilizing and placing units on full alert."

"What does Breitner want?"

"He wants to have a chat with Jack and me, to discuss old times."

"He wants to kill you both."

"He'll kill everyone in the building if I don't come. What choice do I have?"

"What about your wife and kids?"

"That's my next telephone call."

"I can't believe this is happening right under our noses. I'll fill Andy and Noah in, sneak downstairs, and meet you. I've got to think…"

The call disconnected, and Zack dialed his wife, Jennifer.

"This is a nice surprise," she cheered. "You never call me during business hours." She glanced at the television. There was breaking news about a hostage standoff at Dearborn Police headquarters.

"Hey, Zack, honey. Doesn't Jack Dylan work for the Dearborn Police?"

"Yeah, why?"

"There's something on the TV about a hostage standoff."

"That's why I'm calling, Jenny. *Jack* is the *hostage*. He's being held by Bart Breitner."

"The dead guy?"

"I guess he's not dead."

"What do you mean, 'being held?'"

"Breitner is wearing a suicide vest. He will release everyone but Jack as long as I come down there so the three of us can be alone to sort out our differences."

"You're not actually thinking of going, are you?"

"I'm on my way there now. That's why I called. Jenny, I have no choice."

Jennifer Tracey Blake began to cry. "Of course you have a choice!" she screamed. "You can choose your family over some clients and a bunch of strangers. What does this have to do with you, anyway?"

"Mr. Breitner is apparently upset about some of the things I said about him in court."

"He's going to kill you, Zack. You can't go. I forbid it. I lost one husband. I will not lose another. Turn around and come home!"

She was breaking his heart. In the heat of the moment, he'd forgotten. Jennifer was once married to a wonderful man who died in an industrial accident. Zack handled his wrongful death case. Several years later, after a priest abused her children, Jennifer turned to Zack again. While it is taboo to date (let alone fall in love with) a client, nature took its course. They fell in love, and after the case was over, they married. Eventually, Zack adopted Jennifer's boys. Kenny and

Jake were the sons he never had. '*I will not lose another...*' her words were crushing.

"Zack?" Jennifer interrupted his thoughts. "Did you hear me? Turn around, please?"

"I can't do that Jenny," he finally replied. "Are Jake and Kenny home?"

"No!" she screamed. This strong woman who endured so much tragedy in her life was hysterical.

"Please tell them I love them, and I'll see them soon. You too, sweetheart."

"Don't you 'sweetheart' me, Zachary Blake. You come home to me. I'm begging you. Promise me you won't do anything stupid or crazy."

"I'll try not to, Jenny. If it makes you feel any better, besides the three of you, *I* am my favorite person."

"That's not funny. Promise me you will come home to me."

"I promise."

"Liar!" Jennifer screamed.

"I've got to call the police station, Jenny. I have to go."

"I love you."

"I love you more."

"I love you less, you bastard. Come home!"

"Do you want that to be the last thing you ever say to me?"

She was screaming and crying, almost uncontrollably. This 'I love you' game was their ritual.

"I love you most," she finally said. "Come home to me, Zack. Come home to the boys. We love you; we can't lose you."

"I'll be home soon, sweetheart. Bye."

"Don't hang up," she pleaded, as she heard the phone click off.

*\*\*\**

Zack arrived at Dearborn Police headquarters with five minutes to spare. Pandemonium ruled the complex. The place was crawling with cops, FBI, and SWAT from Dearborn and neighboring communities. Zack pulled out his cell and called Shaheed.

"Where are you?" Shaheed answered.

"I'm here, at police headquarters. How the hell do I get by all of these cops?"

"Tell me exactly where you are, and I'll come and get you." Three minutes later, the two men were standing side-by-side at a side door to the building.

"This is Lieutenant Shaheed. I'm here with Zack Blake. Let us in."

A uniformed officer came to the locked and guarded door and opened it for Shaheed to re-enter.

"I can't let you go up there by yourself, Zack."

"Well, you sure as hell aren't going with me. First of all, you're a Muslim, and he'll hate you at first sight. Second, we don't know whether he knows you or not and, besides, he didn't request you. Third, it's me he wants. It's me he asked for, and I'm a great negotiator."

"This is not a lawsuit negotiation. This is a hostage situation. Are you crazy?"

"Maybe. My wife certainly thinks so. Hang on a second. I've got an idea," Zack said as he picked up his phone and began dialing. Upstairs, on the second floor, Jack Dylan's cell phone rang.

"Hello?" Breitner chirped.

"Bart? This is Blake."

"You better be here. You're out of time."

"I'm here, Bart, but I'm not coming up unless you release everyone on the second floor."

"Fuck you, Blake. I make rules, and I say they stay where they are."

"Then I'm not coming."

"Then I'll just kill your buddy Dylan here and enjoy doing it."

"You're going to kill him anyway. You're pissed at Jack. You're pissed at me. I get it, Bart, but no one else up there has anything to do with this. Let them go, and I'll come up. You'll have what you came for-Jack Dylan *and* Zachary Blake. What do you say?"

Breitner paused for a long, deafening moment, total silence on the other end of the line.

"All right, Blake. I'll let them go, but this is my last concession. And if you don't get your ass up here the minute these people leave, I am going to blow this place to kingdom come."

"I hear you, Bart. I'm coming. As soon as I see the whites of everyone's eyes, I'm coming." He hung up the phone and turned to Shaheed.

"Shaheed? How well do you know this place?"

"Like the back of my hand," Shaheed assured. "There's also an architectural drawing over at the sergeant's desk. SWAT brought it in."

"How did Breitner get in here, by the way? How did he get past the desk?"

"Don't ask. The guy who let him by is a basket case over this."

"Where are Breitner and Jack, exactly?"

"I'm not sure."

A stairwell exit door slammed open, and people began pouring into the lobby. Andy saw Shaheed and ran to him.

"Andy, man, I'm glad to see you. You were still on two? How did that happen? Where are the two of them situated, exactly?" Shaheed asked frantically.

"They're in the second-floor waiting room."

"Where in the room?"

"Breitner is seated in one of the chairs lined up against the back wall. Jack is seated across from him." He pointed to the drawing. "Here…and…here."

"Perfect. I've got an idea. People are still coming down. Zack, we are going to split up. I've got to talk to SWAT. When you get up there, I want you to sit next to Jack on the opposite side of this wall, got it?" Shaheed pointed to the location on the drawing.

"Got it."

"Make sure Jack stays seated in that same spot. Don't get up, and don't let him get up." He turned to Andy and put his arm around his shoulders. "Andy, you're coming with me. Zack, whatever you do, make sure you and Jack stay on the opposite side of Bart."

"Will do, Shaheed. Care to share?"

"No. I don't want you giving anything away."

"I'll do as you say. But remember, Shaheed, everyone is counting on you."

"Stall him, Zack. Keep him talking. Tell him you're willing to represent him all the way to the Supreme Court if you have to."

"Will do. Wish me luck."

"Good luck. Now, get out of here before he wonders where you are. Watch where you sit and keep him talking."

"I know, I know," replied Zack as he set off in the opposite direction. "I'm a quick study. I went to law school, you know."

Shaheed smiled. He hoped those were not the last words he ever heard from Zachary Blake.

As Zack ran up the stairs, Shaheed and Andy ran over to the SWAT team leader. He was surprised to see Clare Gibson and Pete Westmore standing alongside the SWAT team.

"What are you guys doing here?" Shaheed asked, mildly perturbed. *Looking to usurp another operation? Not this time! Not on my watch...*

"We received the alert. I couldn't believe my ears. Breitner is *alive*, after all of this? We're here to help in any way we can," replied Gibson.

"Hasn't the FBI *helped* enough, Gibson?" Shaheed asked, caustically. "First, you usurp our sarin operation and screw up the capture. Then, Jack is tried and almost convicted of murder on the evidence you helped collect and process. When it should have been quite apparent he was innocent, you and Alexander doubled down and attempted to secure a conviction anyway. Did I leave anything out? Now, after all of that, you want to *help?*"

"Guilty on all counts, Ali. What can I say? I feel terrible about the way things went down. But all of that was yesterday. *Today*, we have a terrorist with a bomb, holding a cop and an innocent civilian hostage. This is what we FBI agents *do*. Let us help you, *please*," replied Gibson, earnestly.

Shaheed studied Gibson and Westmore. He saw deep regret, sincerity, and determination in their eyes. "Support only," he finally conceded.

"Support only," replied Gibson.

Shaheed turned to the SWAT team leader and motioned Gibson and Westmore over.

"Do you guys have any of that Doppler radar equipment? You know, the stuff that sees through walls?"

"We do," replied the SWAT team leader. "Why?"

"Well, I have an idea. I know this building extremely well. Here's what I would like to do…"

# Chapter Forty

"Hello? Bart?" Zachary Blake arrived on the second floor and walked casually through the exit door.

"In here, Blake. You alone? If I see anyone else, even a rodent, I'm going to explode this thing."

"I'm alone, Bart. Here I come." Zack walked up to the waiting room and saw Breitner. He was seated against the back wall, holding a detonator. Jack Dylan was on the opposite side, his back to Zachary, training a gun on Breitner. Zack walked up to the two men and sat down next to Jack, exactly as Shaheed instructed. He did not want to give Breitner a chance to dictate where he sat.

"I don't think we have been formally introduced, Mr. Blake. I was dead before you got involved."

"I'd like to say it's a pleasure to meet you, but..."

"Real comedian, this one, Dylan. Where'd you find him?"

"Cut the crap, Bart. Get to the point. What do you want?"

Zack wanted to shout at Jack. *Don't cut the crap, Bart. Keep talking. Let's talk about the trial and your so-called death. How did you escape? Want me to negotiate a book deal for you? Let's talk about the weather. How about fishing? We can talk about fishing. You like to fish, right? Let's talk about anything, anything at all. Talk, Bart, talk!*

"Easy, Dylan, easy. It's just the three of us here. We've got plenty of time. Let's talk about the trial. I couldn't be there. I was just *dying* to be there."

"Fuck you, Bart. You're not funny—" Jack started to say.

Zack interrupted him. "I don't mind talking about the trial. I love to talk about my work. I'm a damn good lawyer. I could probably get *you* off, Bart. What do you say?"

"See? I was right. You *are a* funny guy, Blake. So, let's discuss the trial. What was your courtroom strategy? Breitner was a bad guy, so it's justifiable homicide?"

"No, Bart. Actually, it was more complicated than that. I was trying to prove you exploded the grenade, not Jack."

"Cut it out, Zack," said Jack. "*Of course* that was the strategy. It was the truth. I know it, and Bart knows it, too. We were there."

"I don't know, Jack. Maybe it didn't happen exactly the way you said it did. I'd like to hear Bart's side of the story."

"Yeah, Dylan! You got a hot date or something? You're not going anywhere. So, Blake here's the story—"

"Fuck this shit," Jack said, starting to rise, holding the gun steady on Breitner. Zack put his arm on Jack's, silently imploring him to sit. Jack looked into Zack's eyes, and Zack motioned with them for Jack to resume his seat. There was a hint of recognition a plan was in the works.

"Okay, Bart. Why don't you tell me what really happened on the boat? And tell the truth, please?" Zack asked, politely.

"Our *hero cop* lied to the Manistee police. Didn't you, Jack? He claimed he was a fisherman on vacation. He didn't want the locals to arrest me. He wanted to kill me from the beginning. He was planning an execution, Zack. That's illegal, isn't it, Blake?"

"Yes, Bart, it is," Zack said, playing along. "Is this true, Jack? Were you going to arrest him or kill him?"

"What difference does it make? This is the guy who plotted to steal sarin gas and release it in Dearborn. He's a terrorist. If I captured him, I captured him. If I killed him, I killed him. Who the fuck cares? Either way, the world would be better off without Bart Breitner walking the streets."

"He's got a point, Bart."

"He's got no proof I had anything to do with sarin gas. Where's the proof? Because he suspected I was involved, he became obsessed. He followed me to Manistee, planned to kill me and actually tried to do it. *He blew up my boat.* That is stalking and attempted murder and the entire fucking police force *and* the Feds just let him go rogue."

"The Feds have photos of you on-site at the sarin warehouse, scumbag," replied Jack, vehemently.

"It's a free country. For all you know, that was a coincidence. I might have just happened to be walking by. Or, maybe I have a doppelganger."

"But you weren't, and you don't, Bart. The FBI has photos of you pulling up in the transport vehicle, exiting that vehicle, and entering the warehouse where the sarin was stored. Do you deny this?"

"Absolutely. I was home in bed when those arrests were made."

"No, you weren't. You abandoned your so-called brothers and went crawling through the sewers like the rat you are."

"Objection, Your Honor. Can he talk about me like that in a court of law?"

"Behave yourself, Jack," Zack admonished. "Bart has some valid points."

"Screw this shit, Zack. Let me shoot this bastard and be done with it."

"Not before I detonate this bomb." Breitner held up the detonator and began to slowly depress the button.

"No, no! I want to hear more, Bart. Tell me what happened on the boat."

Breitner relaxed again. "Well, we went fishing. First, we went out with these frat-boy air-traffic-controller guys. I've taken them out before. All those assholes ever wanted to do was get laid and get drunk. They were never really there to fish. They weren't serious fishermen by any stretch of the imagination. But hey, their money was good, and they always have plenty of it. That's when your boy Jack here steps up and pays for their fishing trip. He just met them, yet he pays for the whole thing. And that's when I first knew something was up. That's how badly he wanted to hang with me. He was obsessed, I tell you. He wanted to kill me."

"Sounds like he *was*, Bart. Please continue." *The more he talks, the less he'll think about blowing himself up.*

"After the first fishing trip, Jack stays behind, and we get to talking. He tells me he's heard some of the things I'd been saying to others around town, and he wants me to know he agrees with many of my positions. He'd like to get involved, he says. How about it? He asks. That's *entrapment*, isn't it? Anyway, I tell him to come back tomorrow so we can talk some more."

"Did he come back?"

"Oh, please kill me, Bart. I can't take any more of this bullshit," said Jack irritably.

"Dylan shut the fuck up!" Zack was furious. "I said I would listen to Bart's story, and I want to hear this. I listened to your whining and bellyaching for all those months in Manistee, didn't I? Now, if you don't mind shutting your mouth for a few minutes, I'd like to hear Bart's version of the story."

Jack shot him a furious glance. *Is he serious? What the fuck is going on here?*

"Thank you, sir," replied Breitner. *I like this kike. He's probably a great lawyer.*

"Please continue, Bart," said Zack, politely.

\*\*\*

On the opposite side of the building, Shaheed, Andy, the FBI, and SWAT operatives silently climbed the parallel staircase that led to the second floor. Upon arrival, they carefully and quietly opened the exit door. The SWAT team was carrying Doppler radar equipment. Team members removed their shoes and continued to move in virtual silence west to east toward the waiting room where Bart Breitner was holding Dylan and Blake.

The journey seemed to take forever. Their steps were methodical and deliberate. In actuality, they covered a distance equal to half a city block. As they traveled down a narrow corridor that led to the offices, they could hear voices. One of those offices was located directly behind the waiting room. The office and waiting room shared a back wall. A door on the opposite wall provided entry to the inside office.

*Keep him engaged, Zack. Keep him talking,* thought Shaheed Ali as they continued to move forward. They heard a voice: "Please continue, Bart."

Bart Breitner continued his outrageous version of events. "So, he comes back the next evening and meets the whole gang. We all get along great. Finally, everybody is leaving and dickhead Jack stays behind like he did the night before. He wants to chat me up a bit. Only he slips up and calls me 'Bart' instead of 'Bert,' my Manistee name. I'm a sharp guy, Blake. This slip up only confirmed what I already knew. 'Jack Manning' was really 'Jack Dylan,' Dearborn cop and huge asshole. Jack had, what do you lawyers call them, *ulterior* motives. That's what they were, *ulterior* motives. He wanted to get me alone so he could *kill* me.

"He never wanted to hang out with me. He was there for a different reason. I asked him, 'What the fuck?' and he tried to tell me he made an honest mistake. I told him his flimsy explanation broke my bullshit meter. Do you know what he did then?"

"No, what?" Zack replied, egging him on.

"He pulled a gun on me! Can you believe that? Just like he did today. He carries a concealed weapon. That's illegal, isn't it?"

"Sure is, Bart. Go on…"

"Now, I'm not going to lie, I had some explosives on that boat. But your boy Jack here conducted an illegal search of my boat and found the explosives."

"If he did, that's a Fourth Amendment violation. A cop can't do stuff like that. What happened next?"

"He found a grenade, pulled the pin, and threw it at me."

"Seriously, Breitner?" Jack asked, rolling his eyes. "There's no judge here, no jury. It's only Zack and me. You are a fucking liar, and we all know it. What is the purpose of this exercise?"

*I'm trying to keep him talking until help arrives. Shut up, moron!* Zack was dumbfounded Jack failed to grasp he was trying to stall. Jack would need to understand he needed more time.

"The purpose, Mr. Hero Cop, is to set the record straight before we die. Hey, Blake, can you get one of those, what do you call them, steno-something's down here?"

"Stenographers? Court reporters? I'm not sure they would put someone in harm's way, Bart. It's too dangerous. If you want to make a statement, you could turn yourself in and—"

"You'd like that, wouldn't you, Blake? Tie this all up in a neat bow with no bloodshed, especially yours."

"I admit I don't want to die, Bart. I have a family."

"Then why did you come? Not for this asshole."

"I was hoping you would release some hostages in exchange for me, and you did."

"Mighty white of you, Blake. You're okay in my book. Are you sure you're Jewish? Most of your people are pussies. Like all of those people who marched to the gas chambers for Hitler."

Zack thought about arguing with Breitner about Jewish resistance and resilience during the Holocaust, but he knew he was wasting his breath. *Would it keep him talking?*

"Jack says *you* threw the grenade, Bart. He says you purchased a bunch of grenades and hid them on the boat. You admitted that. He says you were the only one who knew they were there and where to look for them."

"That's bullshit, Blake! Dylan searched the boat. I'm telling you. He got his hands on one of those grenades, tossed it, and jumped in the water. I loved that boat. It was my livelihood and my home away from home. Why would I deliberately destroy it?"

"That's a valid point, Jack," replied Zack.

"The asshole did it to escape, Zack!" cried Jack. "What the fuck is *wrong* with you? Maybe he didn't anticipate getting his hand blown off, but he knew what he was doing. He had no other choice!" Jack turned to Bart, enraged. "Did it hurt you fucking prick? I sure hope it hurt like a motherfucker!"

"If I'd been in control of the grenade, I wouldn't have gotten hurt. I'm an *expert*, like that bomb guy who found my prints and DNA."

"If that's true, Bart, how did the grenade pin get your fingerprints on it?"

"That bomb guy lied, of course. I never touched the damned thing."

"How were you able to follow the trial, Bart?" *Keep him talking…*

"Who gives a shit?" Jack raged. He was ready to blow. "I've had about enough of this crap. Kill us or walk the fuck out of here and take your chances. I don't care which. An explosive death is ten times better than being bored to death."

"Maybe I'll let Blake go," said Bart. "He may be a kike, but he seems like a good guy."

"He is a good guy, asshole. He's a great guy, in fact. Why else would he be sitting here listening to your shit?"

*Why indeed?* Bart Breitner leaned back in his chair, placed the back of his head against the back wall, and began to contemplate that question. It was the last conscious thought he would have on this earth. Multiple shots rang out, and pieces of drywall and blood exploded into the room from the other side of the wall. Debris went flying this way and that. Breitner slumped forward. He was hit from behind and had no gunshot wound visible to Jack or Zack. As Breitner began to move his thumb toward the detonator button, Jack pumped two rounds into his head and grabbed the detonator in one quick motion. There was no question this time. Bart Breitner was seriously dead. All the building occupants were safe. *But where's Zack?*

"Zack, Zack! Where are you? Are you alright?"

"I'm over here, Jack. I'm fine, I think." Zack Blake poked his head out from behind the second row of chairs. He jumped the opposite way. Only first responders are trained to run *into* trouble. Ordinary citizens like Zachary Blake tend to run *away* from it.

"Are you hurt?" Jack asked, concerned.

"I'm fine," said Zack, dusting himself off. "You?"

"Fine."

"What the hell was that?"

"That was our task force's definition of *backup*. You knew they were coming, didn't you? Why didn't you tell me something was up?"

"Are you kidding me? What kind of cop are you? I gave you hint after hint to allow me to continue to engage him, to keep him talking, and you kept trying to shut both of us up. What's the matter with you?"

"I completely understood your signals, Zack. But I also knew Breitner better than you. If we both tried to keep him talking, he would have smelled a rat. Why do you think I kept telling him to shut up?"

"Brilliant, Jack. That is fucking brilliant. I never even considered that. He kept talking to me out of spite for you?"

"Exactly," replied Jack sporting a self-satisfied grin. "I *am* brilliant, aren't I?"

Zack was livid. "Are you out of your fucking mind? What if it didn't work? What if he said, 'I'm sick of this Dylan guy,' and pressed the button?" Zack asked, incredulous.

"Then, we'd be dead, but so would he. It was a gamble I was willing to take," Jack confessed.

"With *my* life? I have a wife and kids!"

"I knew he'd keep talking to spite me. He was enjoying the exercise, and he wanted to piss me off. In fact, the whole thing was pissing me off. He believed he convinced you his story was true or, at least, felt you were beginning to believe it."

"How sure were you?"

"Pretty damned sure. Seventy-thirty, maybe."

"Seventy-thirty? A thirty percent chance of *my* death was acceptable to you? You're crazy. You know that?"

"Well, then, how does eighty-twenty sound? Better? Everything worked out in favor of the good guys, didn't it?"

"No thanks to you, asshole." Zack started to calm down.

"Not a scratch on either of us. We had a pretty good result, I'd say."

"I almost had a heart attack. Can you imagine the headlines? Famous lawyer survives bomb scare, pees pants and dies of a heart attack."

"You saved my life, man, more than once now. I was only returning the favor."

Zack glared at him, started to reply, and then heaved a sigh of relief.

"It's over, Zack. It's over, man, and you and I are fine. We survived. Now, call Jennifer."

Shaheed, Andy, and several SWAT team and FBI members stormed through the back door of the waiting room. "Everyone, freeze!" Shaheed commanded.

"Shaheed! We're fine. Breitner's dead. Stand down!" Jack shouted. The words sounded like orders as if Jack was resuming command. "You guys were amazing! You saved a lot of lives today, ours included."

"We have got to get some of these Doppler gizmos for the Dearborn P.D. These things are really cool," said Andy. "Are you guys sure you're okay?"

"We're both fine thanks to you guys. Who cooked up this half-baked plan to shoot blindly through the back wall and put an innocent civilian at risk?" Jack winked and nodded at Shaheed.

"It was all Lieutenant Ali, Dylan. He cooked up the plan and all of us executed it," replied Gibson. She turned, hesitantly, to Shaheed.

Jack grimaced and turned to Shaheed. "What is *she* doing here?"

"The FBI responded to your APB for assistance. Gibson and I were the agents they dispatched," Westmore explained.

"You're not welcome here," Jack seethed. "We didn't need you before, and we don't need you now. You've been nothing but a pain in my ass since the very beginning."

"Jack," Shaheed reasoned. "Their assistance and equipment were invaluable to this rescue operation. They didn't have to respond, but they did, even though they knew that you would probably be hostile toward them. They came. They did the job and did it well. How about a little cop to cop appreciation for a job well done?"

"*NFW*, Shaheed. I'm a forgiving man, especially to fellow law enforcement brothers and sisters, but this was a bridge too far. These two put me on trial for *murder*, man!" He pointed at Gibson. "She was part of the team that gathered evidence and prosecuted me. I cannot easily dismiss or forget what she did."

"I don't expect you to, Dylan. I'm just pleased you guys are okay." Gibson turned and acknowledged Zachary Blake as well as Jack Dylan. "I was happy for the opportunity to assist you guys today." She turned back and faced Jack. "I want you to know I'm terribly sorry for my role in this whole affair. If I could do everything over, I would do things very differently. For now, all I can offer is a sincere apology. I hope, someday, you'll find it in your heart to forgive me. You have a friend for life at the FBI. We're all in this together."

Jack softened. "I appreciate the apology, Gibson. I know it's sincere. But an apology doesn't erase several months of hell. Given some time…"

"Not a problem, Dylan," she interrupted. "We'll get out of your hair." She motioned to Westmore. "Let's go, Pete." Zack, SWAT, and the Dearborn task force watched Gibson and Westmore walk away.

"She's probably a good friend to have, Jack," Zack suggested, ever the mediator.

"Probably," Jack grunted, staring off into the distance. Suddenly, he snapped to and turned to Shaheed. "So, Lieutenant Ali—let's get back to this half-assed plan that endangered everyone, including an innocent civilian."

"I am guilty of saving your sorry ass, Jack," said Shaheed. "Of course, I had a little help from our FBI and SWAT friends. It helped I knew the building."

As Zack stared at the bullet-ridden wall, Shaheed got Jack's attention and winked at him.

"As to your so-called innocent victim, he was already at risk, and we figured he could handle himself. Besides, he was expendable. One civilian casualty in a hostage situation is a good result, don't you think? This Doppler stuff is so good it wasn't difficult to determine who was who and where each person was from behind the wall. The risk was sufficiently minimized."

Zack exploded. He was unaware of the ruse. "Expendable? Sufficiently minimized? I've got a wife and two teenage boys, and I'm *expendable*? I should sue the city for this. You scared the crap out of me. Breitner was happy and talking. You guys are as crazy as Dylan is."

"He's kidding, Zack," Jack smirked. Zack looked over at Shaheed, who began to laugh. "You are extremely important to us. You must know we cops love you scumbag defense lawyers. After all, you're the guys who fight to put criminals back on the streets after we have worked so hard to arrest them and get them *off* the streets."

"Or nice young women who cops wrongfully arrest," replied Zack caustically. "Or hero cops wrongfully accused, you unappreciative assholes."

"Or situations like the ones you mention," said Jack, smiling. He turned to Zack and earnestly added, "Zack, I am forever in your debt, man."

"You're welcome."

"And we're terribly sorry we made you pee your pants," Shaheed snickered.

"Great, more comedy," Zack grunted.

"Don't you need to do something, Zack?" Jack prompted.

"What?"

"Call Jennifer!"

"Shit! I've got to call Jennifer!"

"I said that. Didn't I just say that?"

"Another damn comedian!" Zack shouted.

They all laughed and began to exit the room. Zack pulled out his phone and dialed.

"Zack? Thank God! Are you safe? Are you hurt? What's happening?" Jennifer asked frantically.

"Everybody's fine, Jen, except Breitner. He's dead. It's over, Jenny. It's all over. You were right. I was crazy to come. These guys aren't worth it." He glanced at the cops, chuckled, and returned to the telephone call. "It's all about you and the boys. I love you. I'll be home soon."

"Aw, isn't that sweet?" Jack chided. "Boys, that's what it looks like to be in love."

Zack gave Jack a middle finger salute while he listened to the love of his life at the other end of the line. Jack was correct. This *was* what it looked like to be in love.

"I love you, too," said Jennifer. "And remember, I'm *always* right. The boys are here. They want to talk to you. Hang on."

"Dad! This is so cool! Are you hanging with the SWAT team? We were watching on TV. You weren't hurt, were you?" It was his youngest, Jake.

"I'm fine, Jake. It is great to hear your voice! Yeah, I guess it was pretty cool. If I weren't involved in it, I would have noticed how cool it was. Still, it was pretty frickin' cool!"

"Are you telling us the truth, Dad? You're not hurt?" Kenny asked. They were both calling him 'Dad.' Tears formed in his eyes.

"I'm great, Kenny. Not a scratch on me thanks to these fabulous Dearborn police professionals." He again glanced at the police contingent and gave them the thumbs up sign.

"The television people are calling you a hero, Dad."

"I'm no hero, son. I did what anyone else would have done under the circumstances."

"I'd say 'hero' is an appropriate term here, Zack," Jack said. "Thank you for what you did today. It was above and beyond the call of duty. You're damn lucky it was Shaheed who made the call because I wouldn't have let you do it."

"Then we're both damn lucky Shaheed made the call because if I didn't do it, you might not be here. You're welcome, by the way."

"Here we go…" Jack sighed.

"Are you coming home now, Dad?" Kenny said into the receiver. Zack almost forgot Kenny was still on the phone.

"Yeah, son. I'll be home soon. We'll grab some dinner. Put Mom back on the phone, please."

"Zack, will you be home for dinner?"

"I'll be there soon. We'll go out."

"Good, because with all of this excitement, I didn't start anything."

Zack stepped away from the group and turned his back to them, whispering, "God, Jenny. You were so right! What was I thinking? This guy had a bomb big enough to take out the whole floor. I could have been killed. How could I do that to you and the boys?"

"No, you were right, Zack. How could you not? Please, come home now! And Zack?"

"Yes, honey?"

"Don't ever do anything like this ever again."

"Yes, dear. Whatever you say, dear."

"I love you, Zack."

"I love you more."

"I love you less."

"I love you the most."

"No, I love *you* the most."

## END

## Connect with Mark

Email: info@markmbello.com
Website: www.markmbello.com
Facebook: MarkMBelloBooks
Twitter: @JusticeFellow
YouTube: Mark M. Bello
Goodreads: Mark M. Bello

If you enjoyed this or any other novel in *The Zachary Blake Betrayal Series*, please consider rating and reviewing them.

Other books in the series:
*Betrayal of Faith* (Book 1)
*Betrayal of Justice* (Book 2)
*Betrayal in Black* (coming soon)

To request a speaking engagement, interview, or appearance, please email 8GrandPublications@gmail.com.

Printed in the USA
CPSIA information can be obtained
at www.ICGtesting.com
LVHW091053090324
774009LV00001B/148

9 781732 447103